The man couldn't seem to take his eyes off her

And Lisa couldn't take her eyes off him, either. But then, it wasn't every day that a man who looked like this strode into the TV studio. "Can I help you?" Lisa finally got out.

"Actually I'm just here to see a friend. But I'm not in any big hurry...." He smiled, Lisa smiled back, and for a moment they just stood there, grinning at each other.

"Dan! Dan Ashley! I don't believe it!" Lisa spun around. Fiona Parker, the station femme fatale, was sweeping down the hallway toward them.

"Ah, Fiona. How nice—" Dan Ashley looked as if he would have said more, but Fiona had already made her move. Darting forward like a praying mantis, she clutched her victim and brought her fire-engine-red lips down on his.

So it was Fiona he'd come to see. Lisa should have guessed. Turning her back in disgust, Lisa silently wished the next time Fiona launched herself at a man, she'd trip and break her leg. And maybe Lisa would do the tripping!

ABOUT THE AUTHOR

Dawn Stewardson lives in Toronto with her husband, John, an array of pets and a garden that thinks it's a jungle. *Across the Misty* is her tenth novel for Harlequin.

"I only wish," she told us, "that they got easier to write with each one. No such luck. They still take an incredible amount of work. But then, it's a labor of love."

Books by Dawn Stewardson

HARLEQUIN SUPERROMANCE

329–VANISHING ACT
355–DEEP SECRETS
383–BLUE MOON
405–PRIZE PASSAGE
409–HEARTBEAT
432–THREE'S COMPANY
477–MOON SHADOW

HARLEQUIN INTRIGUE

80–PERIL IN PARADISE
90–NO RHYME OR REASON

Across the Misty

DAWN STEWARDSON

Harlequin Books

TORONTO • NEW YORK • LONDON
AMSTERDAM • PARIS • SYDNEY • HAMBURG
STOCKHOLM • ATHENS • TOKYO • MILAN
MADRID • WARSAW • BUDAPEST • AUCKLAND

Published May 1992

ISBN 0-373-70498-4

ACROSS THE MISTY

To Bob, who gave me the idea for this book
and who proves that finance types
aren't all as dry as unbuttered toast.
And to John, always.

CHAPTER ONE

"THAT'S ABOUT IT, then, Saint-John," Jake said, tossing the ratings sheet onto his desk. "Obviously, we yank *Love in the Afternoon.*" He glanced across at Lisa, apparently expecting her to nod agreement.

Instead, she settled more firmly into her chair. This was shaping up to be one of their longer post-ratings week Thursday afternoons. Because she certainly wasn't going to sit here like Little Miss Mouse and let Jake ax *Love.* But she'd have a better chance of changing his mind if she could put him into a happier mood. "The *Fiona* ratings are still right up there," she offered.

"Yeah. Fiona's done a good job of grabbing audience share. The show could be even better, though. There's one change I'd like to see immediately."

Right. There was one change a lot of people at the station would like to see immediately. Unfortunately, whatever Jake was about to suggest, it would hardly be replacing the host.

"I want Fiona to lighten up," he continued. "We're going to start losing the viewers she's pulled in if she keeps treating the topics so seriously."

"Lightening things up sounds good to me, Jake. But Fiona isn't exactly Joan Rivers."

"Well, I want to see more of her cute-and-fluffy routine. You know the one I mean."

Lisa nodded. She knew only too well. He meant the nauseating act Fiona put on every time an interesting man came within ten feet of her.

"And the show definitely needs an injection of humor," he added. "Why don't you slate some frivolous themes? And maybe booking a few off-beat guests would help. Now, getting back to *Love,* canceling it is going to leave us an hour short on our local broadcasting commitment. Let's handle that by going with Fiona's idea. She's itching for more exposure, so we'll give her a second weekly time slot."

We'll give her? As in, he'd definitely decided? Several choice, four-letter words popped into Lisa's mind. And for the hundredth time she vowed that if she ever got her hands on that friend of Jake's in Manhattan— the one who'd introduced him to Fiona Parker—Jake would have a dead friend in Manhattan. Until six months ago, before Fiona had left the Big Apple for Walkerton, Ohio, life at television station WALK had been far sweeter.

"So, how does that strike you?" Jake pressed. "In addition to Friday, she could have Tuesday at eight. And all it would mean is some rescheduling."

"Jake, maybe for *you* all it would mean is some rescheduling, but for me..." Lisa paused, ordering herself to make her point without using any four-letter words other than Jake. "Jake, trying to produce two segments of *Fiona* every week would turn me into a candidate for a rubber room."

He shot her a quizzical look. She gave him a black one in return, just in case he had any idea that she was joking. He saw *Fiona* as part of the answer to his dream of sky-high ratings. But she saw it as a producer's nightmare. And it had her crew members feeling as if they were working in the television Middle Ages.

In the 1990s, only a host from hell would insist on doing a talk show live. They always taped, anyway, to have a record of the segments, and even minimal editing made shows much smoother. But Fiona refused to accept that going out live was just plain stupid.

Of course, some viewers *were* watching solely in the hope of seeing Fiona or one of her guests make unedited fools of themselves. So she'd been right about the live angle boosting her ratings. And the fact that there was nothing in the world Jake liked better than good ratings made criticizing Ms. Parker a tricky proposition.

Lisa forced a smile. "Jake, even setting aside my fear that I'd end up on a trip to the funny farm, I have problems with Fiona's idea."

"Saint-John," he said, grinning, "be honest. What you have problems with is Fiona."

"That simply puts me in the vast majority, Jake. Everyone who works with her has problems. All the women, at least. During last Friday's show, the makeup girl actually began twitching."

"I can't for the life of me see why you don't like our top talent," Jake teased. "She's an absolute pussycat with me."

"Right. I've noticed her purring whenever you're in the same room. But you don't suppose that routine has anything to do with your being the boss, do you? Or the fact that you're a man and she drools at the sight of any male younger than eighty?"

"She does?" An obviously feigned expression of naiveté appeared on Jake's face.

"Well, maybe *drools* is an exaggeration. But she does make a point of checking out every man who has a discernible pulse." Lisa decided she'd just exceeded her cattiness quota for the day and bit back the rest of the unkind remarks she was tempted to make.

"Any man younger than eighty, huh?" Jake muttered. "That's downright depressing news. I figured she simply had the hots for divorced men with receding hairlines."

Lisa merely shook her head at him. Jake was no fool. He had foxy Fiona pegged.

"Well," he went on, "if you aren't going to tell me Fiona thinks I'm the second coming of Paul Newman, why don't you elaborate on the problems you have with her wanting an additional time slot?"

"Jake, the main one is that there are only twenty-four hours in a day. And that's not enough time to produce twice as many segments of *Fiona* as we're doing now. They take forever to put together because she meddles in every detail of production. She drives my crew nuts. You know what they call her behind her back?"

Jake grinned again. "Yeah. Nosey Parker."

"That's about their kindest name for her. I'm surprised one of them hasn't murdered her by now."

"You don't think you might be exaggerating again, do you?"

"Well, if not murdered, at least seriously maimed. Jake, we can do a segment of *Love* in exactly half the time it takes us for one of Fiona's. And all those extra hours are because of her interference."

"She's after ratings, Saint-John. And she's doing a good job of getting them. I've never seen a host so conscious of audience share."

"Jake, I can't argue with you about that. But if you want to double her airtime I'm going to need *at least* one more production assistant."

Jake cleared his throat—uncomfortably, Lisa noted with satisfaction. He might have a vault full of musty old family money, but he was a tight man with a buck. Even hinting about needing additional staff was a guaranteed way to shut him up.

"Besides," she added quickly, deciding she'd gotten as close as she was likely to get to winning that particular argument, "I don't agree with you about canceling *Love*. You haven't given it a fair shot."

"No? Well, I'd say I've given it more than a fair shot. You know, maybe part of our problem was going with Crystal as host. She's just a kid."

"Jake, she's not. She only looks young. She's actually twenty-six. That's only three years younger than your precious Fiona, only two years younger than me. Besides, I think her looking young is a plus in this instance. We don't want an old hag hosting a program about romance."

"Saint-John, I don't want *anyone* hosting a program about romance. *Love* has had three months to attract an audience and—"

"Three *summer* months, Jake. You can't attract an audience when everyone's on vacation. Besides, we've done nothing to promote the show. Not a darned thing."

"Forget it, Saint-John. *Love* is history."

Lisa took a deep breath and decided to ignore the slitting gesture her boss was making across his throat. "Look, Jake, it's September. People are watching television again. Why not give Crystal a few more months? All we need is something to pique viewer in-

terest, something that'll get people to tune in and give
Love a chance. Give *Love* a Chance! How about that?
We could run promos with that as our catchphrase."

The dim expression on Jake's face clearly said what
he thought of Give *Love* a Chance.

"All right, so this needs work. But I still say there's
a potential audience. We just haven't tapped it. And
I'm sure Crystal and I could come up with a gimmick
that would catch people's attention." She waited while
Jake considered the idea.

"I'll make you a deal," he finally said. "If you can
actually come up with a good gimmick—and I do mean
good—I'll give you till year-end to turn *Love*'s pitiful
ratings into something believable."

"Great! I guarantee you won't regret—"

"I'm not finished. This is a two-sided deal."

Lisa's elation began to dissipate. Whatever the other
side of the deal was, she had a feeling she wasn't going
to like it.

"If Crystal doesn't have decent ratings by Christmas," Jake said, "we cancel her and go with doubling
Fiona's airtime."

"Oh, no, Jake, I—"

"That's the deal, Saint-John. And it's the best one
I'm going to offer."

She nodded slowly. She'd done well even to buy *Love*
a few more months. And surely they could pull its ratings out of the doldrums.

If not, though... Well, she simply wouldn't consider that possibility. Why should ostriches have a mo-
nopoly on sticking their heads into the sand?

"Thanks, Jake," she murmured. "Crystal and I will
think of a promo idea that'll absolutely knock your
socks off."

"Don't get too carried away, Saint-John. I said it had to be good, not that it had to leave me naked." He glanced at his watch. "It's four-thirty. Let's call this a wrap so I can catch Crystal before she leaves. Then I'll talk to Fiona, tell her she's going to have to wait a few months before she gets her additional hour."

"Ahh... but she'll only get it if *Love* doesn't start doing well, right?"

"Yeah. Right."

Lisa gazed out the window for a moment, wondering if she'd be able to hang pictures in that rubber room at the funny farm. Clearly, Jake didn't believe *Love* had a prayer of doing well. And if it didn't, Lisa Saint-John would be producing two weekly segments of *Fiona*. Of course, she'd only have to do it until it drove her crazy.

Erasing the mental image of herself attempting to hammer nails into rubber walls, Lisa began to concentrate on thinking up the promotional idea of all time for *Love*.

AHEAD, IN THE DISTANCE, bright morning sunlight danced off the immense stone pillars guarding the entrance to Walkerton University. On impulse, Dan slowed his rented Dueler and made a nostalgic detour into the grounds.

He headed slowly down the poplar-lined main drive, trying to see the campus as he'd first seen it sixteen years ago. Way back then, he reflected, glancing at a couple of students wearing freshie beanies and dazed expressions, one of those kids might have been Dan Ashly. An eighteen-year-old Dan Ashly who'd been accepted by Walkerton's prestigious School of Business and had found himself utterly intimidated by this campus.

He'd spent the first few days of classes desperately wishing he was back home in Spokane, feeling certain that he'd never make any friends here. He had, of course. Good friends, on both sides of Walkerton. Except for Jake, though, he'd lost track of them over the years. An inevitable result of passing time, geographical distance and life's changes.

But Jake had begun working at his family's television station after graduation. And his visits to network headquarters in New York had made it easy for them to keep in touch.

Dan grinned to himself, thinking how much he and Jake had enjoyed the old days. They'd been the only two in their class who'd spent their leisure time on the other side of the Misty, drinking beer with the real people of Walkerton, rather than in the student hangouts on this side of the river. Those had been good days, before he'd ended up amid the crassness of Wall Street, before Jake had assumed the responsibilities that went with inheriting control of an NBS-affiliate station.

Dan turned off the road that led to the stately old brick buildings of the main quadrangle and onto a side drive leading down to the river. He drove along until he spotted the broad stretch of grassy bank where he'd spent countless hours studying, then pulled half off the road, cut the Dueler's engine, and sat gazing across the gray water of the Misty at the sprawling buildings of the auto plant.

There had always been two distinct faces to the city. On this side of the river, even beyond the confines of the campus, it was a university town. But the east side was predominantly blue-collar, home to Quality Motors' Plant W.

He focused on the huge QM logo blazed across the top of the tallest building, wondering how many of the guys he'd known, way back when, still worked there. They'd been fellows who'd started at the plant about the time he'd started university.

Undoubtedly, he'd see some of them in the next month or so. Because come Monday morning, like it or not, he'd be over there at the plant. And odds were a million to one that he wasn't going to like it. Despite what the Quality Motors brass wanted to believe, having gone to school here wasn't going to make his presence in Plant W the least bit palatable to its employees.

If he'd had any real choice in the matter, he'd never have agreed to take this assignment. But he hadn't had a choice. If he'd refused, he'd have been out pounding the pavement on Wall Street, looking for another job.

So here he was, and brooding about what he had to do was pointless. And, hell, QM only had him from nine to five. He'd just damn well make the best of his free time. Beginning right now.

With a final glance along the Misty, he restarted the all-terrain Dueler. Once outside the campus gates he turned north, heading for WALK. Barely ten minutes later, he was pulling into its parking lot, grinning to himself once more.

After all their cloak-and-dagger efforts to keep his assignment under wraps until Monday, the big boys at QM would have a million fits if they knew he was about to drop in on the owner of Walkerton's local television station.

But Jake could keep secrets with the best of them if he was asked to. And there was no way Dan was going

to pass up a chance to surprise the devil out of Jake
Forrest.

Inside, the reception desk was unmanned, so Dan
started along the corridor that led to Jake's office. The
last time he'd been in the station, years ago, the manager's office had belonged to Jake senior. But now—

A woman stepped into the hallway and smiled at
him.

He stopped midstride and stood gazing down at
her...at her captivating smile. She wasn't wearing lip-
stick but she had the most luscious-looking lips he'd
seen in an awfully long time.

"Can I help you?"

Her voice matched her appearance—soft and gentle. He glanced at the door of the office she'd come out
of, looking for a clue to her identity. The tiny plate on
it read Lisa Saint-John, Entertainment Producer.

"You're Lisa Saint-John?" he asked, searching his
memory. Jake had definitely mentioned that name at
one time or another.

She nodded.

"You...you're a producer here."

Her smile took on a teasing little tilt. "That's what
the sign says, all right. And you're...?"

"Ashly. Dan Ashly." He eyed her for another moment, liking what he saw. Her fluffy yellow sweater
and casual skirt were a far cry from the power suits that
Wall Street women favored. And she curved in all the
right places, instead of being as anorexically thin as a
fashion model.

And those enormous gray eyes were—

"Well, Dan Ashly...can I help you?" she asked
again.

"Thanks, but I'm just here to surprise a friend. I know the way." His feet didn't want to move on, though, and he simply stood gazing at her for another second, thinking how soft her tawny, shoulder-length hair looked. It hadn't been teased into an impossible shape or sprayed into a solid mass. A man would actually be able to run his fingers through that honey-colored hair. Although he certainly didn't know why that thought had occurred to him.

"Dan! Dan Ashly! It's really you. I don't believe it."

The second woman's voice was anything but soft and gentle. Reluctantly, he pulled his gaze away from Lisa Saint-John and focused on an anorexically thin woman in a navy power suit. For a puzzled moment, he simply stared at her. Then the recollection of her sprayed-almost-to-death red hair helped him push the right memory button. "Fiona. How nice—"

He'd have said more if her fire-engine-red lips hadn't closed over his surprised ones.

Lisa stared in disbelief as Fiona made her move—like a praying mantis darting forward to clutch her victim. So this Dan Ashly, whoever he might be, had come to the station to surprise Fiona. Lord, that woman had to know every gorgeous hunk in North America. And know them intimately.

For the tiniest instant, as Fiona wrapped her arms around her prey's neck and began devouring him, Lisa felt a pang of disappointment. The moment she'd seen this particular gorgeous hunk, she'd felt an unusual tug of attraction.

Of course there was nothing unusual about considering chiseled good looks and broad shoulders attractive—not to mention the way his jeans hugged his lean hips. It certainly wasn't every day that a cowboy strode out of a Levi's ad and into WALK.

But her instincts had told her there was more to the cowboy than physical appeal, that he was someone she'd like to know.

So much for her instincts. They were apparently in dire need of an overhaul. She didn't want to know *any* man who was as familiar with Fiona Parker as this man clearly was.

She stood watching the two of them for a moment, almost embarrassed by the way they were kissing the daylights out of each other. And then an unexpected surge of anger swept her. But it was an absolutely ridiculous surge of anger.

Why on earth should she be angry at a man she'd exchanged no more than a dozen words with? Because, she silently answered her own question, men who were so blind that they didn't see through women like Fiona made her blood boil. That was why.

And the fact that her first impression of this character had been so completely off base made her angry with herself to boot. She'd thought she'd seen intelligence in his slate blue eyes, but she'd thought wrong. Mr. Dan Ashly was simply a male version of the proverbial dumb blonde.

Well, no, dumb blonde wasn't precisely right, she corrected herself, glaring at the way Fiona was twisting a strand of his hair around her finger. His hair was actually light brown.

But regardless of its color, he was simply a male bimbo, ready and willing to have Fiona wrap him around her little finger, just the way she was doing with his hair. And he'd obviously been well and thoroughly wrapped before this.

Lisa turned on her heel and started down the hall. After Jake's ultimatum yesterday, she and Crystal were going to have a brainstorming session over lunch to come up with an absolutely brilliant idea to promote *Love in the Afternoon.*

They'd go out for pizza. No. Burgers and fries. With a side of gravy. And double-thick chocolate shakes. And maybe hot fudge sundaes for dessert. For some reason, she suddenly felt an overwhelming craving for chocolate.

"DON'T WORRY about it, Crystal," Lisa offered, pausing outside her office door. "When we finally do come up with an idea, it's going to be a terrific one."

Crystal managed a wan smile. "You sure about that? I mean, if even that second round of chocolate shakes didn't give us inspiration, what will?"

"I don't know. Pizza, maybe? If you're not doing anything tomorrow night we could get together and have another go."

"Oh, that would be great, Lisa. I know I'm not going to get a second of decent sleep until we think of something."

"Well, why don't you come over to my place, then. That'll give me incentive to do something about the two-inch layer of dust in my apartment."

"Okay. And I'll bring some wine. About eight?"

Lisa nodded and turned into her office. There was something fundamentally wrong with the male population of Walkerton when Crystal had nothing better to do on a Saturday night than sit around trying to brainstorm a promotional idea for a TV show. She was a really sweet person. And, in the looks department, she could double for Christie Brinkley.

Of course, her being a television host probably intimidated a lot of men.

And what about you, Saint-John? a little voice inside her head asked. *What's your excuse for Saturday night? Producers aren't celebrities.*

She told the little voice to shut up. She'd concluded, years ago, that her girl-next-door looks appealed to only the odd man. And there hadn't been any odd men on the horizon lately.

Propped in the center of her desk was a note, written in Jake's scrawl. It read: "Saint-John, where the hell are you when I need you?"

"Oh, great," she muttered, starting for his office. They likely had another Fiona-instigated Friday crisis on their hands. For hours before each show, the woman was a basket case.

Jake glanced up as Lisa reached his doorway. "Where on earth have you been? There was someone here I wanted you to meet."

"I went out for lunch, Jake. You know? The meal between breakfast and dinner that most people have time to eat every day? The one I manage to squeeze in once or twice a month?"

"Eating lunch every day would make you fat. And make you miss what's happening around here. While you were out enjoying yourself, I had the local news of the decade dumped into my lap."

"What local news of the decade?" Lisa took a close look at the expression on Jake's face and decided he was serious.

"Saint-John, what I'm going to tell you is in the strictest confidence."

She nodded.

"Okay, then. Have you heard any rumors about Plant W? Has your father mentioned even a word?"

"I don't have the foggiest what you're talking about."

"Rumors. You know. About something unusual happening."

"I was at the house for dinner only last night, Jake. And Dad didn't say a thing."

"And he would have if he'd heard something, right? I mean, he'd have wanted to know if we'd heard anything at the station, wouldn't he?"

"He'd have wanted to know if we'd heard anything about what? Look, you're going to have to fill in some of the blanks if you expect answers."

"Damnation. Then Dan was right."

Dan? Who the heck was Dan? Jake was still speaking, so she forced her attention back to his words.

"They've actually managed to keep the lid on this," he was muttering. "Dan said that Ken Woody was the only one who knew about it, but I couldn't believe they'd really kept it that quiet."

"Jake, *who* kept *what* quiet? What does only Plant W's manager know about?"

"Hold on to your hat, Saint-John. And swear you'll keep this under it. What's happening is going to mean changes in next week's programming, so I'm letting you in on it. But until Woody makes the formal announcement on Monday, you can't tell anyone. And that definitely includes your father."

"All right. My lips are sealed. Now, what?"

Jake took a deep breath. "QM's top management in Detroit has hired an outside analyst—one who specializes in the auto industry—to study Plant W. He starts on Monday and figures his report will take about a month to complete."

Lisa sank into a chair and stared at Jake. With a father who was president of the union local, she knew perfectly well what management's "studying" a plant for a month meant. They were considering closing it. And an outside analyst was nothing more than a hired gun.

The specter of how plant closures had practically destroyed Flint, Michigan, forced its way into her mind. She forced it right back out. Walkerton, Ohio, wasn't Flint, Michigan. And closing Plant W would be unthinkable. It was one of Quality Motors' major assembly plants. And the only plant turning out Duelers.

"Jake, there can't be anything to this rumor. Not if even my dad hasn't heard it."

"Saint-John, I don't know how the hell they kept the news under wraps, but this isn't a rumor. It's a fact. I got it straight from the horse's mouth. Or more accurately, from the analyst's mouth."

"The analyst?"

"Right. He's one of my closest friends."

Lisa struggled to rein in her thoughts. They'd begun racing in all directions. If the analyst was both Jake's friend and his source, then there was actually going to be a study. And if there was, her father had to be told. She'd have to let him know what was going on, warn him what the company was up to before Woody simply sprang the news on the workers. But she'd just promised Jake she wouldn't say a word. So what the hell should she do?

Right this moment, she realized, she should listen to what Jake was saying about his friend. She picked up on his words midsentence.

"...so when Dan got in from New York this morning he dropped by the station to see me. But he wouldn't tell us what he was doing in Walkerton until he'd sworn us to secrecy."

"Us?"

"Fiona and me."

Fiona? Why on earth would Jake's friend tell Fiona about something that was top secret? Lisa's mind shifted into overdrive, and the name *Dan* began flashing on and off inside her head. The Dan who Jake was talking about was his analyst friend. But surely Jake's Dan couldn't be the Dan whatever-his-name-was who'd been making a spectacle of himself with Fiona earlier. No, of course he couldn't. Fiona's Dan had been jeans and cowboy boots. Jake's Dan would be pinstripe New York. But two different Dans appearing at WALK this morning would have been an incredible coincidence.

"Jake? This friend of yours? This Dan? He isn't a friend of Fiona's, too, is he?"

"Yeah. Dan Ashly. I'm sure I must have mentioned him to you. He's the one who introduced Fiona and me in New York last spring. If it wasn't for him, we wouldn't have her here."

Lisa slumped farther into her chair, only partially listening to Jake start in about how his friendship with Dan went back to their university days.

Dan Ashly was the man who'd made that fateful introduction. And for the past six months, she'd been fantasizing about killing him because he had. Of course, in her fantasies, he'd been nameless and faceless. She'd merely thought of him as that friend of

Jake's in Manhattan. But now he had a name. And now she had an additional reason to contemplate murdering him.

Directly or indirectly, Quality Motors employed half the people in town, including her father and brother. She might live and work on the west side of the Misty these days, but her roots were firmly on the east side. And she knew precisely how the auto workers would react to this news. They'd assume the absolute worst and be so upset that—

"Are you listening, Saint-John?"

"Of course I am, Jake." *Just don't quiz me on what you've been saying,* she added silently. She breathed a tiny sigh of relief when Jake simply picked up where he'd apparently left off.

"Lord, I wish we could blow the story wide open tonight on *Friday at Six.* Then we could follow up by bumping Fiona's scheduled guest and having Dan appear instead. He's agreed to be on Monday's news broadcasts and to guest on next Friday's segment of *Fiona,* but Lord, I wish—"

Apparently, there was a higher gear in Lisa's mind than overdrive because her thoughts began whirring so fast and furiously that she could no longer hear Jake speaking.

He'd asked Dan Ashly to be on *Fiona?* Oh, God! The news that there was going to be this study was bad enough. And it would practically put her father into cardiac arrest. But if Quality Motors' hired gun appeared on the show that *she* produced, Dad would hang her for treason. Or maybe he'd have her drawn and quartered. Well, at the very least, he'd disown her.

Of course, they'd have to have Dan Ashly on the news once the story broke. But they certainly didn't have to have him on *Fiona.*

"Jake?"

"What?"

"Jake, I've already got next Friday's show booked. We're doing that story about the underwater expedition that's planned for Lake Erie. You remember, the ship graveyard bit? Some of those warships have been on the bottom for almost two hundred years, and I've got a marine archaeologist who's alarmed that they might end up damaged. He's agreed to come all the way from Toledo, and I'd hate to ask him to reschedule the trip."

Jake stared at her as if she'd lost her marbles. "I assume you mean Toledo, Ohio. Not Toledo, Spain."

"Of course."

"And you'd hate to ask him to reschedule the trip? Hell, we're not asking him to trek to Timbuktu and back. Even if he drove at half the speed limit he could make it here within an hour."

"Well ... well, he's usually busy on Friday nights. And those ships are a great local-interest story. I'd hate to lose it."

"Saint-John, do you figure folks around here are going to be more concerned about some dumb old sunken ships or about what's going on at Plant W?"

"Jake ... Jake, listen. You know as well as I do that television appearances give people credibility. And the auto workers are already going to feel terribly threatened by your friend's study. So I don't think we should be doing anything to foster the impression that he's credible."

"What the hell are you talking about? He *is* credible. Eminently credible. He's a financial analyst with a major Wall Street firm."

"Jake, what I'm saying is that local feelings are going to run awfully high about this, so I think it would make sense to play the story down instead of up."

"Play it down? Saint-John, did whatever you ate for lunch bring on premature senility? Considering the number of Walkertonians working for Quality Motors, when Dan guests on *Fiona* everyone in town will tune in. Our ratings will go through the hole in the ozone layer."

"Ahh...right. But sky-high ratings aren't everything."

"Since when?"

"Well, I mean we have to think about the overall picture here. You know what auto industry *studies* are. Especially ones conducted by outside analysts. They're nothing more than whitewashes to produce reports justifying plant closures."

"Whitewashes? Plant closures? Saint-John, let's not start leaping to conclusions. Dan's simply doing an analysis for QM, giving them an outside expert's opinion about their operation."

"Oh, Jake, don't pretend you're that naive. The only conceivable reason they've got a Wall Street wizard here is to have him play hatchet man. His report will recommend closing Plant W. Then the company bigwigs will innocently hold up their hands and claim they're only following the recommendations of an esteemed and impartial analyst. And if we have him guest on local television we'll just be reinforcing that image of him."

"So what? He *is* an esteemed and impartial analyst. And you, Lisa Saint-John, are all wet. I know Dan. His report will be factual and fair. He's not the type to act as anybody's puppet. And he's a definite go for next Friday's show. I just hope to hell Detroit doesn't tell him to clam up. He said he'd have to let them know he's agreed to do a talk show. And if they're not happy with the idea of his discussing the study in detail, the segment could drag a little.''

"Drag a little? How about it could be downright deadly? And even if he doesn't clam up, how am I supposed to make the segment light and humorous and all those things you want when you're sticking me with a topic the viewers will find threatening and a guest who probably suffers from terminal accountancy?''

"Get your facts straight. Dan's a financial analyst. Not an accountant.''

"Same boring school. Money people are dry as unbuttered toast. So the only reason viewers will watch is because Mr. Dry Toast is going to be talking about Plant W.''

"But they *will* watch. And ratings are ratings.''

"Oh, hell, Jake, I know you'll get your ratings. But the viewers are going to hate both your Mr. Ashly and what he has to say. Jake, I produce *Fiona*. It seems to me I should have had some input before you—''

"You were out for lunch when the matter came up," he interrupted smugly.

Lisa glared at him, desperately racking her brain for more arguments. Not a single fresh one materialized. "Jake, I don't like this idea. I think—''

"Take it down a thousand, Saint-John. We're only talking one segment. And I'm not positive what's got you this upset but I have a darned strong suspicion. So, if I'm right, you'd just better remember that you promised you wouldn't breathe a word about this to your father.''

"I remember." But, oh damn, she'd made that promise without knowing what they were talking about. And now that she did, there was no way she could keep it. Under normal circumstances, she might be the most trustworthy employee Jake had. But these weren't normal circumstances. Promise or no promise, she was going to call Dad at dinnertime. Then at least he'd have the weekend to decide how the union should react when Woody dropped his bombshell.

"And you'd also better put aside your preconceived ideas about whitewashes and plant closures," Jake ordered her. "A study of Plant W is big news, and we're going to give it the coverage it deserves. The *fair* coverage it deserves. Hell, this is the type of local story that the network likes to pick up for rebroadcast. Part of the segment with Dan and Fiona might easily make the national evening news. So, when you're working on the interview ideas with them, keep in mind that you're paid to be an unbiased professional."

"I'm perfectly aware of that." But she wasn't paid to be a blasted traitor. She was Bert Saint-John's daughter and Roy Saint-John's big sister. And that meant she couldn't help having biases.

She pushed herself up from the chair. "I'd better get going. I told Fiona I'd be dropping by to talk about tonight's show."

"You'll see she keeps it light?"

"I'll certainly try."

Lisa left Jake's office and started along the corridor, sorting through everything he'd said. Maybe Jake was right. Maybe Dan Ashly wasn't QM's puppet. Maybe he would prepare a fair report. Maybe she was leaping to conclusions. But there were far too many maybes involved for comfort. And Jake wasn't seeing that.

Of course, Jake had grown up in a wealthy family on the west side of Walkerton. There was no way he could truly comprehend what a catastrophe it would be if

Plant W was shut down. But she comprehended perfectly. And the thought that it could happen scared the hell out of her.

So unless what Ken Woody had to say on Monday was both logical and reassuring, she intended to do everything she could to lessen that study's impact. And she'd start with next week's show.

Jake was definitely right about one thing. That segment was going to be exactly the kind of local coverage that NBS liked to use spots from. And how impressively Mr. Dan Ashly came across would depend, to some extent, on the way she handled production details. And whereas a report prepared by an esteemed expert would be accepted as gospel, one done by a fool wouldn't.

Not that she could make Dan Ashly look foolish without cooperation from him. But she could certainly have a shot at seeing that he didn't look like an esteemed expert. And if he did *happen* to come across with a whole lot of egg on his face, especially if his eggy face appeared nationally... Well, Quality Motors could hardly justify whitewashing Walkerton into oblivion on the report of a fool.

She turned down the hall that led to Fiona's office, her thoughts still racing. Now she not only had to think up a plan to make *Love* work, she also had to think up a plan to make Mr. Ashly look inept. Lord, for the next while, she was going to have to spend a hundred hours a day thinking.

But right this instant, all she seemed able to think about was that Dan Ashly represented a threat to the future of her family and her hometown. And about how that made him her enemy.

CHAPTER TWO

LISA CHECKED HER WATCH. Almost seven-thirty. Just over half an hour to air. The studio audience would be admitted in a few minutes, so she had to stop sitting here at her desk, worrying about that study, and get out on the floor for tonight's show.

If only her memories of the Long Strike, as the town still referred to it after seven years, weren't so vivid that they might have been clips from a movie. If only she could stop imagining how much worse a permanent plant closure would be.

She closed her eyes, picturing snow and ice. The workers at Plant W had gone out on strike in early February and stayed out until the following January. A face formed in her mind's eye, her father's face, raw from the cold of the picket line.

He hadn't been union executive then. So every day, he'd done his stint. At first, it had been during one of the coldest winters in Ohio's history. Then under the sizzling summer sun... then back to the bone-chilling cold of another winter. She could recall, so clearly, how it had hurt to watch him age before her eyes, to see her mother growing increasingly worried about him.

A second face appeared. One she hadn't thought of in a long time. The image caused her throat to tighten. It was the father of one of her closest friends. He'd grown so depressed during that year he'd committed suicide.

A blur of women's faces replaced the man's. Women she'd baby-sat for that summer when she couldn't get a job. They'd been wives of striking workers. Women like her own mother, who'd always stayed home with their children. But when the strike began, they'd quickly taken any available job.

As the women faded, she saw a collage of people lined up at a bank, withdrawing savings. Her father was in that line, forced to cash in the certificates he'd bought as her brother's college fund.

And then she was no longer imagining him in the line but at home, standing in her room, his hands jammed in the pockets of his pants. She swiveled from her bedroom desk and eyed him with concern. His face was creased with lines that hadn't been there a month ago.

"Lisa," he said, his voice forced, "baby, I have to talk to you about your birthday present."

She shrugged, trying to look nonchalant. "I don't need anything, Dad. Really."

He simply ignored her protest and pressed on. "Baby, I know I promised you that computer months ago. And I realize how much help it would be with all those papers you have to do for your courses but...Lisa, I thought the strike would be over by now. That things would be getting back to normal."

"Dad, it's all right. Honestly. I managed to get through high school and half of university with just a typewriter. If I got a computer, I probably wouldn't even be able to figure out how to use it."

He tried to smile but it didn't come off. "I...I just wanted to explain, baby, because I...because I've always been able to give you and your brother what you needed. I've always figured I was a pretty good father. Now, though..."

His voice cracked and he quickly looked away. But not before she realized his eyes were growing moist.

"Oh, Daddy," she murmured, pushing herself up out of the chair, throwing her arms around his neck and hugging him with all her might. All she could think about was that father of her friend, committing suicide. "Oh, Daddy, you're not just a pretty good father, you're a wonderful father. And the union's dumb old strike can't do anything to change that."

He hugged her so hard she couldn't breathe, then murmured a gruff thanks and released her, turning away quickly. She was certain that was so she wouldn't see his tears.

Lisa swallowed hard, back in the present. She'd wanted to help out more than ever after that, to get a job instead of going back to university for the next term. But her parents had argued against the idea until she'd given in. Her scholarship paid her tuition, and, even if she'd quit school, there were no jobs to be had in Walkerton.

All there were were sad farewells—people giving up and leaving when the months stretched endlessly into one another. And now, if Plant W was shut down for good, it would be even worse. Half the people in town would be out of work. One by one, they'd pack up and leave. Walkerton would practically become a ghost town.

"Hi," a male voice said from her office doorway.

Lisa glanced up and stopped breathing for an instant, her unhappy reminiscences dissolving in the warmest pair of blue eyes in the world. If they'd belonged to any other man, she'd probably be melting into her chair. But these eyes belonged to the enemy.

Enemies, she thought fleetingly, shouldn't be allowed to look the way this one did. He was standing casually in her open office doorway, all masculine broad shoulders, muscled leanness and carved-from-granite features. An errant lock of straight brown hair fell across his forehead.

His personality would undoubtedly turn out to be the dry toast she expected, but his appearance was pure chocolate éclair. This morning's cowboy look had been replaced by casual cords and a turtleneck sweater. It was the precise slate blue of those eyes that seemed intent on holding her gaze forever.

He stood smiling at her as if he'd stopped by for a neighborly chat. "We kind of met earlier," he offered.

She nodded. Did he actually think she didn't know who he was? Well, if that was the case, she could certainly play along. "Yes, I recall. You're Fiona's friend."

He laughed a deep, quiet laugh that started her stomach doing nervous flip-flops. Seeing this man again, she realized, was making her very anxious. No. Anxious wasn't right. The word was guilty. Seeing him was making her feel guilty about having told her father what was happening. But that had been, she assured herself for at least the thousandth time, the only thing to do under the circumstances.

"Actually," her guilt-provoking visitor said, "I'm Jake's friend. I barely know Fiona."

Sure he didn't. What was the saying? Know thine enemy? Lisa made a mental note that Mr. Ashly was a man of extreme understatement. Having seen him in action this morning, she had a pretty good idea of what his "barely" knowing Fiona involved. Likely, he was into word games and *barely* was the key word.

"Jake said he told you why I'm in Walkerton," Dan added when she didn't speak. "I hope you're as good at keeping secrets as he swears you are."

She pasted a smile onto her face. Jake wouldn't be swearing things *about* her if he learned she'd told. He'd be swearing *at* her. And amid the obscenities would be statements like, "I'm going to kill you, Saint-John" and "You're fired, Saint-John."

"I won't let the cat out of the bag," she managed to say, telling herself that wasn't exactly a lie. She wouldn't *be* letting the cat out. She already had.

Lisa glanced everywhere but at Dan Ashly, wishing he'd go away. He'd taken her by surprise. She'd assumed she'd have until sometime next week, until the preinterview for next Friday's segment, to figure out how to act toward him.

By then, news of the study would be public knowledge, and she might have a better idea about its true purpose.

"I came down with Jake tonight," Dan volunteered. "To watch Fiona."

Lisa tried to decide whether he meant watch the show or the woman. She thought back to the morning once more and decided it was the woman he wanted to see. He probably intended to pick up from wherever he and Fiona had left off when she'd moved from New York to Walkerton. And it didn't take much imagination to figure out where they'd left off.

What did that matter, though? It didn't. Not in the least. All that mattered was whether Mr. Ashly's study was going to be the fair analysis Jake claimed it would be. If it was, then the workers weren't being set up. But talking with her father had only deepened her suspicion that this "analysis" wasn't going to be the slightest bit aboveboard.

Far more likely, QM had given its outside analyst specific instructions about what his "findings" should be and what his "report" should conclude. After all, the company was paying the bills. So, logically, it would also be calling the shots.

What had her father said? She recalled his precise words: "Lisa, baby, you know what a dismal track record the QM management has when it comes to openness and honesty. Do you really think they'd give this guy carte blanche?"

Dan cleared his throat, making her realize he expected her to say something. She scrambled to recall what his last comment had been. He'd come to the station with Jake. That was it.

"Ahh... I thought Jake had to drive down to Columbus tonight."

"He does. Bad timing, huh? I came in early to surprise him, figuring we could spend some time together this weekend, and he's got a conference out of town. But he said it doesn't matter what time he gets away tonight."

Lisa merely nodded once more. Surely, if she didn't hold up her end of the conversation, Dan would take the hint and leave.

"And," he continued, apparently oblivious to her silence, "I want to see *Fiona* air before I'm the guy in the hot seat. So Jake offered to come along, in case I have any questions about what to expect next week. I've never been on a show that broadcasts live."

"No. No one except a Neanderthal has."

Dan laughed again, this time appreciatively. "Jake mentioned that you considered the live angle prehistoric."

Lisa smiled uncertainly. She didn't know whether she liked the fact that Mr. Ashly had tuned in so quickly to her warped sense of humor. Normally, that was something that attracted her to a man. But she definitely wasn't attracted to this one.

Of course, she recognized that he was darned good-looking. She wasn't blind. But recognizing a fact and feeling an attraction weren't the same things at all. She just wished that laugh of his wasn't so engaging. And that his eyes weren't so blue.

"The prospect of appearing live is a little scary," he admitted. "I sure hope I don't come across as a jerk."

"I can't imagine you will." And that was true. Clearly, Dan Ashly would come across as appealing, sincere and intelligent. Unless Lisa did something to prevent it.

She checked her watch again. "I'm afraid I have to get going. My production assistant's away, so I'm on the studio floor tonight instead of in the control room. And when I'm working down there, I like to be on hand for the audience warm-up."

"I'd better get back to Jake's office, then, and collect him. See you again." Dan flashed her a distinctly interested smile before turning away.

Any woman who *did* feel the slightest attraction to him, Lisa realized, would kill to see him smile that way. She yanked open the bottom drawer of her desk and rummaged under a stack of papers, searching for the box of chocolates one of their suppliers had given her months ago. She opened the lid, chose one of the gooiest of the variety mix and devoured it. Lord, it tasted wonderful. Strange how she was behaving like a chocoholic today. She seldom had a craving for chocolate.

She sat staring at the almost-full top layer, trying to decide if it would be an awfully bad idea to put a couple of the little beauties into her pocket. They might squoosh. Or melt under the heat of the studio lights. But the way she was feeling at the moment, she'd probably eat them before they could do any damage.

She pocketed a couple of foil-wrapped ones, then ate another gooey-center for good measure, before heading to the studio.

LISA GLANCED AWAY FROM the set to check audience reaction and almost wished she hadn't. Both Jake and Dan, sitting in the front row, looked as if they were interested in the show. But she doubted the sincerity of their expressions because the young man sitting on Dan's right-hand side was yawning. Thank heavens one of the technicians was already holding up the "sixty seconds" cue card.

Quickly, she scribbled a note and passed it to the floor director. Apparently, Fiona had completely forgotten the talk they'd had about lightening the mood. If Hank didn't give her a reminder during commercial, the home viewers would start switching channels in droves.

Having a sexologist as their guest practically guaranteed people would tune in. And as a bonus, Dr. Hershberg's carefully cultivated beard made him look a fair bit like Freud. That should be enough of a subliminal cue to glue viewers to their sets. But they weren't going to give the show much longer if Fiona didn't steer the conversation away from scientific generalities and on to the nitty-gritty of sex.

The technician raised a hand above the time card and dropped his fingers one by one, counting off the last five seconds to commercial.

"And we're clear," Hank muttered as the lead-in to the first ad appeared on the monitors. "I'll go straighten her out." He started across the set, the bright studio lights making his bald head shine.

Fiona patted Dr. Hershberg's knee with one perfectly manicured hand, then fluffed her long mane of red hair. Hank reached her side and started talking, but she glanced into the audience and shot a lascivious smile at Dan before turning her attention to the director.

The young man sitting beside Dan perked up noticeably. Apparently, Fiona's smile had hit a wide mark.

Lisa's glance involuntarily wandered away from the young man and back to Dan. Absently, she pulled one of the chocolates from her pocket, unwrapped it and popped it into her mouth. She was savoring the sweetness, her gaze still on Dan, when he caught her watching him and flashed his million-dollar smile.

Damn. What had she been doing? Why had she been staring at him? And why was his smile sending this peculiar rush through her? It felt akin to a surge of adrenaline. She realized her face was flushing and quickly turned away, her heart racing because she'd been caught looking.

Of course, she hadn't actually been looking at all. Her thoughts had simply been straying. She'd really just been scanning the studio, not seeing anyone in particular.

But if that were true, why was she standing here with a picture of Dan Ashly in her mind's eye? And she was visualizing him perfectly—from the way he was sitting with one lanky leg crossed over the other to the way his face was a fascinating study of angles and planes.

Why was she picturing him at all, perfectly or otherwise, when she should be paying attention to her job?

She focused on Hank for a moment. He was cuing that they were almost back. The makeup girl brushed a final touch-up of powder onto Fiona's nose, then dashed off the set.

Lisa stood watching camera one as its red light flashed on again, deciding she must be coming down with something. She seemed to be breathing faster than usual, and she was definitely having trouble concentrating.

"Welcome back," Fiona said, smiling at the audience and then at her guest. "Let's pick up on what we were talking about during the commercial, Dr. Hershberg." She paused to wink at the camera. "The good doctor was telling me that what we commonly refer to as 'chemistry' between two people actually *is* a chemical reaction. Tell us all about this chemical Cupid, Dr. Hershberg."

"Well, Fiona, it's an amphetamine that occurs naturally in our bodies."

"And does it have a name?"

"Yes. It's called phenylethylamine."

"Ooooh." Fiona wrinkled her nose. "I think I'll just keep calling it Cupid. And exactly what does it do to us?"

"Well, basically it simply lurks inside you, waiting for the right person to come along."

"The right person? As in Mr. Right?"

Lisa shot Hank a smile. Fiona had clearly listened to him. She'd done an abrupt about-face and switched to her Miss Cute and Fluffy mode.

"Mr. Right?" Hershberg said, chuckling. "Well, I guess that if you're lucky, it's Mr. Right who causes your chemical Cupid to fire his little arrows. Unfortunately, though, it's just as often Mr. Wrong. You see, phenylethylamine—or P.E., I should perhaps call it for simplicity—doesn't react to personalities. All it cares about is physical attraction."

Fiona winked at the camera again. "And exactly what happens, Dr. Hershberg, when I see a man I'm physically attracted to?"

As in, Lisa thought, nine out of every ten men she sees.

"Well, Fiona, as I said, P.E. is an amphetamine. And amphetamines release adrenaline. So basically what happens when you see someone you're extremely attracted to is that you experience an adrenaline rush."

"Ooooh... You know, I recall a sexy song with the refrain, 'What a feeling, what a rush.'"

"Precisely. Now, we experience various types of adrenaline rushes in various situations. When we're angered, for example, that surge puts us into fighting mode. But the rush that P.E. causes is all mixed up with sexual desire. That adrenaline acts as a sexual stimulant."

"My goodness, Doctor. How do we tell whether we're sexually attracted to someone or angered by them?"

Hershberg laughed. "The physical reactions your chemical Cupid causes are unmistakable. They're what we've come to think of as the symptoms of love at first sight. You look at a person and your face flushes. You notice your heart is racing. And if he does as much as smile at you, you find yourself breathing faster than normal and have difficulty concentrating. Often, you even notice your hands trembling.''

Lisa was only half concentrating. Then, suddenly, her brain jolted to attention. Why was Hershberg describing what she'd been feeling only a few minutes ago? She was coming down with something. A cold, at least. Maybe even a killer flu. But he'd just enumerated her symptoms as being . . . she struggled to recapture his words. He'd said, *"Symptoms of love at first sight."*

Her gaze flashed to Dan Ashly. He smiled at her, just like he had earlier, and all of a sudden her heart was racing and her face was flushing and...oh, no. Oh, no, no, no! Her hands were trembling.

But there was no way that what she was feeling had anything to do with love at first sight or second sight or any other sight. Absolutely no way. Just the thought of it was insane. She had no intention of even liking a man who was on a search-and-destroy mission for Quality Motors.

So, since she wasn't even going to like Dan, she couldn't possibly...

She forced her eyes away from him and back to the set. Her symptoms were symptoms of a killer flu. Yes, she was certain they were. And thank heavens. She'd rather have killer flu than a ridiculous attraction to Dan Ashly. Much rather.

And as far as love at first sight was concerned, Dr. Hershberg must be a quack if he actually believed in it. She tried to remember what his credentials were. As she recalled, they included not only an M.D. but a whole slew of postgraduate training at Harvard. Well, even Harvard probably produced its share of quacks.

"So," Fiona was saying, "what should we do to protect ourselves if we aren't in the mood for love? If we want to avoid being hit by Cupid's little arrows?"

"I'm afraid protecting yourself is virtually impossible, Fiona, because, as I said, we all have P.E. lurking in our systems, just waiting for that special person to come along and trigger its release. That's why people can't help who they fall in love with. Try as we might, we can't fight biology."

Lisa stood staring at Hershberg, wishing the set would open beneath him and swallow him whole. Every time he spoke she heard something more that she didn't want to hear. You couldn't protect yourself? Couldn't help who you fell in love with? Couldn't fight biology? She wasn't buying any of that for a minute. Maybe the doctor was a defeatist, but she certainly wasn't.

"But what can we do, then," Fiona asked, "when we realize it's a Mr. Wrong that we're attracted to?"

"Good question," Hershberg said.

Good question, Lisa silently echoed. Stealthily, with her hand inside her pocket so that the foil's crackle would be inaudible, she unwrapped the remaining chocolate, then snuck it into her mouth.

"The interesting thing about falling for a Mr. Wrong, or a Ms. Wrong as the case might be," the doctor continued, "is that it's often a person's subconscious that first recognizes a fatal attraction and tries to fight it."

"Fight it how?" Fiona prompted.

"Well, one of the most common behaviors we see is someone—more often than not a woman—going on a chocolate binge. Of course, she isn't consciously aware of any relationship between eating chocolate and trying to avoid an involvement that her head knows would be foolish. But the relationship definitely exists."

"A relationship between eating chocolate and falling in love?"

"Not exactly, Fiona. It's a relationship between craving chocolate and subconsciously trying *not* to fall in love. You see, chocolate contains P.E. So eating chocolate floods our systems with that specific amphetamine. And the flooding throws our reactions off kilter and actually works to diminish the symptoms of love at first sight."

Fiona laughed. "You mean that all the fellows who bring chocolates for their dates are doing the wrong thing?"

"Definitely. They should stick to flowers."

"Fascinating, Dr. Hershberg. Absolutely fascinating. We have to break for a moment. When we come back, I'll be taking audience questions. And while we're away, anyone who pigged out on chocolate today can think about who you might have a subconscious, fatal attraction to."

Hank leaned closer to Lisa. "Fatal attraction to," he whispered as a commercial appeared on the monitors. "Fiona's dangling her prepositions again."

Lisa nodded. But Fiona's dangling prepositions were the last thing she'd been thinking about. She'd been too busy recalling her lunch with Crystal—the lunch they'd had scarcely half an hour after Dan Ashly had first walked into the station. Two rounds of double-thick chocolate shakes, then hot fudge sundaes for dessert. And then there'd been the chocolate tonight.

What if this theory of Hershberg's was right? What if it was a scientifically proven reality? If she'd really been chocolating-out all day to avoid...

Lord, if she had, she was going to gain ninety pounds before that blasted QM study was completed. Because she didn't have to dig into her subconscious to figure out who she was at risk of having a fatal attraction to.

Oh, rats. Now *she* was dangling prepositions. Lisa took a deep breath and ordered herself to calm down. Hershberg was probably talking nonsense. And even if she actually *was* having a stupid, physiological reaction to the enemy, there was no reason to get worked up about it. Just because Dan Ashly was going to be in town for a month didn't mean she'd be seeing him.

They'd have a meeting or two before next week's segment. Then, after the show itself, he'd be gone from her life again.

A bumper appeared on the monitor, indicating that they were coming out of commercial. She'd concentrate on the show. In half an hour it would be over and the audience—including Dan Ashly—would leave.

"AND WE'RE BACK," Fiona gushed at the camera. The show was heading into its final five minutes, and she'd almost worked her way to the rear of the audience.

Lisa shuddered as Fiona shoved her mike within millimeters of a man's face. The way she flailed that thing around, it was simply a matter of time before she smacked someone in the teeth with it and Jake had a lawsuit on his hands.

"You wanted to ask Dr. Hershberg something about our chemical Cupids," she prompted.

"Yes. What happens to them after we get married? In most cases, they seem to disappear."

Several audience members laughed their agreement, and Fiona grinned back at Hershberg. "Well, Doctor?"

"I'm afraid that's often true," he said. "The P.E. has done its job by encouraging mating. But once that's happened . . . Well, in most marriages, sex eventually becomes pretty boring."

Fiona looked as if she'd just made an instant decision never to marry. "I know there's a gentleman in the back row who has a question," she said, moving up to the second-last step of the raised audience seating. She thrust her mike at the mop-haired fellow standing in front of the uppermost aisle seat.

And suddenly Lisa was paralyzed by disbelief.

Fiona's body followed through the forward motion of her arm and she stumbled up onto the final step. Her knees hit the low barrier behind the back row. A resounding crack split the air, instantly followed, as the barrier gave way, by a shocked, ear-splitting scream.

Then incredibly, as if in slow motion, Fiona toppled forward and disappeared behind the seats. Her scream ended abruptly. Simultaneously, there was a thud of flesh hitting the floor.

The audience seemed frozen in place, every head swiveled toward the back of the studio, one giant, collective breath held in horror. Only the faint whir of cameras broke the deathly still shrouding the studio.

A second passed . . . another . . . then Jake jolted to his feet. "Pan the audience," he hollered to camera one. "We're at three minutes, Saint-John! Give me audio till I cue you. Follow me," he shouted, pointing at camera two and taking off at a run.

Vaguely, Lisa heard his words and noted that Dan was on Jake's heels. Then someone thrust a mike into her hand. She stared at it uncertainly, sound and activity exploding around her. A million things were happening at once.

"Ambulance," Hank was yelling. "Someone call an ambulance. And is there a doctor in the audience?"

"I'm a doctor," Hershberg cried out. His voice rang with surprise, as if he'd just remembered the fact. He leaped up and raced after camera two.

It was rocking along at full tilt on its dolly, the cameraman following Jake and Dan up the corridor that ran beside the seating section. A technician was scurrying along after the dolly, desperately trying to keep the camera's trailing power cord from catching on anything.

"Audio, Lisa!" Hank screamed. "You're on audio!"

His shout jerked Lisa out of her fog, and she realized what the mike was doing in her hand. She glanced at a monitor. Camera one was picking up the pandemonium of audience reaction. Some people were still in their chairs, clearly stunned. Those in the back row were peering down behind their seats. Most of the others had started along the side corridor after camera two. Several women were crying.

Lisa swallowed hard, trying to relieve the tightness that was constricting her throat, and began a voice-over. "You've just witnessed a terrible accident on WALK's set of *Fiona*. Our host, Fiona Parker, lost her footing and plunged from the back of the raised audience seating. The drop is at least ten feet onto the concrete studio floor." As she said that, the full realization of what had happened hit her. A wave of nausea washed over her.

"Lead to the accident scene," Hank hissed. "Jake's going live to Fiona with camera two."

Oh, no! Lisa mouthed.

"What the hell did you think he was doing? And you've got dead air!"

She fought back her revulsion and started speaking into the mike again. "In just a moment, one of our cameras will be in place and we'll be taking you behind the seating to check on Fiona's injuries. Fortunately, as you're aware, our studio guest this evening is a medical doctor. Dr. Hershberg is now on his way to Fiona's aid."

"We're staying with it," Hank whispered, relaying a message from the rear of the studio. "Jake says we're going to keep rolling past slot."

Lisa swallowed again. "We'll be staying live with this emergency, ladies and gentlemen. Our nine-o'clock programming will be delayed until after we've been able to bring you Dr. Hershberg's report of Fiona's injuries."

"Switching to Jake...now," Hank muttered. "And you're off. Good work, Lisa."

She stared at the monitor as camera two closed in on Fiona's body. It lay, crumpled and motionless, on the studio floor. Her eyes were closed and one of her legs was bent at an unnatural angle.

Off camera, Jake began his audio coverage, but Lisa didn't listen to his words. All she could do was gaze at the image on the screen and pray that Fiona wasn't as badly injured as she appeared to be. Audience members began coming into view on the monitor, pressing closer to her.

"Get back! Everyone get back," Dan's voice ordered loudly. "Let the doctor through. And somebody open the doors. We need cooler air."

Dan appeared in one corner of the monitor, his arms stretched protectively to either side of where Fiona lay, as if he were a human police line.

Still, people beyond his reach pressed forward.

"Give me a hand," he snapped to someone off screen. "Clear a path for the doctor."

A moment later, Carl Gustavson moved into camera range and began to make shooing motions at the crowd. But the janitor's help wasn't very effective. Along with half the others in the studio, he seemed to be in shock, his normally ruddy face as pale as his mane of white hair. He looked, Lisa thought, like a ghost.

Ghost. "Oh please," she whispered, the word echoing in her mind, "please don't let Fiona be a ghost." But no, surely that fall wasn't enough to kill someone.

Hershberg burst onto the screen, panting. He knelt down beside Fiona and undid the top buttons of her dress.

Lisa turned away, her stomach churning, unable to watch any longer.

An eternity of minutes later, she heard a faint moan and looked back at the monitor. Fiona had regained consciousness. Her face was distorted with pain.

"Definitely a broken leg," Hershberg was saying. "Possibly internal injuries, but we'll have to get her to a hospital to check that. I'll go with her in the ambulance," he added, taking her hand.

As if on cue, a distant siren's wail floated in through the door that had been opened on to the street.

Jake picked up the voice-over once more, saying something about Fiona's leg being broken and an ambulance on its way.

Lisa could scarcely make out his words for the buzzing inside her head. And she really didn't want to listen to whatever gory details he was providing. She wandered across the set, slumped into Fiona's wing chair, and stared out at the audience section.

Almost all the seats were empty now. Those who weren't at the rear of the studio, watching Fiona's pain live, in person, were standing near the monitors, watching it live on air.

Lisa sat alone on the set, watching nothing.

Soon, the ambulance arrived and took Fiona away. Eventually the last of the audience members were sent out into the evening. All of them, Lisa noted absently, except for a short, silver-haired woman who was nattering to Jake.

Hank headed slowly across from the side of the studio, perspiration glistening on his bald head. His shoulders were slumped. His face was strained and gray, making him look every one of his sixty years.

He sank onto the guest couch and shrugged his shoulders at Lisa as if he couldn't believe what had happened. But then, she doubted that any of them could.

"I think Fiona's going to be okay," he offered. "By the time they left, both Hershberg and the ambulance attendants seemed to think it was just her leg, that there was nothing serious, nothing internal. But a broken leg's going to put her out of commission. So what'll we do for a host?"

Like it or not, Lisa realized, there was only one logical answer. She had a solid background in broadcast interviewing. "I guess," she told Hank, "the obvious solution would be for me to fill in on air until Fiona's back. Our only other real option is Crystal, and she's not going to want to be stuck trying to cover a second show when *Love* is in trouble."

"Fiona's not going to like being replaced, Lisa. Not even for a few weeks."

"Let's hope a few weeks is all it takes, that she really did get off with nothing more than a broken leg." Lisa caught a motion with her peripheral vision and glanced up. Dan Ashly was walking slowly down the steps of the audience seating section, his hands in the pockets of his cords, his expression deadly serious.

He reached them and stood gazing at her, his eyes troubled.

And he was troubled, she knew instinctively, about more than the accident.

"What?" she murmured.

He slowly shook his head. "I'm afraid Fiona's fall wasn't quite what it seemed. There's a trip-wire stretched across that top step."

CHAPTER THREE

JAKE HUNG UP the receiver, grinning broadly. "Fiona's going to be okay. No serious injuries except the broken leg."

Lisa closed her eyes for a moment, a flood of relief washing over her. Then she glanced, in turn, at the others. Hank's face had lost its gray, strained expression. Mrs. McMurry, the silver-haired woman from the audience, looked as if she'd just been told she'd won a lottery. And Dan...well, looking at Dan was a bad idea.

Each time she did that, she wanted to get up from the conference table, leave the room and get far away from the station. At home, in the freezer of her fridge, was a frozen chocolate layer cake with her name written all over it.

She dragged her gaze away from Dan and focused hopefully on Kurt Kusch. Now that they knew Fiona was all right, maybe he'd let them leave.

He was scratching his head thoughtfully. The gesture, she decided, glancing again at the unbelievably rumpled trench coat he'd tossed onto a spare chair, was something he'd picked up from watching *Columbo*. The Kurt Kusch she'd known in high school, Kurt Kusch, star quarterback, definitely hadn't been the thoughtful type.

Of course, she'd only known him slightly. He'd been a couple of years ahead of her. She recalled his reputation, though—all brawn and no brains. In fact, players on the rival teams had called him Mr. Moron because he had trouble remembering plays. Now he was Detective Moron.

"Well," he finally said, "that's good news. But there's no getting away from the fact that Fiona could have ended up in far worse shape. Now, where were we before that call came in?"

He sounded as if he honestly didn't remember, and Lisa rolled her eyes at Jake. How had Kusch ever made detective? Maybe because he'd done his best to turn himself into an oversize Peter Falk look-alike. Or maybe it had something to do with the push for equal rights. Yes, that was more likely the answer. The Walkerton police force must have been ordered to promote a token idiot.

And now he was in charge of this investigation. The responsibility for catching whoever had injured Fiona was in the hands of a man who shouldn't be put in charge of a bowling ball.

Mrs. McMurry cleared her throat. "You were asking me if watching that tape again helped me recall anything else."

"Right. Of course. And did it?"

"I'm afraid not. I've told you everything I can. I looked down beside my seat and there the man was, out of his chair and hunched over in the aisle. So I asked him, 'What are you doing?' And he said he was a technician, said he was running a length of wire for the sound system, that it had to be threaded across up there just before the show began.

"Then I didn't pay any more attention to him until Fiona fell. But after she did, I thought it was strange he ran off the minute people began moving around. Because everyone else in the back row was looking down behind the seats, trying to see if she was hurt."

Kurt nodded. "You've been very helpful, Mrs. McMurry. And I appreciate your staying. There's no point in keeping you here any longer, though."

She looked disappointed but collected her coat and left.

The door closed behind her and Kurt glanced around the table. "Maybe we oughta rerun that tape again."

"Detective Kusch," Jake snapped, "I've got a two-hour drive to Columbus ahead of me tonight. I don't want to be on the highway at four in the morning. And we've already run that damned tape three times."

"Yeah...well, I've never had a case before where we had such a clear picture of the per...per...."

"Perpetrator?" Lisa supplied.

"Yeah. The perpetrator." He grinned at her.

Good grief. This man's job was protecting the citizens of Walkerton. Come tomorrow, she was going to install an extra bolt on her apartment door.

"I mean," he elaborated, "the only crime-in-progress pictures we generally get are bank and convenience store videos. And their quality stinks."

"Look," Dan said, "it's clear your perpetrator was disguised. His wig was pretty obvious. And his mustache and glasses were probably fake. So watching the tape again won't help. Wouldn't it make more sense to talk to Fiona? See if she has any idea who might have been out to get her?"

Kurt gave his head another scratch. "Makes a whole lotta sense. And I'll be doing that tomorrow. But right now, she's lying in a hospital bed, pumped full of drugs. So let's start with what you people can tell me. Is there anybody you know of who particularly dislikes Fiona?"

Lisa studiously examined her hands. No one else spoke.

"So," Kurt pressed, "you can't think of anyone who hates her? Or is jealous of her because she's a star? Or has a grudge against her? Or who's had a run-in with her lately?"

Jake cleared his throat. "Detective Kusch, Fiona isn't exactly Miss Popularity around WALK. But there's certainly no one working here who'd . . ."

"Who'd try to kill her?" Kurt said.

His words hung in the air.

"Kill her?" Hank finally repeated. "You don't really think someone was trying to *kill* her . . . do you?"

Lisa glanced at the director. His expression told her he'd been assuming the same thing she had, that Fiona had been the victim of a sick, perverted, practical joke, but that whoever had strung the wire hadn't actually expected the barrier to give way.

She turned back to Kurt. He didn't look as if the possibility of Mr. Last Row being a particular joker had even entered his mind.

"A ten-foot fall?" he said. "Onto concrete? Yeah, I think someone was trying to kill her, all right. I think she was just damned lucky. And I've assigned a couple of men to her hospital ward for the night. To be on the safe side."

Lisa stared at the detective, a queasy feeling settling in her stomach and an icy, tingling sensation creeping up her spine. Was it really possible that their tape had captured a murder attempt? Could someone actually have been trying to kill Fiona? No, that couldn't be. Detective Moron was simply getting carried away.

"Let's talk a little more about the incident," he said. "You four all witnessed it. And all played parts in the aftermath."

Kurt shoved back his chair, rose and sauntered around the conference table to stand beside Lisa and directly across from Dan.

"You, Mr. Ashly. You don't work at WALK—you were only here to watch the show. So how did you end up in charge of crowd control?"

Lisa swallowed uneasily, wondering if Dan felt intimidated. She certainly did, and Kurt wasn't even paying any attention to her.

Dan merely shrugged. "I didn't stop to think about what I was doing. Jake took off for the back of the studio and I took off after him. And then I just did what made sense."

"I see." Kurt paused, referring to his notebook. "So you know Fiona. From New York."

"Yes."

"And how well do you know her?"

"Not well at all. I was seeing her roommate for a couple of months. That was about it. But I knew Fiona was dying to host a talk show and wasn't getting any breaks in New York. So I introduced her to Jake when he was in town."

Lisa stared across the table. What Dan had said earlier had been true, then. He really didn't know Fiona well. So that display this morning must have merely been a typical Fiona production number. And maybe that meant Lisa Saint-John's instincts weren't in dire need of an overhaul, after all. Maybe her initial impression of Dan had been on target. Maybe...

Oh, Lord! She was forgetting reality. Dan Ashly might not be a male bimbo but he was still a hired gun. How on earth could she have forgotten he was the enemy? Even for a second?

Just as she glanced back at Kurt he turned to her and spoke—so suddenly that she jumped.

"Anything unusual about the show tonight, Lisa?"

"No. I mean not until . . . not until the end."

"So everyone was where they usually are during a broadcast? Doing their normal jobs?"

"Ah . . . well . . ." Damn. She hadn't done anything wrong, so why was her anxiety level heading upward at breakneck speed?

"Yes?" he pressed.

"Well, generally, I'm in the control room, that long, narrow room above the back of the studio. But tonight I was working on the floor."

"Why?"

"Filling in. My assistant's on vacation."

She watched uneasily while Kurt wrote something in his book.

"And you?" he asked, glancing at Hank.

The director shook his head rapidly. "I just did what I always do."

"And you, Mr. Forrest? You come in every Friday evening to watch *Fiona,* do you?"

"Actually, no. I usually watch it at home."

"I see. But tonight you were here. Any particular reason?"

"Yes. Dan was interested in seeing it broadcast."

Kurt smiled. But it wasn't a friendly smile. "Curious, isn't it? Of the four of you, two of you aren't normally here for Fiona's shows. And another one of you was doing a different job than usual, was out front tonight, instead of in the control room.''

Lisa glanced at the others, wondering if Kurt was making them as uncomfortable as he was making her.

Jake cleared his throat. "Look, Detective, we all want to get to the bottom of what happened. But I don't like the insinuation that any of us might have had something to do with Fiona's accident.''

"It was hardly an accident, Mr. Forrest. It was a trip wire.''

"Yes. Yes, of course. I simply meant that none of us was involved in what happened. You've got the action on film, got the tape of that man.''

"I doubt he was working alone.''

"What?'' The word slipped out before Lisa even realized she'd opened her mouth, and that icy, tingling sensation started up her spine again.

"I said, I doubt he was working alone,'' Kurt repeated. "I doubt that would even have been possible unless he was on staff here. Which isn't likely. There'd be too much chance that one of you would have recognized him, even with a disguise. I'd say that whoever we've got on tape was simply doing the dirty work for someone who *is* on WALK's staff.''

"That's preposterous,'' Jake snapped.

"Is it? Mr. Forrest, you said earlier that you normally keep your studios locked.''

"We do.''

"And that only station staff have access to them unless they're being used.''

"Of course, but—''

"Mr. Forrest...about the barrier that gave way when Fiona stumbled...''

"Yes?''

"Well, sometime earlier today, someone who had access to the studio sawed almost entirely through that board. Then they filled the cut with plastic wood and touched up the paint. The area around the break was still tacky when my men checked."

Lisa's breath caught in her throat. Kurt wasn't as much of an idiot as she'd been giving him credit for. Someone really *had* tried to murder Fiona.

"So I'd say," he continued, "the logical conclusion is that someone at WALK had a lot to do with what happened tonight."

Lisa tried to speak but her voice wouldn't work. "And you think it was one of us?" she finally managed to say.

He shrugged. "Not necessarily."

Not necessarily? Not necessarily was a far cry from *no*. It was closer to *maybe*. Or possibly even to *yes*. But the idea was ridiculous. Wasn't it? Of course it was. Except that, until a minute ago, she'd thought the idea of a murder attempt was ridiculous.

"Now, let's follow through on that conclusion," Kurt continued. "Would anyone at WALK benefit from something happening to Fiona?"

"Absolutely not," Jake said. "She's our top talent. And the show's ratings are going to plummet while she's away."

"Yeah? You think so?"

"Of course."

"You don't think this little incident might just give your ratings a boost? Might make people watch your channel for the next few weeks in case anything as exciting as this happens again? On *any* of the local shows?"

Jake's face went pale. "That doesn't even deserve a comment."

Darn right it doesn't, Lisa silently agreed. High ratings might be Jake's favorite thing in the world, but surely no one, and certainly not Jake, would do such a despicable thing simply for ratings.

Of course, Kurt was bang-on about what would happen to them. After tonight, WALK's audience share was bound to soar. She glanced at the detective again, wondering if he could have been taking smart pills since high school. So much for him being Detective Moron.

But just because he was right about the ratings didn't mean he should be eyeing Jake as if he expected to see a smoking gun—or a smoking trip wire, as the case might be—in his hand.

"What," Kurt asked no one in particular, "will you do about Fiona's show until she's back?"

"Lisa will host it," Hank blurted out.

Kurt gazed at him curiously.

"I asked the same question earlier," he babbled on, his words tumbling out, revealing how upset he was. "And Lisa said she'd be the obvious one to do it."

"Oh?" Kurt's expression grew twice as curious. "Exactly when did you ask?"

"Right after the...right after it happened. Lisa was sitting on the set, in Fiona's chair. And I went over and started talking about the show and she said that she was the obvious one to take over."

"That's how we'll be playing it," Jake agreed. "Lisa's had on-camera experience."

She barely registered Jake's words. Hank's were still too horridly vivid in her mind. He couldn't have realized how what he'd said had sounded. But she certainly had. And if she had, then Kurt had as well.

Lord! She could practically read his thoughts. He was imagining her sitting on the set, in Fiona's chair. Before it had even grown cold. And he was wondering whether she'd rather host the show than produce it. He was wondering whether she might want that badly enough to plan a murder.

Fearfully, she snuck a peek at him. What she saw did nothing to alleviate her fear. Far from it. The way he was looking at her left no doubt that she'd just replaced Jake as number one suspect.

LESS THAN TWO MINUTES away from WALK, Lisa began shivering. The warm September day had turned into a cold September night, and she'd raced out of her apartment this morning without a jacket. She hadn't expected still to be at the station at midnight.

She hesitated, glancing back, trying to decide whether she should retrace her steps and call a cab.

No. She was so relieved Kurt had finally let them leave that she'd rather turn into an icicle than go back. Besides, she was incredibly wound up, and the walk home might help wind her down.

She started off again, striding rapidly through the darkness, feeling more uneasy with each step. But that was just plain silly. This was a safe town, and she wasn't normally nervous. Tonight there was even a full harvest moon, hanging in the sky like a huge yellow balloon, lighting her way.

But didn't full moons bring out werewolves? What if there was one on the loose in Walkerton? Maybe there was, and he was to blame for what had happened tonight. Maybe he'd sneaked into the studio and sawed through that barrier. Maybe the disguised man in the audience had actually been a disguised were-wolf.

"Oh, Saint-John," she murmured, "get hold of yourself."

She walked on, trying to force away the image of Fiona falling, trying to forget about Kurt Kusch. She couldn't manage to do either. Fiona had almost been killed. By whom? Someone, Kurt said, who worked at WALK. But who?

Not Jake, nor Hank. That was for sure. When there'd been mice in the station, neither of them would even set a trap. And certainly not her, despite Kurt's suspicions.

How could that man possibly believe she was capable of murder? Ludicrous as it was, he did. Not that he'd come right out and said so, but his thoughts had been written all over his face.

She resisted the urge to scream at the insanity of her situation. And it was only going to get worse. If he already suspected she was guilty, he was going to be downright positive when he learned that, way back when, she and Jake had discussed the possibility of *her* hosting the Friday evening show.

That had been practically a year ago, of course. Back in the planning stages. And she'd had mixed feelings about returning to the other side of the camera. So she hadn't really minded when Jake had hired Fiona. At least, she hadn't minded him hiring someone else as host. She'd just minded that the woman had turned out to be such a . . .

She pushed the remainder of the sentence from her mind. Fiona was lying in a hospital bed. She deserved compassion, not insults.

Lisa turned her thoughts back to Kurt. When he learned that she'd been considered for that job he'd assume . . . well, maybe he wouldn't find out.

Ha! snorted an imaginary little voice. Just because Jake hadn't volunteered the information tonight, that didn't mean somebody wouldn't mention it. Several people at the station probably knew about it. Hell, Fiona herself undoubtedly did. And she'd be only too happy to fill Kurt in. And dammit, there was no doubt what he'd conclude.

Wow, Jake was going to be up to his eyeballs in silver linings. Behind the dark cloud of having temporarily lost his top talent, his ratings were going to shoot up because of the way he'd lost her. And in a few days, they'd shoot up even further—when the news broke that his entertainment producer had been thrown into jail on attempted murder charges.

But she was going to look so dreadfully fat in prison stripes! And jail cells were so awful. And Ohio was a death-penalty state. Did people get sentenced to death for *attempted* murder?

Oh, why was she even thinking about that? She was getting absurdly carried away. She'd had nothing to do with Fiona's fall. And innocent people didn't get arrested. Well, not very often. And surely Kurt would discover who actually tried to kill Fiona. She just hoped he managed it quickly. Very quickly.

In the meantime, when she got home she'd have a hot shower and a cold Scotch. Hopefully, the combination would make her feel better. She was trying to decide which order to have them in when she heard a car. An instant later its headlights captured her from behind. And then it slowed.

Without looking back, she quickened her pace. The way this night had been going, abduction, rape and murder would provide the perfect finish.

The car pulled abreast of her, barely moving now. She glanced at it out of the corner of her eye. A dark Dueler with tinted windows. She didn't recognize it. Her heart began racing and she started walking even faster.

"Lisa?" a male voice called.

She whirled toward the car and almost sagged with relief. Dan Ashly was smiling at her through the open driver's window.

"Sorry," he said, "I didn't mean to startle you."

Startle? Well, she'd already pegged Mr. Ashly as a man of extreme understatement. "I . . . I wasn't really startled. I just didn't know the car."

He laughed. "I assumed you'd think I was any one of ten people you know. From what I saw today, every second person in town drives a Dueler."

"Just about. That's what we make here." Which wasn't exactly a news flash for the auto-industry analyst. Dan probably already knew more details about what went on at Plant W than she did.

"This is the first one I've driven," he offered. "There's not much call for all-terrain vehicles in Manhattan."

"Like it?"

"Yeah. So far it's handled impressively."

"Good." Well, telling her father that might make him feel marginally better. At least the hired gun wasn't proclaiming that Plant W's products were tin trash.

"I'm glad I caught up with you. I didn't realize you walked home until Hank mentioned it. And by then, you'd left. I didn't like the idea of you walking alone this late."

Lisa shrugged. Now that her heart had stopped pounding, the night no longer seemed half as menacing. "This is Walkerton, Dan, not New York."

"Well, I just figured after that guy being at the show tonight...well, I'm not entirely sure I buy Kusch's theory that he was part of a conspiracy to murder Fiona. He could simply be a crazy. And if there's a loose cannon roaming around town you shouldn't be on your own."

At Dan's words, the night seemed more threatening again.

"I...I was thinking he might be a werewolf," she admitted. "You know, with the full moon and all."

Dan grinned at her. "Whatever he is, I'd feel better giving you a lift home."

A lift home. In that nice, safe car. She was awfully tempted. Surely accepting a ride home wouldn't qualify as fraternizing with the enemy.

"Come on," he pressed. "I'll take you for coffee, then home."

Coffee. No, coffee was getting too close to fraternization for comfort.

"Lisa, you're shivering. Get in," he added, shoving the passenger door open from inside.

The overhead light flicked on. The red interior looked warm and inviting. And so did Dan Ashly. Dangerously warm and inviting.

She hesitated for another second, imagining what her father would think if anyone saw her in the enemy's car. Of course there *were* those tinted windows. And besides, almost nobody knew who Dan was yet. "Well, a ride would be great, thanks. But it's a little late for a caffeine jolt.''

"Fine. Just a ride home, then."

Dan shot her a devastating smile that started her feet moving toward the car. Thank heavens he'd suggested taking her for coffee rather than hot chocolate. She doubted she'd have been able to resist chocolate.

"IT'S THE NEXT STREET," Lisa said. "Misty Drive."

Dan slowed for the turn and glanced at her once more. Her hands remained clenched in her lap. It had been one heck of a night, and he'd probably just added the icing to the cake by suggesting there might be a lunatic wandering around town. But hell, there very well could be. New York hadn't cornered the entire market on weirdos. So her walking alone in the middle of the night . . . well, he was just relieved he'd caught up with her.

She looked across at him and almost smiled. She had, without the tiniest doubt, the most kissable-looking lips in the world. And her perfume . . . the moment she'd closed the car door, that perfume had begun working magic on him. He certainly hoped she was planning to invite him in.

"You really figure the guy's a crazy?" she asked, picking up the conversation where they'd left off. "That choosing Fiona as his target was just a random decision?"

"Well, the more I think about Kusch's murder theory, the less sense it makes. I mean, if someone actually wanted to kill Fiona, why do it that way? A professional hit man would break into her apartment or get her alone in a dark alley. And surely even an amateur—a sane one, at least—would recognize it was ridiculous to try killing someone while the television cameras were rolling."

"It definitely increased his odds on being caught, didn't it."

"Hell, he was damned lucky not to be. Instead of Mrs. McMurry, he could easily have wound up with someone sitting across the aisle who realized his story that he was laying a wire for the sound system made no sense. But what about Kusch figuring someone at WALK was behind things? What do you think about that, Lisa?"

"I guess it's possible. I don't know who it could have been—certainly not Jake or Hank or me—but I guess someone could have been involved. Otherwise, how did the guy get into the studio? To rig that barrier, I mean."

"I don't know. I just know that the idea of a murder attempt doesn't ring true to me."

She nodded slowly, then glanced out the window. "It's that one with the porch." She pointed ahead to a rambling old two-story on an enormous riverbank lot. No lights were on, but moonlight bathed the house in silver.

"Nice place," he said, pulling to a halt. "Living in Manhattan, you forget that some people actually own houses."

She smiled fully this time. It started a warm sensation tickling his groin.

"I wish I did own it, Dan. But I'm only a tenant. The owners live downstairs, and I have the second-floor apartment."

"It still must be nice. Backing onto the river, like that. How did you luck out and find it?"

"Jake knows the Cramstons, the couple who own it. And the apartment became vacant when I was looking for one. And . . . well, you're right. It was pure luck." She pushed the door lever down.

"You must get a terrific breeze off the water," he said quickly. "Must be great on hot summer days."

"Yes. I have a deck. Just a big balcony really, overlooking the river. It's a relaxing place in the summer. And the view's lovely all year round."

He concentrated on thinking about how much he'd like to see that view, hoping Lisa had ESP.

"But there's nothing to see at night, of course," she added.

"No. Of course not." There probably was, though. In fact, tonight, with the starry sky and that moon, her view was undoubtedly gorgeous. Not to mention romantic as hell. Moonlight on the Misty. It even sounded romantic.

He smiled to himself, wondering where the thought of romance had come from. Probably, it was a reaction to getting out of the Big Apple. There, millions of power-hungry, hard-nosed money worshipers had trampled romance out of existence decades ago.

Or maybe being back in Walkerton, after all these years, had triggered something. Maybe he'd regressed, emotionally, to his late teens or early twenties.

But whatever was going on in his subconscious, the moment he'd gazed into Lisa Saint-John's beautiful gray eyes this morning he'd begun thinking about things he hadn't thought of in years. About walking hand in hand through fall leaves, going nowhere. About sipping wine in front of a crackling fire, with a woman who had a soft, gentle voice. About simply relaxing with a woman like this one. No, not *like* this one. He'd been thinking very specifically about this particular woman.

She'd been on his mind all day. Hell, he'd even fed Jake that malarkey about wanting to see *Fiona* being broadcast, had been willing to sit through the stupid show, just so he'd have another chance to see Lisa.

She opened her door. "Well, thanks for the ride, Dan. I'll call you early next week to set up a preinterview for the segment. Which hotel are you at?"

"The Pritchard House. I . . . your place is dark. I'll walk you to the door."

She hesitated. But only for a moment. "Well, if you wouldn't mind. The Cramstons usually leave the porch light on, but they're in Florida for a couple of weeks. And my entrance is at the back."

They got out of the Dueler and started up the walk, Dan racking his brain for a line that would get him invited in. But the only ones that came to mind were transparently obvious.

They reached the back door in silence.

"Well, thanks again for the ride." Lisa opened her purse and pulled out her keys.

"You're not nervous about going in alone, are you?" he finally tried. "After all the excitement tonight? And with the Cramstons not home?"

"No. I'll be all right, thanks. I have a guard cat."

"A guard cat? Somehow I can't imagine that's as reassuring as having a guard dog."

She laughed her quiet, gentle laugh. "Not quite. In fact, Tiger hides under the bed whenever anyone except me is in the apartment."

"Ah. So he only qualifies as a guard because you know you'd better check the closets if he's not in sight."

"Something like that."

She laughed again, and Dan stuck his hands into his pockets to keep from touching her. He stood gazing down at her for a moment. The moonlight was coloring her honey hair a paler shade of gold, was making her look positively ethereal.

"Well, good night, Dan." She turned halfway to the door, then suddenly froze and stood staring past him.

He whirled around and gazed into the darkness of the yard, searching for whatever she saw, seeing nothing.

"What?" he whispered, glancing back.

Her eyes had grown frightened. "A man," she murmured.

He scanned the yard again and saw it—the almost invisible figure of a man, standing motionless against the trunk of a huge tree.

Standing motionless... and then he started forward.

CHAPTER FOUR

INSTINCTIVELY, Dan stepped in front of Lisa, his body tensing.

The other man paused, his shape still almost indistinguishable in the tree's black shadow.

A cricket chirped. The man started forward once more, moving into the moonlight.

He was about Dan's height, at least six feet, but younger, in his mid-twenties. Despite the cold, he was wearing only a short-sleeved T-shirt with his jeans. A T-shirt that revealed he was probably into weights. A whole lot of weights. And his shaggy dark hair... God, maybe Mr. Last Row hadn't been wearing a wig after all.

Dan wiped his palms against his thighs and adjusted his stance. "Lisa, get in the house," he ordered out of the side of his mouth.

He heard the noiseless noise of damp grass beneath her feet. Then she stopped, exhaling audibly.

"It's all right, Dan," she murmured, stepping forward and resting her hand lightly on his arm.

"Roy," she called. "Roy, you scared the devil out of me. What on earth are you doing here at this time of night?"

The young man's face broke into a crooked grin. "Just waitin' for you, Sis. Gotta talk ta you."

"Oh, Lord," Lisa muttered quietly, "he's drunk. My little brother," she added, "has taken to spending Friday nights at the local tavern. And my mother's been threatening to bolt the door on him if he comes home in this shape again. Maybe tonight she did."

Roy continued weaving his way across the yard toward them. Not at all steadily, Dan realized once his heart had stopped racing.

"You didn't drive here, did you?" Lisa demanded.

Roy stood in front of them, swaying slightly and looking as if he wasn't sure. "Yeah," he finally admitted. "Didn't you see my Dueler on the street?"

Without waiting for an answer, he glanced at Lisa's hand, still on Dan's arm, then at Dan's face, then back at his sister. "Who's he?"

Lisa removed her hand. "A friend. What do you want, Roy?"

"I gotta talk ta you. About..." he paused, glancing uncertainly at Dan, then cupped a hand to his mouth and carefully leaned closer to Lisa. "Gotta talk ta you about the secret," he whispered loudly.

"Oh, geez," she murmured, grabbing his arm. "Come on. Let's get you inside before you freeze to death."

Dan grinned. From the looks of things, Roy had enough alcohol in his system to prevent freezing at forty below.

Lisa jerked him toward the door, so hard he stumbled.

"Here," Dan offered, taking Roy's other arm, "I'll help you get him up the stairs."

"No! I mean, no, that's all right. I don't want to keep you any longer, Dan."

"It's okay. I'll hold him while you unlock the door."

Lisa hesitated, then released her brother and began fumbling with the key.

"I'm in no hurry," Dan added. "I've got nowhere to go but back to the hotel."

"Hotel?" Roy repeated, focusing on Dan's face. "Who are you?"

"Dan Ashly's the name."

Roy gazed blankly at him for a moment, as if he'd just said he was the man in the moon, then looked back at Lisa. "This is the guy?" he asked, his voice ringing with disbelief.

"No. It isn't. Let's go, Roy. Dan, I can manage. Really. I've got the door unlocked and—"

"This is the guy!" Roy exclaimed. "You're him!" he added, shaking his arm free from Dan's grasp and lurching back a couple of steps. "Why, I oughta... what're you doing with my sister?"

Dan glanced curiously at Lisa. She looked as if she'd just been caught with her hand in the cash box. "Lisa, what's your brother talking about? What guy does he think I am?"

"I'll tell you who you are, you dirty, rotten bastard. You're—"

"Roy," Lisa snapped. "That's enough."

"Enough? I'm gonna show you enough!" Roy lunged at Dan, crashing against his shoulder and knocking him half off balance, then falling onto the lawn. He simply sat there, clearly dazed. "Dad is gonna kill you, Lisa," he finally muttered. "How could you go out with—"

"Roy! Shut up."

"Go out with QM's hired gun?"

Dan cleared his throat uneasily. Apparently, news of his trip had leaked out. He glanced at Lisa. She shot him what he assumed was supposed to be a smile, then began staring at her shoes.

What the hell was going on here? Only hours ago, just before the show, Jake had assured him that Quality had actually managed to keep their little secret quiet, that nobody was going to learn about the study until Monday morning. Well, obviously Jake's sources weren't as good as he'd claimed. Because someone had spilled the beans. And undoubtedly, QM's outside analyst had just had his first confrontation with an upset Plant W worker.

"Ahh . . . you work for QM, Roy?"

"Whadda you think?"

"Roy," Lisa said, "for Pete's sake, get up off the ground and come inside. You can sleep on my couch."

"I don't wanna sleep on your couch. I just came to ask if you'd heard anything more. If you had any more to tell us about the study."

Dan glanced from Roy to Lisa, feeling his unease turning to anger, aware his blood pressure was rising. If she had any more to tell? Dammit to hell! He was standing here with the bean spiller herself.

So much for Jake's assurance that she could be trusted. And so much for her saying she wouldn't let the cat out of the bag. She'd told her damned brother, and her damned brother had probably told everyone in the tavern who'd cared to listen. And if he had, the level of hostility at Plant W would be sky-high before Ken Woody even made his blasted announcement.

Hell, the minute the autoworkers heard there was going to be a study they'd jump to the worst conclusion they could think of. And if they had the entire weekend to let their paranoia run riot, he could be facing a lynch mob by Monday morning. He glared at

Lisa, willing her to look up. She didn't. "You told your brother," he finally said to her bowed head.

"Nope," Roy corrected him from his seat on the grass. "She told Dad. And Dad told me."

Dan turned his glare to Roy. "Your dad tell anyone else?"

"Whadda you think? You expect the president of the union local ta sit on a ticking time bomb?"

President of the union local? Oh, terrific. Just terrific. Good old Jake had forgotten to mention that minor fact. But it made his confiding in Lisa even stupider. Every autoworker in town was going to know about the study before it was officially announced. He'd kill Jake for this. That's what he'd do. Hell, he'd do it tonight if Jake wasn't halfway to Columbus.

Dan forced himself to count to ten. "So...Lisa," he said as nonchalantly as he could, "your father's president of the union local."

"And I'm a steward," Roy announced.

Dan glanced at him, barely surprised by the news. At this point, he wouldn't be particularly shocked to learn that the entire assembly line was manned by Lisa's relatives.

He focused on her once more. "So your father's president and your brother's a steward and you're...what, Lisa? Honorary union informer?"

She finally looked up, then gave him a guilty shrug. "Sorry, Dan. I just...I just couldn't let Dad be surprised."

"You couldn't let Dad be surprised? Well, that's great. That's damned great. So rather than let Dad be surprised, you've laid the groundwork for a major misunderstanding. What the hell were you thinking of? Don't you know what you've done? Look how upset your brother is. And every other QM employee is going to be in the same shape by Monday."

"Whadda you expect?" Roy muttered. "We're gonna lose our bloody jobs."

"You're not! I'm only here to analyze things, not to get anyone thrown out into the street."

"Ha," Roy snarled. "I'll bet."

"You see?" Dan growled at Lisa. "You see what you've done? If you'd allowed Woody the chance to give out the news himself, maybe he'd have explained things without getting people worried. But now they're going to show up at the plant on Monday morning with fire in their guts and a hundred misconceptions in their heads. They'll be in no shape to listen to a single word of rational explanation. Hell, I come here to do an honest job, and you've just made it about a million times harder than it needed to be."

Lisa stared at Dan blackly for a long moment, her hands on her hips. When she finally spoke, he couldn't believe his ears.

"Don't stand there blaming me, Mr. Ashly," she snapped. "Whatever happens will be your own damned fault."

"What?"

"I said, it'll be your own damned fault. If you didn't want anyone to know about the study, you shouldn't have told anyone about it, should you?"

"What? *You* were the one who told your father. So how the hell is anything going to be my fault? What kind of crazy non-logic is that?"

"It's perfectly logical logic. If you hadn't told Jake why you were here, he wouldn't have told me and I wouldn't have told my father."

Dan started to reply, realized he was merely sputtering and stopped. This absurd woman had set him up for a barrel of grief and now was telling him it was his own fault? He'd have to be as nutty as she obviously was to buy that line of garbage.

He stood scowling at her, trying to remember what he could possibly have seen in her. Whatever it had been must have resulted from temporary insanity on his part. Because Lisa Saint-John was the least appealing, most infuriating woman he'd ever met.

He turned on his heel and stomped off along the side of the house, leaving her glowering at him and her brother unsuccessfully trying to get to his feet. To hell with both of them. He'd seen her home safely and that was the last thing he intended to do for her. Ever. And if Roy couldn't walk up the stairs without two people supporting him, he could damn well crawl.

LISA PAUSED halfway down the corridor to Fiona's room and stood gazing at a bulletin board. Not that she had the slightest interest in the collection of official notices and thank-you notes from patients, but she needed a minute to gear up for this visit.

She took a deep breath, only to be rewarded by air stinging the linings of her nose and throat. Over the years, antiseptic fumes must have permeated every crack and crevice of the old hospital.

The smell and irritating sensation made her wish even more that she was still in her apartment. Her blasted brother was liable to make good his escape while she was out—before she had a chance to rake him over the coals for his performance last night.

He'd still been on her couch when she'd left, still sleeping off the effects of the beer. But she wanted to be there when he woke up because he deserved to have at least nineteen strips torn off him.

How could her own brother have blown the whistle on her? How could he have stood there—or sat on the ground, actually—and told Dan what she'd done?

Roy's damned indiscretion was bound to cost her her job. She might even be out of work by tomorrow night. Well, no, not likely that soon. Jake had mentioned he'd be late getting back from Columbus.

But odds were a million to one that, first thing Monday morning, Dan would be on the phone telling Jake she'd let the secret out. And odds were two million to one that Jake would fire her because she had. And, focusing on an even more immediate issue, odds were three million to one that she wasn't going to get in and out of Fiona's room this morning without having to discuss what would be happening with the show.

So what should she say? That they'd decided she'd be filling in as host or that, long before next Friday's segment, she and WALK would undoubtedly have parted company?

Well, no, she could hardly say that. Not when there was an infinitesimal chance Jake would be understanding. The last thing she wanted to do, though, was admit she was slated as substitute host. But maybe she'd be able to simply avoid the subject. And avoid Fiona's wrath.

Sure you will, muttered a sarcastic little voice inside her head.

Much as she wanted to get back onto an elevator and flee, she gritted her teeth and started along the corridor again. Someone from the station had to show concern for Fiona. And for the time being, at least, she was still someone from the station.

The door of room 743 was open. Lisa walked through the doorway, then froze, her spirits slipping impossibly lower. Not one, but two people glanced up at her—Fiona Parker and Dan Ashly. Neither of them smiled.

And Fiona... Fiona wasn't merely sporting the leg cast Lisa had expected to see. Fiona was in traction. She was lying in the bed, bandages wrapped around her head and one wrist, with her right leg strung up at a forty-degree angle.

Lisa stared at the plaster-encased leg, unable to drag her eyes away from it. Finally, she swallowed hard and managed a "Good morning."

Fiona mumbled a response but Dan said nothing. Lisa's gaze slipped to him for an instant, and she fleetingly wondered why he was here.

He was sitting in an armchair beside the bed, looking cool, calm and collected while she was anything but. Merely seeing him made her feel guilty all over again.

You did the only thing you could have, she silently told herself. Her father had a right to know what QM was up to. And Dan Ashly's opinion of what she'd done didn't matter the slightest bit. He was the enemy. Doubly so, now that she was going to lose her job because of him.

She looked back at Fiona. Her body seemed to be entirely covered by either the sheet, bandaging or bruises.

"Ahh...how are you feeling, Fiona?" The moment the words left her mouth, she realized how inane the question sounded.

Fiona's expression confirmed that the question was indeed as stupid as they came. "I ache all over," she snapped. "My entire body is black and blue, my leg is broken in two places, my wrist is severely sprained, I'm absolutely racked with pain, and I can scarcely lift a finger. But I'll live. At least, that's what they tell me."

"Right. We were all awfully relieved to hear that last night. We were really worried about you."

"Where's Jake?" Fiona demanded. "Why isn't he with you?"

"He . . . he's gone to Columbus for the weekend. He had a conference to attend, remember?"

"He still went? After what happened?"

"Ahh . . . well, we'd heard before he left that you'd be okay. And I guess he knew he couldn't be any help. But I'm sure he'll be in to visit on Monday. And he asked me to send you flowers today. From him personally, I mean."

"He did?"

"Yes."

Fiona smiled slightly, reaffirming Lisa's belief in the value of little white lies.

"I guess I'll get going, Fiona," Dan said. "Now that you've got other company."

"Oh, no, Dan. Don't leave. Lisa won't be staying long."

He hesitated, half in and half out of the chair.

Lisa briefly eyed him again, trying to decide if she'd rather he stay or leave. Stay, she decided. As much as she wished he'd disappear from the face of the earth, if he stayed, Fiona was less likely to explode when they got around to talking about her show. "Fiona's right, Dan. I won't be here long. I just dropped by for a minute to—"

"To tell me what you're thinking of doing about my broadcasts?" Fiona asked.

"Ahh . . . not really." Damn. She hadn't thought Fiona would press the issue immediately. And she wasn't quite ready to address it. She glanced at Dan as he sank back into his chair, hoping he'd say something to change the subject. He gave her a knowing look, telling her he recalled precisely what had been said about her being the one to fill in, then pointedly looked away from her.

Well, she should have known that hoping for any help from him was futile. She turned her attention to Fiona once more. "I just wanted to see how you were," she tried lamely.

"Okay, now that you've seen, let's get to the important topic. What's going to happen with *Fiona* while I'm laid up? Jake thinks Crystal should take over, doesn't he?"

"Ahh—"

"That's a really bad idea, Lisa. *Really* bad. And I want you to tell him so the instant you see him. I don't want Crystal within fifty feet of either my set or my guests. She's completely screwed up *Love in the Afternoon,* and I won't have her running my ratings into the ground."

"Ahh . . . well . . . I don't think Jake's intending to have Crystal take over. In fact, I know he isn't."

Fiona looked distinctly relieved. "Oh. So the plans are still up in the air, huh? I guess I should have realized that. I don't know what got me thinking I was replaceable. Must have been all the drugs they gave me last night. Well, listen, things aren't as bad as they seem because I've come up with a terrific solution. We'll do the next couple of weeks from here. Until I can get around with a walking cast, I mean."

"Pardon?"

"We'll do the next couple of weeks from here," Fiona repeated impatiently. "From this room. You know, in the best tradition of the show must go on? These damned breaks in my leg aren't clean so I'm going to be in traction for at least the next two shows. Now, I realize I won't look great. In fact, I think you'd better get me an extra makeup girl to help out. And I'll need a good hairdresser brought in, of course. But just imagine my ratings when we run promos about the victim of a murder attempt carrying on from her hospital bed. Between that and Dan guesting to talk about his study, we'll have a ninety share next Friday."

Lisa tried to look as if she thought Fiona was talking lucidly. But aside from the fact that coverage of even a nude beauty pageant wouldn't draw a ninety, the idea of trying to broadcast from a hospital room was crazy.

"Don't you think it's a fantastic plan?" Fiona pressed.

"Well…it's certainly something to consider. I'm just not sure the hospital administration would go for it. I mean, we'd be disturbing a lot of awfully sick people. And even if we could get around that somehow, there'd be so many technical difficulties that—"

"Technical difficulties? Lisa, you're worried about having to deal with a few minor production problems when we can have the ratings of the century? Look, if I'm prepared to broadcast from this bed of pain, the least you can do is not worry about having to overcome a few technical difficulties. Just think of the pathos. Me lying in the hospital, practically at death's door but still carrying on. Jake will love the idea."

Yes. As a matter of fact, Jake just might. *Ratings are ratings,* he always said. Hell, maybe being fired wasn't the worst thing that could happen, after all.

"So, Lisa? Why don't you start the ball rolling this morning? You could go talk to the hospital administrator while you're here."

"Fiona, I don't think hospital administrators are generally in on weekends."

"Well, you'd better call him at home, then. You're going to have to get this okayed so we can move on it. I mean, if Jake doesn't want Crystal taking over—and he's perfectly right not to—but if he doesn't want to go with her and I don't do the show, who will?"

Dan grinned evilly at Lisa, so evilly that she almost squirmed. He was obviously enjoying the prospect of her having to answer Fiona's question. He knew darned well that Fiona would want to rip her substitute's throat out.

Of course, as long as she stayed a couple of feet away from the bed, Fiona wouldn't be able to reach far enough to do any throat ripping. But she certainly wasn't going to take the news lying down.

Ahh...bad choice of words. She certainly wasn't going to take the news gracefully, though.

"Who *will* do Fiona's show if she doesn't, Lisa?" Dan pressed, sounding as if he didn't have the slightest idea who the replacement might be.

She glared at him. He was positively relishing this. Dan Ashly was, without doubt, the most vile man she'd ever met.

"So the gang's all here," a male voice said from behind Lisa. "I didn't expect to find a full house this early."

She whirled around and saw that the voice belonged to Detective Kurt Kusch—and that he was looking at her with the same suspicious expression he'd been wearing last night.

Well, possibly Dan Ashly was the second most vile man she'd ever met. At least Dan didn't suspect her of attempted murder.

"AND THAT'S EVERYTHING I remember," Fiona concluded.

Kurt, who'd commandeered the bedside chair to conduct his interview, glanced across the room at Dan. He continued to stand gazing steadily out of the window, apparently oblivious to the proceedings.

Fleetingly, Lisa wondered if he had any more idea than she did about why the detective had insisted they stay. Then Kurt shifted in his chair and looked at her, as if he expected she'd have something to offer from her seat in the corner.

Or maybe something to admit, she thought uneasily. Sometime during her long, sleepless night, she'd decided that she'd been imagining he was suspicious of her. Well, maybe not exactly imagining, but at least vastly exaggerating. Now, though, her intuition was telling her she hadn't been.

The detective frowned, then turned his attention back to Fiona. "And the fellow in the back row didn't look the least familiar?"

"No. And Kurt, I just can't imagine why anyone would possibly want to kill me."

Exactly when, Lisa tried to recall, had Fiona switched from "Detective Kusch" to "Kurt"? Probably about the same time she'd begun patting his arm possessively as she spoke. Lucky for her it was her left wrist she'd sprained in the fall, not her right. Apparently, even being in traction wasn't enough to completely cramp the famous Fiona style.

"Well, let's just consider possible motives for a minute, Fiona," Kurt suggested. "Is there anyone at the station who doesn't like you?"

"Oh, no. I don't think so."

Lord! She was actually batting her lashes at him. The woman was too much.

"Well," he tried, "what about someone benefiting from your not being able to host your show? Is there anyone waiting in the wings, eager to take your place? Eager enough to arrange for your little accident?"

Lisa swallowed uneasily, only too aware of where Kurt was heading. But wasn't there some law against leading the witness? Or did that only apply to the courtroom scene?

"I guess that could be it," Fiona murmured. "Much as I hate to think it of her she just might . . . I mean she certainly had a motive . . . I know she once wanted my job."

Oh, geez. Just as Lisa had feared, the long-ago possibility that she'd be the show's host had come back to haunt her. Fiona was about to add fuel to Kurt's fire. And once he figured he had a solid motive, Lisa Saint-John would be learning how bad prison food was.

"She?" Kurt pressed, leaning forward in his chair.

"Crystal Stafford, of course."

Fiona's words took a moment to sink in. "Crystal?" Lisa echoed incredulously, once they had. "Crystal? You don't honestly think Crystal ever wanted your job, do you?"

Fiona gave Lisa a withering look. "Of course she did. Why would she have settled for hosting a silly old afternoon program if she could have gotten prime time?''

"Fiona, Crystal was never interested in the Friday night slot. I was there when that show was being planned, and she didn't express the slightest desire to host it.''

"That just proves you don't know everything, Lisa. Because Jake once told me that he'd talked to someone already working at WALK about taking on the show. Before he hired me, I mean. And obviously, the only person it could have been was Crystal.''

Lisa stared at Fiona. She didn't know the truth. Jake had never told her precisely whom he'd considered. He'd said *someone,* and Fiona had assumed the someone was Crystal.

"And now,'' Fiona continued, focusing on Kurt once more, "Crystal would have a very pressing reason to want me gone. She's about to lose her show, *Love in the Afternoon.* Its ratings are in the cellar, and she's only hanging on by her fingernails. So if she could steal *Fiona,* I'm sure she would. Any way possible.''

Kurt was writing rapidly in his notebook. "So you think this Crystal might actually have rigged the barrier?''

"Well, she had access to the studio. And just on Thursday afternoon, Jake told her he'd likely be canceling her show. It certainly adds up, doesn't it?''

"No, it doesn't,'' Lisa snapped. "You're being ridiculous, Fiona. Crystal wouldn't thank you for a shot at your spot. And she wasn't the person Jake initially considered having host it. I was.''

"You?'' Fiona asked, her expression saying she didn't believe Lisa could host her way through a commercial break.

"So," Kurt said, stretching the word into three syllables, "way back when, Lisa, you wanted to host that show. Then, after Fiona was injured, you immediately volunteered to take over."

"She did what?" Fiona demanded.

"Volunteered to take over," Kurt repeated. "Didn't she tell you? They decided last night that she'd be replacing you."

"Replacing me?" Fiona shrieked at Lisa. "*You* are going to replace *me?*"

"No! Not replace, Fiona. Don't be silly. I'm merely going to fill in until you're back."

"Over my dead body!"

"Maybe," Kurt said, eyeing Lisa closely, "that's what she had in mind."

"That's enough!" Dan snapped.

Lisa's gaze shot to him. He'd been quiet for so long she'd forgotten he was there, but now his presence seemed to be filling the room. He was clearly about two seconds away from punching the detective in the nose.

"That's enough," he repeated more quietly. "I may not be a lawyer, Kusch, but I know you're out of line. Way out of line. And if you want to talk about this again with Lisa, advise her ahead of time. So she can arrange to have legal counsel present."

Dan strode across the room and stopped in front of Lisa's chair. "Let's get out of here."

He extended his hand. Without even thinking, she took it and rose.

"See you, Fiona," he offered, glancing back toward the bed. "Hope you start feeling better soon."

Lisa wasn't certain she could manage to speak, but decided she'd better try. "I...I'll mention your idea to

Jake, Fiona. About broadcasting from here, I mean. We'll see what he thinks.''

Fiona merely glared at her.

An instant later, Dan was propelling her out of the room and down the hall toward the elevators. He said nothing until they reached them and he'd pressed the call button.

"In New York," he finally offered, "that detective would be in uniform, walking a beat—if he'd even made the force to begin with."

Lisa managed a smile, but the effort almost made her teeth chatter. She realized she was shaking. That didn't entirely surprise her. Mere seconds ago, she'd been visualizing Kurt Kusch handcuffing her and dragging her off in a police car. "He...Dan, do you think Kurt actually believes I'm his man? His woman, I mean?"

"I don't know. But I was serious about having a lawyer present if he wants to talk to you again."

The elevator door slid open and Dan hustled her inside. He was, she noticed, still holding her arm. She stared at his hand, wondering why his touch didn't make her feel even slightly uncomfortable and wishing it did. Wishing, deep down, that she didn't have to admit that Dan Ashly wasn't even close to being the most vile man in the world. In fact, he probably couldn't make it onto the vileness scale at all. Her situation would just be easier if he could.

The door opened on to the lobby, and Dan ushered Lisa from the elevator. She'd stopped trembling during their trip down from seven, so he no longer had any excuse to hold her arm. He released it, silently berating himself for not wanting to let go of her.

Hell, only last night he'd sworn that he'd never again do anything for her...ever. But here he was, desperately wishing he could say or do something to make her feel better.

He started toward the front entrance with her, wondering what on earth was going on inside his head. Lisa Saint-John was the woman who'd spilled the beans about his study, who'd set him up for a pack of trouble. So why should he care if she got some trouble of her own? Why the hell had he jumped into the Mr. Protector role upstairs?

Because that damned detective was such a jerk. That was the only reason. Well...almost the only reason. Of course, there was also the way Lisa had leaped to Crystal Whatever-her-name-was's defense, even though she must have known she'd find herself up to her ass in alligators for her trouble.

And even before that, there'd been her story about the flowers. He'd heard every word Jake had said last night and sending Fiona flowers certainly hadn't been mentioned. Lisa probably needed her head read for wanting to be kind to someone like Fiona but...well, it did say something about her...trying to spare Fiona's feelings when the woman probably didn't even have any.

He pushed open the main door, glanced down at Lisa and caught her eye.

She smiled at him, and he began to wonder what he'd have done yesterday if he'd been in her shoes. If *his* father was the president of the union local.

They walked down the front steps, and she paused when they reached the sidewalk.

"Dan, thanks for the rescue. I was lucky you were there...why *were* you there?"

The instant she asked the question, Lisa's face colored, as if the words had slipped out by mistake and she desperately wished they hadn't.

Dan couldn't help grinning, which merely turned her face from pink to crimson. But dammit, if she was curious about his relationship with Fiona, then she must be interested in him. And that was a news flash he liked.

To hell with her father and last night. If she could admit she was interested in him, he could admit that her interest made him feel good.

"I was visiting Fiona sort of by default," he offered. "With Jake in Columbus, I didn't have anything special to do this morning. I decided to take a walk, and I figured, since the Pritchard House is close to the hospital, I might as well take a walk with a destination."

"I . . . I'm glad you did."

Her words seemed so tentative that he wanted to give her a reassuring hug. Instead, he told himself not to push things.

"And about what I said last night," she went on, "about whatever happens on Monday being your own fault. Well, I know it won't be. It'll be mine. And I'm sorry about leaking your secret. I really am. I mean, I had to do what I did, but I'm sorry it's going to cause you problems. I hope they're not terribly serious ones."

He nodded. "I can understand why you told your father. Kind of."

He stood looking at her for a moment, wondering if he was insane to be thinking what he was thinking. But hell, when he'd asked, Jake had said that she wasn't involved with anyone at the moment. And insane or not, he couldn't convince himself there wasn't something special about her. Besides, he couldn't convince himself to walk away without at least trying. "Look, Lisa, I was wondering, if you're not busy tonight, that is—"

"Oh. I am."

"Oh. Of course. I mean it's Saturday and all. I should have realized you'd have a date."

"Well ... it's not exactly a date. I'm spending the evening with Crystal. What Fiona said about *Love in the Afternoon* being in trouble is true. Crystal and I are trying to come up with a way of saving it."

She smiled again, but anxiously, he thought. Did that mean she was lying about having made plans with this Crystal? That she simply didn't want to go out with him?

Maybe her question about why he was visiting Fiona had been simple curiosity. Maybe he'd read more into it than he should have. Damn. That was probably the case. Likely she didn't have the least bit of interest in him. Last night, she certainly hadn't been intending to invite him in, even before her brother had appeared.

He nodded, feeling like a total fool. "Well, some other time, maybe."

"Right. I ... well, I'll see you," she said, starting to back away. "Thanks again for saving me from Kurt."

"Any time."

She turned and began almost running down the block. Dan watched her until she disappeared around a corner, telling himself he'd been an idiot.

Well, hell, what did it matter? What did he want with a woman while he was in Walkerton, anyway? Nothing. Nothing at all. He wasn't going to be here long enough to make starting anything worthwhile. So the most sensible thing he could do was forget about Lisa Saint-John.

He had a million more important things to think about than her. Like, for example, how he was going to handle that lynch mob when it materialized at Plant W on Monday.

CHAPTER FIVE

"WHAT'S WITH the early-bird routine?" Jake demanded, eyeing Lisa from behind his desk.

"Oh, just couldn't sleep." *So,* she added silently, *I figured I might as well come in and see if I still had a job.* She sank into a chair, managing to keep from glancing at the phone. She must have spent half the weekend worrying that Dan would call first thing this morning to let Jake know she'd tipped off her father.

Most of the other half, she'd spent replaying that parting conversation outside the hospital. When she'd apologized for leaking his secret, Dan had said he understood. Rather, he'd said he "kind of" understood.

Did that mean he'd decided to let her off the hook as far as telling Jake was concerned? That her job wasn't at risk? She'd been praying that was exactly what it meant. But over the years, her prayers hadn't always been answered.

"The last time you made it into the station before eight," Jake muttered, "hell, you've never been in this early, have you?"

This wasn't, she told herself, forcing a smile, the moment to remind the boss how many evening hours she put in. "How was the Columbus trip? Useful conference?"

"Not bad. It's always good to hear what everyone's up to. How was your weekend?"

"Fine," she lied. When she hadn't been worrying about Dan blowing the whistle on her, she'd been worrying about whether Kurt Kusch might actually throw her into jail. And then there'd been the depressing Saturday evening she and Crystal had spent brainstorming—still unable to come up with a decent promo idea for *Love*.

"You talk to Fiona?" Jake asked.

"Yes. I went to see her on Saturday."

"And?"

"Well, the fall didn't do anything to quell her...her spirit. But she looks worse than I expected her to. And they have her in traction, so she may be off work for quite a while. We're going to have to set up some sort of semiofficial visiting schedule so she doesn't feel neglected. But, Jake, she's got this crazy idea about broadcasting from her hospital bed."

A gleam of interest sparkled in Jake's eyes, and he gazed at Lisa with a question on his face.

She shook her head and the gleam slowly died.

"I guess," he finally said, "that would be just too tacky, wouldn't it?"

She nodded, grateful she hadn't had to fight him. She was running on so little sleep that she probably couldn't win a fight with a three-year-old.

Her gaze wandered to the phone. Then she snuck a peek at her watch. It was after eight. The day shift would be in Plant W by now. And Woody was supposed to make his announcement first thing. Dan would be on hand...which meant her job was safe for at least a few more hours.

DAN STARTED ACROSS Plant W's floor with Ken Woody, heading for the makeshift raised platform.

Any Duelers that hadn't passed muster on the customer inspection line must have been driven to another part of the plant. Because this morning there wasn't a single vehicle parked in the finalizing area. It was wall-to-wall people.

The assembled autoworkers cleared a path for the two men, shifting out of their way as if they were lepers. And that was a fair assessment of the way Dan felt.

His gaze drifted over the hostile crowd, searching for familiar faces, hoping in vain for even a single friendly one.

Approximately one in fifteen or twenty were women, most wearing navy coveralls. Only about half the men were, though. But whether they were day-shift workers or not, practically all three thousand Plant W employees must have come in to listen to Woody.

If he'd actually believed his announcement was going to be a surprise, his delusion couldn't have lasted longer than it had taken him to glance around.

Dan spotted a face from the past and paused mid-stride. "Craig. Craig Bradstock," he said, offering his hand to the man who'd been one of his drinking buddies, years ago.

Every other person within hearing range turned to stare at Craig. He colored slightly, nodded an acknowledgment, but jammed his hands into the pockets of his coverall.

Dan slowly dropped his own hand, trying not to let the hurt show, telling himself not to take the rejection personally.

He walked the rest of the way to the platform and joined Woody, without focusing on faces in the crowd. There was no point in making anyone else he might know feel uncomfortable.

Woody introduced Dan to the silent assembly, then launched into a spiel about the study. Dan concentrated half on the plant manager's words and half on the sea of faces before them. He picked out Roy Saint-John, standing right up front. And he'd be willing to bet that the grim-faced trio to the side of the crowd, dressed in suits, were union executives.

Two of them were in their early forties, so the dapper-looking fellow in his mid-fifties, with the gray hair and mustache, had to be Lisa's father. *Bert,* Woody had said the local president's name was. Bert Saint-John.

He tried to see a resemblance to Lisa, but the man had none of her delicate features. He did look like an older version of Roy, though. He had the same muscular build. And dark eyes, rather than the delectably deep gray of Lisa's. Dan forced her image from his mind. For a woman he'd decided to forget about, she seemed to be front and center in his thoughts an annoying percentage of the time.

"So that's pretty well it," Woody said, giving a nervous little laugh. "That's about all there is to say."

That was about it? Dan felt his spirits sinking even lower. He'd been hoping those empty platitudes the man had been spouting were merely preamble, that he'd been saving the meat for later. But apparently not.

The workers weren't going to buy Woody's verbal pat on the head and his "don't worry, management knows what's best" tone. They were going to demand specific reasons for why Detroit wanted their plant studied. And if they didn't get them, there'd be trouble.

Woody began mumbling something about everyone cooperating, and Dan wondered if even the plant manager knew what this study was actually all about, what top management's real agenda was.

Because Dan wasn't sure they'd told *him* everything there was to tell. Oh, he knew Bill Wireton, QM's president, was a straight shooter. But in a situation like this, there was often a lot of behind-the-scenes activity—or behind the president's back activity, as the case might be.

He just hoped to hell nobody was planning to twist and turn his final report to fit whatever Detroit wanted it to fit.

He glanced at Ken Woody, far from delighted that this man was his local liaison with the top brass. Woody, with his gangly build, nondescript coloring and almost rodentlike features, wasn't the sort who inspired trust and confidence. And for a man who'd said, "That's about all there is to say," five minutes ago, he was certainly droning on.

"So you'll be seeing Dan's face here and there, but don't let his presence concern you in the least. Now, are there any questions?"

Amazingly, the response from the floor was absolute stony silence. In a building that generally rang with the constant rhythmic roars and clanks of assembly lines, the sound of the proverbial pin dropping would have been ear-shattering.

Three thousand pairs of the most unfriendly eyes in the world stared at the two men on the platform. And Dan found himself wishing he'd never heard of Walkerton, Quality Motors or, most especially, Plant W.

BERT SAINT-JOHN watched Ken Woody and Dan Ashly leave the platform and start in the direction of the management offices. The brothers and sisters began to disperse, muttering angrily among themselves. It was probably a miracle that some hothead hadn't disregarded his instructions about keeping quiet this morning.

He caught sight of Roy and frowned at the scowl on his son's face. The boy was right up there with the hottest of the hotheads. Dammit, by the time your kids were in their twenties, you shouldn't still be worrying about them. Not that he and Helen worried much about Lisa, of course. Oh, they were old-fashioned enough to wish she were married by now, but that was their only nagging concern.

Their son was a different story, though. His drinking was getting his mother more upset by the day, and, from what he'd said about Friday night, he must have actually taken a poke at Ashly.

Bert shook his head. If he hadn't been so darned tied up with union business all weekend he'd have called Lisa and found out exactly what had happened. Just for starters, what the hell had she been doing out with that Ashly character for half the night? Damn. Maybe they *should* be worrying about her. For all her surface sophistication she was still a small-town girl. And some hotshot from the Big Apple just might figure she was fair game.

He glared at Dan Ashly's retreating form, feeling that old familiar concern for his only daughter, then told himself to relax. Small-town girl or not, Lisa was twenty-eight and no fool.

He focused on Roy again, grateful he'd at least kept his mouth shut when Woody had invited questions. The last thing Bert wanted was his membership going off the deep end before he determined precisely what Detroit was up to. And if *any* steward, let alone the local president's son, had started asking questions from the floor, it would have unleashed the floodgates.

There was little doubt that Woody's answers would have been as vague as his speech, which would have escalated the simmering unease to a rapid boil.

Woody was going to get those questions he'd asked for. He was going to get all kinds of them. But they were going to come in private, from the union executive.

Bert glanced, in turn, at Dave Canovic, the local's vice president, and the secretary, Gary Kraemer. They were both watching the workers—the day shift straggling to their lines, the graveyard shift heading for the exit.

Thank God the Silver Dollar tavern wasn't open in the morning. If it was, there'd be a parade directly from here to the union hangout. But the Dollar would be crowded this afternoon, before the late shift came on. A lot of his members would be fueling their anxiety with beer.

He had to get a handle on things fast, then get the message out so the next shift wouldn't arrive loaded for trouble. If they were going to give management grief, he wanted it to be planned grief, not wild-cat eruptions.

"What do you think, Bert?" Dave asked.

"Strikes me it's as bad as we figured," Gary muttered.

Bert shook his head. "I can't see that we know anything more now than we did before Woody started talking. Let's go and find out what's really happening."

The three men strode across the finishing area, headed up the stairs and along the hallway to Woody's office.

His secretary glanced at them, then at the closed office door. "I'm afraid Mr. Woody has someone with him, Mr. Saint-John."

"Dan Ashly?"

She nodded.

"Good. Tell Woody we'd like a meeting with them both."

The young woman hesitated.

"Now," Bert added.

She pressed an intercom button and repeated his message. A moment later, she was ushering them into the plant manager's office.

"Morning Bert...Dave...Gary," Woody offered from behind his desk. "You haven't formally met Dan Ashly."

Dan rose and shook hands with each of them in turn. A firm grip, accompanied by an easy smile and a friendly "pleased to meet you," Bert noted.

Lisa had been right. The fellow came across as sincere and likable. But appearance could be deceiving. And neither sincere nor likable had anything to do with why he was at Plant W.

"Have a seat, fellows," Woody invited. Despite the closed door that had greeted them, the three empty chairs he gestured at said they'd been expected.

"So, what's happening?" he asked once they were sitting down.

"That's exactly what we've come to find out," Bert said. "What are the cold, hard facts about this study?"

"Bert, I said everything I had to say downstairs. Detroit's just doing one of its senior management things. Probably wants something to impress the shareholders with at annual report time. Nothing at all to worry about.''

"That's not good enough, Woody. Not nearly good enough. I get elected to protect the interests of our members. And I've got three thousand brothers and sisters who are worried about job security. I want hard and fast answers.''

"Bert . . . Bert, Bert, Bert. Let's not create problems where there aren't any. Dan's just here to look things over and tell Detroit what he thinks.''

Bert glanced at Dan. "You ever done anything like this before?''

"Of course he has,'' Woody said quickly. "Dan's area of expertise is the auto industry. That's why Detroit hired him.''

"That so?'' Bert asked, still watching Dan. "You an expert?''

He shrugged. "I guess I'm as expert as the next guy who's specialized in the field. And yes, I've done studies like this before.''

"Studies like this,'' Bert repeated. "Good. Then you can tell us exactly what you're planning to do and why, which is more than Woody seems willing to do.''

"Now just a minute,'' Woody snapped. "You know better than that, Saint-John. You deal with *me*. You got questions, you ask me. I'm management and Dan's an outsider. He's simply doing a job for the company. He's not here to answer your questions, and he doesn't speak for Detroit.''

Bert could feel his temper beginning a slow burn. "Fine. Ashly doesn't speak for Detroit but you're supposed to. So *you* damned well tell us exactly what he's here for and what he figures on doing. And make it good and specific, Woody, or you can forget about him getting the slightest cooperation from my people.''

"Look, Bert, I just told you exactly what he's here for. He's here because Detroit wants an outsider's opinion on the plant. That's as good and specific as it gets.''

"Yeah? Well, you and I both know that every time he asks a question on the floor he's probably going to contravene some clause in the union agreement. We could play the grievance game from now till next summer, and he'd never get his damned study finished. But how about we just cut the crapola. The way I hear it, your Mr. Ashly's here to recommend whether or not QM shuts us down.''

Bert stared evenly at Woody, watching his face for clues. There was no faster way of finding out what a man really knew than to throw a rumor at him and see how he reacted.

The plant manager paled a little. "That's not what's happening, Saint-John.''

"No? Then why are we sitting with a two-year assembly horizon? Why aren't there any parts scheduled into the plant beyond that?''

"I...Bert, you know as well as I do we haven't been given the answer to that one yet. But you also know Detroit's thinking about investing a lot of bucks in retooling and computerizing some of the plants.''

"Right. *Some* of the plants. But who's to say this is one of them? Look, Woody, I read the trades as closely as you do. And *Autofacts* says that 'at least' as many assembly plants will be permanently closed as will be opened in the next few years. So what's Detroit got planned for us a couple of years down the road?''

"Bert, I honest-to-God haven't heard anything about a closure. Hell, what are you so worried about? The Dueler's a hot model, and we're the only plant in the country producing it."

"Right. We're the only plant in the country. But what's the company up to off-shore? What's happening in Asia? And never mind even that far away. What about Mexico? Some of the rumors I'm hearing," Bert pressed, keeping his face expressionless, "say that QM's thinking of moving assembly out of the States entirely."

"Oh, come on, let's not be—"

"And other rumors," he continued, cutting off Woody's protestation, "say that Detroit's looking at restructuring, that it's not going to continue supporting six separate car divisions. Hell, maybe we've got no parts scheduled down the line because the Dueler's being phased out of production. It's hot now, but practically every competitor is coming out with an all-terrain vehicle. And we know how fickle consumers are."

Woody stared across the desk at the union officials. "Boys, I can only tell you what I know. And what I know is that I haven't heard a word about anyone even considering a shutdown."

Bert eyed the plant manager closely. Over the years, he'd learned to read the man pretty well, and right now he looked as if he was telling the truth. But Detroit's left hand didn't always tell its right hand what it was doing, let alone tell the managers scattered in plants all over the U.S.A. So what Woody knew or didn't know might not mean a damned thing.

Dave leaned closer. "I think it's major show time, Bert," he whispered.

Almost imperceptibly, Bert nodded his agreement. They could either frustrate the hell out of Woody for the next while, by flooding him with grievances, or they could roll out the heavy artillery and force Detroit into a corner. And it was the big boys who had the answers.

They'd waited and worried about the ever-shortening production horizon for months now. But this outside expert arriving put a whole new wrinkle in that worry. Whatever the company had up its sleeve, the union had a right to know.

Bert eased to his feet and leaned forward, planting his palms firmly on the manager's desk. "Okay, Woody, I'll buy your story that you haven't heard anything about a closure. But we want to know what this plant analysis is all about. I want answers from the company. I want to know what's going to be looked at and why. And I want guarantees. I want a guarantee that we get to see Ashly's final report within twenty-four hours of Detroit receiving it, that we see the entire report, not just the parts the company wants to show us. And I want a guarantee that Plant W's future is absolutely secure."

Woody cleared his throat uneasily. "Bert, nobody's... nothing's future is absolutely secure."

"I want answers and guarantees, Woody. By Wednesday. Let's say by six o'clock, Wednesday. So you'd better get on the phone. Because if I don't get what I want—in writing—I'm pulling the plant."

"You can't," Woody snapped.

"Just watch me."

"That would be an illegal work stoppage, Saint-John, and you know it as well as I do."

"Call it what you like. But I'd call it a labor dispute caused by a management problem." Without waiting for a reply, he straightened up and turned toward the door, glancing long and hard at Ashly.

What did the expert know? Something even Woody didn't? That wouldn't be at all surprising. Bert started across the office, barely aware of Dave and Gary scrambling to their feet.

What were the odds that the expert had been told, word for word, what his report was supposed to say? That he knew what Detroit's true reason was for sending him here?

Pretty high, Bert decided, opening Woody's door. The odds were pretty high that Mr. Dan Ashly knew what was up. So, while Woody was talking to the company, somebody should be talking to Ashly.

Two versions of a story were always better than one. That way, if they didn't match, you smelled a rat fast. Yes, somebody should be talking to Ashly. And there was only one logical somebody.

Bert started down the hall toward the exit, Dave and Gary on his heels, ignoring their running commentary about how they figured Detroit would react to the strike ultimatum.

He glanced at his watch as they left the building, wondering if Lisa would be at work this early, feeling a twinge of guilt about the idea of asking her to spy. But when she'd called him on Friday, she'd said that if this study turned out to be a threat, she'd do anything she could to help diffuse the fallout.

Well, the first thing that had to be done was to establish how much of a threat the study was ... why it was actually being done ... whether or not Detroit had Ashly in their pocket ... whether he'd been instructed as to exactly what his report should say. And Lisa was the obvious one to find out.

Strange how things sometimes fell into place. He'd hit the roof when she'd told him she'd be having Ashly on *Fiona*. And he hadn't liked Roy's story about finding the guy with her on Friday night. Hadn't liked it in the least. But maybe he'd been a little fast when it came to not liking things.

The three men reached the parking lot. "I'll see you back at the union hall," Bert told the other two, stopping beside his black Dueler. "I've got a few things to do, a few people to talk to."

He climbed into the car, reached for his phone, and dialed WALK, feeling another pang of guilt. He pressed the final number, reminding himself that Lisa was twenty-eight and no fool. She'd be able to handle this. And there was no reason to feel guilty about asking a favor of his own daughter.

"Lisa Saint-John, please," he said when the receptionist answered.

Yes, he reflected again as Lisa's line began ringing, she was the obvious one to find out what Ashly knew. And the idea she'd mentioned about trying to make him look foolish on *Fiona*...well, it certainly couldn't hurt. He'd have to talk to her about that, too.

"I LOOK FORWARD so much to meeting you, Lisa."

She swallowed uneasily as the words flowed over the phone line. How could a man make such an innocent statement seem as if he were inviting her into his bed? Maybe it was simply the trace of an Italian accent that made his words sound so suggestive.

"Why...why, thank you, I'm looking forward to meeting you as well, Professor Stelle."

"Benedetto," he corrected her a third time.

"Right. Benedetto." She glanced at the open folder on her desk once more. The photograph smiling up at her from the news department's file definitely matched the smooth-as-satin-sheets voice on the other end of the line. Dr. Benedetto Stelle, Walkerton U's visiting business professor, was from one of the reputedly more bizarre universities in Southern California. He appeared to be in his early thirties, with classic Latin good looks—regular, strong features and what in bygone days would have been called bedroom eyes.

Looking at his picture and talking with him, it was difficult to believe the man was as nutty as a fruitcake. But she'd heard the rumors about him. And the copy in his file definitely attested to "Dr. Benny's" unorthodox approach to the world of finance.

And then there was his theory that the success of romantic relationships depended on the compatibility of the couple's astrological signs. But she certainly didn't intend to get into a discussion of that with him. Hearing a bit of what he had to say about his method of predicting business success and failure had been enough.

Had something about his upbringing in Italy spawned his weird ideas? Or was he another result of a peculiarity in the West Coast air? Maybe all those exhaust fumes Californians breathed caused brain damage.

"If you are even half as lovely as you sound," his voice murmured into her ear, "I shall want to become a regular guest on your show. I adore appearing on television."

She managed to keep her laugh cool. "It's not really my show. As I explained, I'm the producer, not the host. I'm simply filling in for a few weeks." She forced her eyes away from his picture. If he looked even half as good on live camera as he did in that still, the viewers would *demand* he be a regular guest. Come Friday night, they'd be drooling in front of their TV sets.

And Fiona... Lord, Fiona would be lying in her hospital bed, watching the duo of this man and Dan Ashly, and wanting to kill Jake for not going along with the idea of broadcasting from Walkerton General. And wanting to kill Lisa Saint-John for sitting in the host's chair.

Oh, she really didn't want to think about Fiona.

"So," Benedetto said, "I shall be at your office at four tomorrow afternoon for the preinterview. And I shall have done my homework on the management of Quality Motors. Then perhaps we will stretch our interview into dinner, no? A little pasta, a little vino. Better yet, more than a little vino."

"I'm afraid we'd better not count on dinner, Benedetto. Things sometimes come up unexpectedly at the station."

"Well, let us hope that tomorrow there is only the expected. I have been here just a few weeks but I have already discovered Trattoria Ricci."

"Then you've discovered the best Italian restaurant in Walkerton."

"*Sì*, the food is wonderful. We must share it. So I shall hope for tomorrow. Ciao, Lisa."

"Ciao," she repeated, instantly feeling foolish. Ciao! Coming from the mouth of a woman who had to ask waiters which was rigatoni and which was tagliatelle. She slowly hung up, wondering for the hundredth time how she'd gotten herself into doing what she was doing.

"Very simply," she murmured unhappily. "You volunteered." That was definitely how it had come about, all right. On Friday, when she'd alerted her father to the study, she'd offered him her help. And when he'd called yesterday morning, her words had come back to haunt her. The very last thing she'd expected him to do was ask her to get close to the enemy and see what she could learn.

Not that she didn't still want to help Dad. And not that she wasn't still worried about what might happen to Plant W. But she was having a lot of trouble convincing herself that, when it came to Dan Ashly, she hadn't pushed the panic button. And that would mean her suggestion about sabotaging his appearance on *Fiona* had been a tad hasty.

Because the more she'd seen of Dan, the more she'd realized that he seemed to be the honest, reasonable man Jake had claimed he was. And if that was the case, then maybe his study was on the up and up. Maybe he wasn't actually QM's hired gun, after all. Or was that merely wishful thinking on her part?

Whichever, he'd certainly made it difficult for her to think of him as the enemy. Even setting aside the absurd issue of her hormones, there'd been that cold, scary walk home that he'd spared her on Friday night. Then he'd rescued her from Kurt Kusch on Saturday. Maybe he'd even frightened the detective away from her permanently. After all, Kusch had been nosing around the station for two days now and hadn't said a word to her.

And apparently, Dan wasn't going to tell Jake that she'd forewarned her father about the study. Because here it was, Tuesday afternoon already, and Jake was still smiling at her. If he was aware the union had been tipped off, he obviously didn't suspect her of being the tipper.

Yes, all in all, Dan Ashly was hardly acting like an enemy, not *her* enemy, at least. And that made her feel like Benedict Arnold every time she thought about the plots she was hatching.

She opened her desk drawer, flipped the top off the box of chocolates and gazed at the collection of crumpled brown wrappers.

On Friday night, that five-pound box had been almost full. But over the past two days she'd demolished the entire contents, had eaten every last...not quite, she corrected herself, spotting a lonely cream center peeking out from the mess of wrappers. She grabbed it and had it halfway to her mouth when a male voice stopped her hand.

"Lisa?"

She glanced up and focused on the station janitor, Carl Gustavson, fleetingly recalling how upset he'd looked the last time she'd seen him. On Friday night, after Fiona's fall, his face had been as pale as his mane of white hair. Today, his normal ruddy color was back.

Reluctantly, she returned her chocolate to the box and shoved the desk drawer closed. "Sorry, Carl, I'd offer you one but that's the last of them."

"It's all right, Lisa. I'm not much for candies. I just wondered whether I could talk to you a minute."

"Of course. Come in."

Carl took a couple of steps toward the desk, then stopped and stood looking at her, his expression anxious.

"What's the problem, Carl?"

"It...it's that detective fellow, Lisa. The way he's been interrogating everyone about what happened to

Fiona. He's been asking me a lot of questions about the backboard that was sawed through...like he thinks maybe...because I have tools in my room here..."

"Carl, don't let him get to you. We all know you had nothing to do with what happened. And I'm sure Kurt doesn't suspect you of a thing. It's just his manner. At first he had me thinking that *I* was his prime suspect. But he hasn't even spoken to me for the past couple of days. So don't worry about what he's up to. You had nothing to do with the incident, so you have nothing to be concerned about."

"No...I had nothing to do with it. It's just..."

"I know, Carl. Somebody got hold of a saw. But whoever rigged that board probably brought whatever tools they needed into the station with them."

He nodded slowly. "I had nothing to do with it, so there's no reason to be concerned."

"Right." Lisa flashed him the most reassuring smile she could, thinking what a creep Kurt Kusch was, recalling how worried *she'd* been, even though she'd had nothing to do with what had happened, either.

"Am I interrupting anything?" a second male voice asked.

Oh, Lord, it was the creep himself, standing in her doorway and eyeing her and Carl as if deciding which one of them to arrest. So much for her hope that the detective had been permanently frightened away from her.

"We were just talking station business, Kurt," she lied. "What can I do for you?"

He stepped into her office and shot a "get lost" glance at Carl. The janitor immediately mumbled a goodbye and hustled off.

"I'd like a list of the guests who've appeared on *Fiona* since the show started, Lisa. And after I've had a look at that, I'll want to view the tapes of some of the shows."

"Okay. That can be arranged. You think one of the guests might have had something to do with what happened?"

Kurt shrugged. "Maybe. Maybe not. But I haven't turned up any solid clues pointing to station staff, so we're going to widen the circle."

Lisa could actually feel tension draining from her body. She wasn't going to be facing an arrest warrant, after all. And neither was Carl. He'd certainly be relieved when she told him that. She glanced at her watch. "It's after two, but if I get someone working on that list right away we could have it ready for you by morning."

"Good. That would be good, Lisa."

"Just ask at reception for it when you come in tomorrow. And Gloria, in the tape library, will run whichever segments you want to see."

"Great. Thanks for the help, Lisa. I really appreciate it."

She nodded, thinking that maybe Kurt wasn't a total creep, after all. It was amazing how not being a suspect changed one's perspective.

The moment he was gone, she called the janitor's room and told Carl the good news. Then she arranged to have the list drawn up and, finally, turned her thoughts to the problem of *Love*'s ratings. She just *had* to come up with something that would make the viewers tune in.

But thoughts of Dan Ashly kept interfering with her concentration. She tried unsuccessfully not to peek at her watch and check on how long it would be until he'd arrive for their preinterview . . . and their date.

How, she wondered for the millionth time, had she actually managed to get through inviting him out? Not that it had been a terribly forward move, considering he'd asked her out on Saturday. And not that it hadn't been a good idea, either. It would be the perfect chance to pump him without being obvious about it.

But merely dialing his hotel last night, to set up their meeting, had started her hand shaking. And asking him if he'd like to catch an early dinner afterward . . . well, of course she'd stressed that they'd just go someplace casual, but she'd still practically choked on the words.

Somehow, though, she'd gotten them out. And she'd even managed to sound friendly. In fact, she had a dreadful suspicion that she'd sounded *too* friendly. *Far* too friendly. Because if Dan figured she was even half as attracted to him as she actually was . . . well, the last thing she wanted was him thinking she'd be receptive to . . . because she darned well wasn't going to be. Not when there was any chance that consorting with Dan Ashly would be consorting with the enemy.

So when he got here she had to be careful not to seem *too* friendly. She reached into her drawer, retrieved that one remaining chocolate, then sat letting it melt in her mouth. And wondering precisely how friendly she'd have to be, to find out what her dad wanted her to find out.

CHAPTER SIX

"HI THERE."

Lisa didn't have to look up to know who'd spoken. The deep voice sent delightful little shivers through her—delightful little shivers she didn't want to be experiencing.

Dan sauntered across her office and sank into the chair on the other side of her desk. He'd taken her at her word about going someplace casual. He was wearing brown cords, a creamy fisherman-knit sweater... and the sexiest smile she'd ever seen.

"Sorry I'm late," he offered.

"Oh, are you? Late, I mean, not sorry," she added idiotically, glancing at her watch and trying to look as if she'd forgotten she even had one. It was almost an entire minute since the last time she'd looked at it. Almost two minutes since the time before that. "I hadn't noticed it was past four," she lied.

"No?" Dan's sexy smile shifted into a teasing grin. A sexy, teasing grin. "I was kind of hoping you would have. Being invited out for dinner by a beautiful woman always gets a man's hopes up."

Oh, Lord! Given that gleam in his eye, her dreadful suspicion that she'd sounded *too* friendly was bang-on. She was going to be walking a damned tightrope between getting close enough to Dan to help her father and not getting so close that she'd fall.

She thought rapidly, trying to make her own smile seem aloof. "Well, at the risk of dashing your hopes, dinner is going to be courtesy of Jake, not me. He decided that since Friday will be my first show, you and I should spend a little time getting to know each other...so I'd feel more comfortable with you on air."

Dan nodded slowly, as if she *had* dashed his hopes, at least a little. Maybe she'd make a half-decent spy, after all. She was certainly getting good at little white lies. She'd just have to remember to cover herself on this one with Jake.

"Hi, Lisa," Crystal said brightly, popping her head into the doorway. "Oops. Sorry, I didn't know you were busy."

"It's okay, we're just doing a preinterview. This is Dan Ashly... Crystal Stafford, the host of *Love in the Afternoon.*

Crystal smiled and Lisa glanced at Dan, expecting to see him falling all over himself, getting up to greet her. Crystal's Christie Brinkly looks generally had that effect on men.

But he didn't seem the least bit impressed by Crystal. He simply gave her a friendly nod from where he was sitting.

Now why, Lisa asked herself, should that please her so much?

"I just wanted to see if you'd had any inspired ideas," Crystal explained.

"Sorry, nothing yet. How about you?"

Crystal shook her head. "The creative side of my brain must be on vacation."

"Well, we'll both keep on thinking. And we're going to come up with something great. You'll see."

"Right," Crystal agreed, not looking the least convinced that they'd come up with anything at all, let alone anything great. "Well, see you tomorrow, then. Nice meeting you, Dan."

"Same here," he offered.

But he didn't, Lisa noted with another rush of that silly, inordinate pleasure, follow Crystal with his eyes.

"I've made some notes about possible approaches we can use Friday," she murmured, searching through the papers on her desk and trying to ignore the way Dan was watching her.

But ignoring those warm eyes of his was impossible. She didn't know how anything the color of blue steel could be warm, but she could certainly feel the heat of his gaze on her body.

And why was his mere presence causing this difficulty she was having breathing? Because seeing him was making her feel even more guilty about what she was planning? Or was it because he was the most disconcerting man she'd ever met? So disconcerting that she couldn't even find her blasted notes.

She gave up trying and glanced across at him. "So, how are things going at the plant?"

"Well, let's see," he said, frowning as if the question actually required some thought to answer. "The workers think I'm a visiting pariah. If looks could kill, I'd have been dead the moment I walked into the building yesterday. And I suspect that my eating or drinking anything from the cafeteria would be downright suicidal."

"Oh . . . so should I take it that you're having an all-around good time?"

Dan grinned at her sarcasm. "Let's just say I was glad you gave me an excuse to duck out early today.

But that was only an analysis of how things are going with me, personally. As far as how things are going over all, I guess we'll have a better idea of that tomorrow, won't we?"

"You mean when Detroit responds to the union demands?"

He nodded. "Your father sure got grilled on the news last night. His strike threat was obviously bigger news than the study itself."

"Well, the possibility of a walkout at Plant W is always big news here. But I'd say you and Dad shared the coverage about equally."

"Oh, I'm not complaining. In fact, I was relieved that the camera was on your father so much of the time. I imagine his ultimatum was just a bluff though, huh? He wouldn't really have his membership hit the bricks, would he?"

Lisa gazed across her desk uncertainly, wondering who was supposed to be the spy here. Dad was probably waiting by the phone, hoping she'd report in on what Dan had to say. But was someone in Detroit waiting by a phone, too?

"I haven't really talked to Dad much about what's happening," she murmured noncommittally. "But . . . but what do you think Detroit's going to do?"

A slow smile spread across Dan's face. "Well . . . I haven't really talked to Detroit much about what's happening. . . ."

Lisa felt herself flushing as he repeated her words. Playing Mata Hari with Mr. Dan Ashly obviously wasn't going to be any piece of cake. And it was clearly time to change the subject.

"Dan...Dan, before we get started talking about the show, I want to thank you for not saying anything to Jake. About me telling Dad."

"Well, there's not much need to thank me. After I'd had a chance to cool down and think things through, I realized it didn't make any real difference that the union learned about the study before Monday. Not any real difference in the long run, at least. I'd still have ended up a pariah."

"Well...any real difference or not, thanks. You know how Jake tends to go bananas about things. And I've gotten sort of used to a paycheck." She glanced down again, her guilt level inching up a notch, almost wishing Dan *had* told Jake on her. Finally, she located the pages she'd been searching for, then took a deep breath before looking up once more.

"Jake mentioned you had to see how much detail Detroit wanted you to go into about the study. On air, I mean. You...ahh, you did talk to them about that at least, didn't you?"

"Yeah. I called them yesterday."

"And what did they say?"

"Frankly, they're not thrilled with the idea of my even being on the program. So I'm afraid we'll have to stick to generalities."

"I see."

"Hope that isn't going to make the show too dull."

She almost smiled with relief. He'd just given her a perfect lead-in. "Well, actually, I've been proceeding on the assumption that they wouldn't want you to be too specific. And I've come up with an idea that should keep things lively."

"Oh?"

The right-hand corner of Dan's mouth, she noticed, quirked up in a most appealing way when he was interested in what she was saying. Of course, his mouth was darned appealing with or without the quirk. His full, sensuous lips that just begged to be—

"Keep things lively?" he pressed, bringing her thoughts back to the discussion.

"Yes. I didn't want you to come across as boring, so—"

His mouth quirked up an additional quarter of an inch.

"Oh, not that I mean you're boring! I simply figured you might appreciate someone more knowledgeable than I am to bounce thoughts around with. So I've invited a second guest. He does yearly predictions on all the major industries, so he'll be able to converse intelligently about what you're doing."

Dan nodded. "Sounds good. Who is he?"

"Oh, he's a visiting business professor—only at the university for the fall term."

"What's his name? I might know him."

Please don't let that be the case, Lisa silently prayed. "Benedetto Stelle," she mumbled, hoping the name would come out sounding like John Smith.

Dan merely stared at her. Or was he glaring. She wasn't certain. "Dr. Benny?" he finally said, his voice cracking on the words.

Rats. She'd have to work on her mumbling. "Dr. Benny? Ahh...well...now that you mention it, I think there *was* something in his bio that referred to a nickname. You do know him, then?"

She sat gazing at Dan, a phony smile on her lips and sixty-three swear words racing around inside her head. There went the element of surprise she'd expected to have on her side. If Dan knew Benedetto, he'd know what was likely to happen on the show. Of course, knowing what was likely to happen and being able to do much about it were two different things.

"I only know him by reputation," Dan finally said, eyeing her with extreme suspicion. "And I've seen him on a couple of network talk shows. From what I've seen and heard, though, Dr. Loony Tunes would be a more appropriate nickname for him."

"Really?" Lisa opened her eyes wider. "But he's a university professor."

"Yeah. He's a professor at some university that sells diplomas through the mail."

"Oh...oh, but the news department's file suggested he was famous." She dug her nails into her palms. If she got through this performance without Dan being certain she was intentionally setting him up, she deserved an Academy Award. Or at least an Emmy.

"Dammit, Lisa, don't you know why he's famous?"

She merely shook her head. Lying aloud even one more time would probably bring a bolt of lightning flashing down.

"He's famous because...hell, infamous would be a better word. But the reason he's well-known is that he expounds some half-baked theory about using companies' natal dates to project their annual profits. And because his approach is so ridiculous, the press gives him a lot of play. Didn't the bio you read mention that his annual predictions are crazy astrological hogwash?"

"Ahh...well, I don't really know much about financial predictions, Dan. I mean, I did notice that he's into astrology. But I only had time to skim the bio, and there was a note in it that he was extremely entertaining and—"

"Entertaining? Hell, Lisa, the man's got loose boards in his attic."

Dan's voice, she realized, had been growing louder each time he opened his mouth. Half the station must be able to hear him by now.

"Look, Lisa, let's just rethink your idea about having two guests. At least two guests consisting of Dr. Benny and me. Because appearing on a serious show is one thing, but I'm not interested in being part of a sideshow. I—"

"Hey, Dan," Jake interrupted from the doorway. "Thought that was you I heard. What's got you so hot under the collar?"

Lisa managed to smile at her boss, thanking her lucky stars she'd made a point of getting his okay before calling Dr. Benny. Actually, she'd gotten more than his okay. She'd gotten his blessing. He'd asked her to start booking off-beat guests, and he'd been thrilled that she'd come up with such a dilly.

She glanced back at Dan. *Hot under the collar* was certainly an apt description. Not that his sweater actually had a collar but—

"Look, Jake," he muttered, "we've got a problem here. Lisa's..." He paused, momentarily looking at her, then cleared his throat. "We've got a problem with the show on Friday. There's a character named Benedetto Stelle who's—"

"Yeah. Having him on's a great idea, huh? Lisa was kind of worried the show might be a downer. Not because of you personally, but because people are upset about the study, and we figured you wouldn't be able to say much to reassure them. But I hear Dr. Benny's completely off-the-wall. He'll add a dash of humor.''

"Off-the-wall?'' Dan practically shouted, riveting Lisa's attention back to him. "Off-the-wall? Jake, Robin Williams classifies as off-the-wall. And Steve Martin, maybe. But Dr. Benny is just plain crackers.''

"Oh, I don't think that could be true,'' Jake said, shaking his head. "I read his predictions every January. Dr. Benny's Stars and Stinkers, he calls them. And hell, he's got a terrific batting average. He does better at picking stock-market winners and losers than most investment counselors. I've made more than a few bucks buying shares he's recommended.''

"Jake, for Pete's sake! The man's as phony as a three-dollar bill!''

Lisa looked back at Dan, beginning to feel as if she was watching a verbal tennis match. *Hot under the collar* was no longer an accurate description of him. At this point, *apoplectic* would be better.

"Jake,'' he went on, a touch more calmly, "Benedetto Stelle is a laughingstock. His terrific batting average can come from only pure blind luck. And I've seen the jerk in action on talk shows. He goes into an elaborate routine about how astrology's the only true indicator of business trends, about how his blasted lucky streak, which he refers to as his 'divine wisdom from the stars,' runs circles around fundamental analysis.

"And not only that. He positively delights in making anyone who's legitimate look like an idiot. Hell, if he appears on the show with me, odds are I'll come off looking like a fool. And a humorless stick-in-the-mud, to boot.''

Lisa felt her guilt level hitting an all-time high. Dan Ashly coming off as both a fool and a stick-in-the-mud was precisely what she and her father were hoping for. But she hadn't expected that the likelihood of its happening would occur to him. Not immediately, at least. He certainly was a fast man on the uptake.

"Oh, come on, Dan," Jake tried, "where's the renowned Ashly sense of humor?"

"Where? Well, I'm afraid I parked it outside the door of Plant W yesterday. Look, Jake, the QM workers have already decided I'm a dirty rotten bastard. All I need is to have my credibility questioned. That would hand the union members a perfect excuse to start giving me zero percent cooperation instead of the two percent I'm getting now."

"Dan, what's Dr. Benny got to do with *your* credibility?"

"Jake, would an intelligent man willingly be part of a televised circus? Am I supposed to sit in front of a camera, trying to talk sensibly to a bozo who revels in poking fun at the analytic process I use to earn my living? I mean, my choice would be between coming right out and saying he was an idiot—being totally rude to him in front of your viewers—or being polite and acting as if I think there might be even a grain of truth to his claim that he can predict business successes and failures by stargazing."

"Dan, you're overreacting to this. I—"

"Look, Jake, I'll admit that maybe my sense of humor is in a bit of a dip at the moment. The last couple of days haven't exactly been a barrel of laughs. But, hell, merely being seen within ten blocks of that character strikes me as a good way to raise credibility questions."

Jake stood rubbing his jaw. "I guess I can see your point," he finally admitted. "But at first thought, it sure seemed like a great idea." He glanced at Lisa. "You talk to Dr. Benny yet?"

She nodded, trying to look as if she honestly wished she hadn't. "He said he'd be delighted to guest."

Jake shrugged. "Well, Dan...it'll be more than a bit awkward to uninvite him...but if you really don't think you can handle him, old buddy..."

Please, Dan, Lisa prayed as the silence lengthened, *please let's hear a typically male response that says you can handle anything.*

"Well," he finally mumbled, "of course I can *handle* him. The idea of appearing with him just took me by surprise."

A chorus of hallelujahs erupted inside Lisa's head and almost drowned out the voice of guilt. Dad was going to love her for this.

Jake's face broke into a relieved-looking grin. "Good. That's settled, then. Say, what are you doing once you and Lisa are finished here? Want to catch a couple of beers with me? Dinner, maybe?"

Lisa held her breath and willed Jake to vanish into thin air. Surely he wasn't going to blow her story.

Dan glanced curiously from Jake to her, then back to Jake. "Lisa's taking me out for dinner...the station's treat."

Jake frowned. "She is?" He turned to Lisa. "What station's treat?" he asked wryly.

Oh, no. Jake *was* going to blow her story. In fact, the trace of a grin that appeared on Dan's face told her it was already blown.

"Yeah," he said slowly, speaking to Jake but watching her, "we're going out so we can get to know each other better…so she'll feel more comfortable with me on the air."

"What? What the hell are you talking about? Lisa's had a ton of airtime. She doesn't need to—"

Jake stopped speaking midsentence, and Lisa could practically see the lightbulb flash on over his head. But it was too late. Dan was grinning broadly at her now, his expression saying he was certain that he was looking at tonight's dessert.

LISA SAVORED her last forkful of The Cajun's famous double-chocolate fudge bourbon cake.

"Didn't like it much, huh?" Dan teased.

"Not even a little. I really had to force down that last bit." She smiled across the table at him, warning herself for the umpteenth time that being *too* friendly could only be hazardous, that she was here to spy, not to enjoy herself. But enjoying herself with Dan Ashly was proving awfully easy to do. And she *had* made a few stabs at asking him about the study.

He'd smoothly sidestepped her questions, though. So smoothly that she wasn't certain whether or not he was actually being evasive. Obviously, she was no natural at espionage.

She reminded herself Dad was relying on her, took a final sip of coffee, then tried again. "I imagine things will be pretty tense at the plant tomorrow. Until they hear what Detroit has to say, I mean."

"I imagine," Dan agreed.

"So…what do you think the company's response is going to be?"

Dan gazed at her for a long moment, a smile playing on his lips. "Lisa, why do I have the feeling you've asked me that question before? In about six different ways? You know, if I was weak in the ego department, I'd be starting to suspect that the only reason you'd asked me out was to pump me."

"Pump you? No, of course not. I was just trying to make conversation."

He nodded slowly, but his smile didn't fade. "Good. Because I'd hate to think it was anything other than my raw animal magnetism that prompted you to invite me to dinner."

She managed a smile of her own . . . but just barely. "What else could it possibly have been?"

"Oh, I don't know. I did have one crazy idea, though."

"You did? What was that?"

"Oh, I thought it was just possible your father had put you up to it."

"My father?" Oh, damn, her voice had squeaked. She definitely wasn't spy material.

"Yeah, your father. After all, he's the local president. And I'd have to be blind, deaf and dumb not to realize the union's suspicious as hell about why QM singled out Plant W for analysis."

Dan drained the last of his cognac and put the snifter back down before speaking again. "Look, Lisa, let's stop playing cat and mouse and lay our cards on the table."

She bit her lip, trying to decide whether to keep up her Miss Innocent act. There probably wasn't any point. Dan had clearly figured out exactly what she was up to and why. "All right," she finally offered. "I'll admit that I'm awfully curious about the study. The whole town's awfully curious about the study."

"Fair enough. What do you want to know?"

What did she want to know? That had to be a trick question, didn't it? Surely he wasn't prepared to tell her. Not the truth, at least.

Her thoughts were apparently written all over her face because he grinned and gave a little shrug. "Lisa, I've been in Walkerton less than a week, and I'm already sick to death of people looking at me as if I were a combination hangman and guillotine operator. And...and I enjoy your company. I enjoy it a whole lot. So why don't you just ask me what you want to know about the study and I'll answer as well as I can. Then we'll forget about QM and spend the rest of the evening concentrating on each other. Okay?"

She gazed at him uncertainly. He enjoyed her company. A whole lot. And she enjoyed his. A quantum leap more than a whole lot. And, Lord, there was nothing she'd enjoy more than forgetting about QM and concentrating on him. But only if the answers to her questions were the ones she wanted to hear, of course.

"What, no questions?" he pressed.

Well, what did she have to lose? Delicately dancing around the issue hadn't gotten her anywhere. She took a deep breath and plunged ahead.

"Just one question, Dan. And...well, before I ask it, I want to tell you that Jake assured me you were your own man...and so I don't mean to insult your integrity. But...well, I can't come up with a subtle way of asking this. Has QM told you what your analysis is supposed to turn up? Has the company told you what recommendations to make?" Her heart stopped for a beat or two while she waited for him to answer.

"No," he said.

Her heart started once more.

"And you cheated, Lisa. That was two questions, not one. But no, QM hasn't told me what my analysis is supposed to turn up nor what recommendations to make."

She couldn't help smiling. Why hadn't she just come right out and asked him those questions last Friday? Why hadn't she spoken up instead of worrying and wondering and feeling guilty that the enemy had started her chemical Cupid firing away?

Of course...of course, it was possible that he wasn't telling the truth. She gazed at him, silently asking for reassurance.

He reached across the table and took her hand in his. It wasn't exactly reassurance, but it was incredibly wonderful. Only it wasn't wonderful at all if he was lying.

"Lisa, I was hired to come in and do an independent study of Plant W's operation. And to project, as well as I'm able, what the market is likely to be for the Dueler over the next five years. That's *all* I was told to do."

"Really?" she managed to say, her voice refusing to rise above a whisper.

"Really. Look, I know people are suspicious that Detroit's up to something. And that I'm involved in whatever it is. But that isn't the case. As far as I'm aware, the company simply wants an outsider's opinion. Of course, I'm not naive enough to swear on a stack of bibles that Detroit doesn't have a hidden agenda. But if there is one, I don't know about it. And I'm going to give management exactly what it's asked for. An honest analysis and whatever recommendations I feel are appropriate."

She nodded slowly, too flooded with relief to even try speaking. He was telling her the truth. She could see it in his eyes. Jake had been right about Dan being his own man. And more important, far more important, her instincts had been right about him.

"So," he continued, "what do you think your father will say when you tell him that?"

"When . . . when I tell him?"

Dan squeezed her hand and grinned at her. "You *are* going to tell him, aren't you? I've kind of figured out that you tend to tell him things."

"Well, I'm not exactly Chatty Cathy. I only..." Oh, heck, what was the point in denial? Her face felt so hot that it was probably tomato red. "Well, I guess I might mention our conversation to Dad. Only in passing, of course."

"Of course. And look, just before we drop this damn topic, maybe you should also mention that Woody thinks your father's pushing Detroit too hard with that strike threat."

A little alarm went off inside Lisa's head. Why was Dan telling her that? "What do you mean, pushing too hard?"

He grinned again. "Stop looking at me as if I'm evil incarnate. I'm merely repeating what Woody said. And only because if there's anything I can do to smooth things out a little, I want to."

"Why?"

"Pure self-interest. The worse things are between the union and Detroit, the tougher it's going to be for me to make progress with my study."

Lisa eyed him warily. He looked as if he were telling the truth but... "So, what exactly did Woody mean?"

"Well, he figures Detroit might call the union's bluff, just to show who's in charge. I mean, a walkout *would* be illegal. And management knows it wouldn't earn your father any points with the national union brass."

"Dan, Dad's far more concerned about what could happen to the local membership than about what the national thinks."

"Of course he is. But the point is that he might make trouble for himself for nothing. Because Woody's sure that the company would be willing to explain what they're up to if the union made even a minor concession."

"Like what?"

"Like easing off on its ultimatum to hit the bricks tomorrow. I mean, if your father doesn't get the answers he's demanded, maybe he should give the company a little more time. That way, Detroit would save face and your father wouldn't really lose any."

"No? I doubt Dad would see it that way."

Dan shook his head. "Lisa, I was there when your father told Woody that he was going to pull the plant. And he didn't actually specify that he'd do it immediately—merely implied he would. So he could easily leave the threat hanging, but offer to negotiate before wildcatting. After all, a strike's expensive for his membership. That gives him a good reason to delay walking out. And it would be a reason the workers couldn't find fault with."

"That... that's true, I guess."

"Well, I just figured it was worth mentioning how Woody was reading the situation. As I said, anything I can unofficially do to smooth things over will only make my job easier."

"Right. Well, I don't know how Dad will take it, but I'll pass it on." Of course she'd pass it on. Her father would be dying to know every word Dan said tonight. But why did she have the uneasy feeling that she was no longer simply a spy...that she'd just become a double agent?

"Hey," Dan murmured, squeezing her hand once more. "It's time to forget about QM. And we were going to spend the rest of the evening concentrating on each other, remember?"

He gave her a smile that made her feel warm all over—and made her certain Dan Ashly would say some things tonight that she wouldn't be repeating to her father.

CHAPTER SEVEN

DAN TURNED ONTO MISTY Drive, glanced across the Dueler's dim interior at Lisa, and immediately broke into an idiotic grin.

Sometime after they'd stopped talking about QM and started talking about themselves, it had become impossible to look at her without smiling. It had happened shortly after they'd left The Cajun and gone walking, hand in hand, through Central Park—a Central Park that was actually safe to walk in at night.

And if she kept on smiling back at him, the way she was doing right now, it would soon be impossible to look at her without touching her.

She was undoubtedly the most desirable woman he'd ever met. And at the moment, with the faint light from the Dueler's dash softly illuminating her face, and pale moonbeams sneaking in through the windshield to dance like silver sparkles on her hair, she was simply irresistible.

He reached for her hand. She folded her fingers over his and squeezed gently, making him want to floor the accelerator and race the final few blocks. But the intoxicating scent of her perfume was making him dizzy, so he carefully kept within the speed limit . . . and covering those few blocks took forever.

Finally, they came into sight of Lisa's rambling old house. He slowed the Dueler and pulled to a halt. The house was dark and the huge lot was bathed in moon-light, just as it had been last Friday.

"Your landlords are still away?" he asked.

"Yes. They're gone for a couple of weeks."

Reluctantly, he released her hand to cut the engine, then glanced across the car once more. "Do I get to meet your guard cat tonight?"

She smiled another of her enchanting smiles. "I thought I mentioned that Tiger always hides under the bed if there's a stranger in the apartment."

"Well . . . I could stick around until he comes out."

"That usually takes awhile."

All the better. The cat could hide forever if it liked. "I've got nothing pressing," he offered, hoping he didn't sound as anxious as he felt. Surely she was go-ing to invite him in tonight. Surely she was feeling what he was. Lord, the way she'd been holding his hand, the way she'd brushed against him as they'd walked, arousing him with her nearness, had told him she wanted to be alone with him as much as he wanted to be alone with her. Well, no, not *quite* as much. That was inconceivable. But he certainly hadn't gotten a "go away" message.

"I have a bottle of Chablis in the fridge," she mur-mured.

His entire body sagged with relief. It was a good thing he was sitting down. "Chablis sounds terrific," he managed, opening his door and practically leaping out.

Relax, he told himself, heading around to her side. *Relax before she decides you're a total jerk.* Hell, he was acting as if he'd left every last trace of savoir faire in Manhattan. But he'd never met a woman who af-fected him the way Lisa did. She made him feel like a teenager. And easy as she was to talk to, he sometimes felt incredibly tongue-tied around her. He wasn't certain precisely what was so special about her, but there was definitely something.

He helped her out, then glanced along the street and pointed at the Dueler that was parked a few doors down in the shadows beyond the next streetlight. "You don't suppose we're going to find your brother in the backyard again, do you?"

Lisa peered into the night. "You know, Roy's car *is* gray." She stared a moment longer, then shrugged. "I can't make out the license, but he wouldn't have the nerve to pull a stunt like that again. Not after I threatened to kill him if he ever did."

Dan merely nodded. But if Roy was actually here, if he interrupted them tonight, there wouldn't be enough left of him for Lisa to kill.

She took his arm, making him forget about her brother, making him forget about everything in the world except how soft and warm she felt beside him.

They walked across the moonlit yard and along the side of the house. As they neared the back, he could hear gently lapping waves. "Sounds as if we're in the country. I didn't hear the river the other night."

"There wasn't as much of a breeze then."

They reached the back door, and Lisa freed her arm from his, dug out her keys, then turned to survey the shadows in the yard.

"I've already checked," he told her. "No visitors tonight."

"Good. I knew that couldn't have been Roy's car."

She smiled up at him...a little uneasily, he thought, and he wanted to fold her into his arms right then and there, wanted to kiss away her nervousness. He managed to resist the urge and, instead, took the keys from her, opened the door and flicked on the inside light switch.

He waited a moment, but she didn't move. "I can almost taste that Chablis," he hinted.

"Right." She shot him another anxious smile, then headed up the stairs. Her hips swayed enticingly, and with each step the slit in the back of her skirt revealed an alluring glimpse of leg.

He simply watched for a moment before starting after her. If she was intentionally trying to be seductive, she couldn't possibly do a more effective job. Lord, he hoped she was intentionally trying.

She paused on the landing at the top to unlock a second door, then pushed it open and gestured him ahead.

Inside, the wall to the left was a row of curtainless windows. Outside, beyond the balcony, the moonlit yard and river lay below.

A table lamp glowed gently in one corner of the room, combining with the moonlight to dimly illuminate a large space decorated in appealing earth tones. The furniture was comfortable-looking, the floor satiny dark wood. A nubby, wheat-colored rug defined the living-room area. Beyond that sat a round pine table with four Windsor chairs. In the center of the table was a ceramic bowl filled with fresh flowers.

The apartment was warm and inviting. It suited her to perfection.

"Dan, the kitchen's through that doorway to the right of the dining room. Would you mind getting the wine? There's a corkscrew in the drawer beside the sink. And the glasses are in the cupboard above it. I'm just going to change into something more comfortable.''

He swallowed hard, his eyes following her from the room. Had she actually said what he'd heard? His imagination conjured up a picture of Lisa wearing a silky black dressing gown . . . with nothing beneath it. He almost groaned, tried unsuccessfully to ignore his arousal, and headed to the kitchen.

It was small. Tiny, even. Two people wouldn't be able to make a meal in it without constantly bumping into each other. He stepped over a little china bowl that was decorated with flowery letters spelling Tiger, thinking how much fun it would be to cook dinner here, with Lisa.

But when he opened the fridge its emptiness told him that not much cooking went on in the tiny kitchen. Aside from the wine, her supplies included only milk, a half-empty can of cat food, a tin of ground coffee and the remnants of what had once been a chocolate cake.

He'd uncorked the Chablis and had just located wineglasses when Lisa spoke from the doorway. ''Find everything all right?''

He turned, his heart suddenly pounding with anticipation. But instead of a black silk dressing gown, her something more comfortable proved to be jeans and a pink mohair sweater that was so bulky it revealed only a hint of her breasts.

The legs of her jeans, though, were skin tight, accentuating the curves of her calves, the shapely length of her thighs. Hell, the way they must be clinging to her behind would probably be enough to put him into cardiac arrest—if he could see her behind. But that darned sweater stretched down to conceal her hips entirely.

She gazed at him curiously for an instant, then broke into a knowing grin.

Oh great, just great. Either his disappointment was written all over his face or she was a mind reader.

She tugged the hem of her sweater down even farther. "It gets chilly on the balcony in the fall. But I thought you'd like to sit outside and look down at the river."

He nodded a lie. All he wanted to look at was her. And actually, he didn't want to do much looking. What he wanted to do was hold her and kiss her. And he'd lay odds that, on the balcony, she had a couple of uncomfortable outdoor chairs. Outdoor chairs that held only one person each.

He picked up the glasses and open bottle, and reluctantly followed her across the living room, glancing longingly at her well-padded couch. He stepped through the French doors after her, back into the coolness of the evening. The two wooden chairs, separated by a small table, were exactly what he'd expected.

Despite her sweater, Lisa shivered a little in the breeze. She gestured at the table, indicating Dan should put the wine and glasses on it. But when she started to sit down he captured her hand, enclosing it firmly in his own, and drew her over to stand beside him at the railing. Her heart began beating faster at his nearness.

Then, in one motion, he released her hand and dropped his arm casually over her shoulder, pulling the length of her body against him, banishing the evening chill.

"Let's just admire your famous river view," he murmured, gazing down at her for a long moment before glancing out over the yard.

Admire the view. Right. Only she couldn't manage to force her gaze away from his face. Her pulse was racing and there was a fluttering sensation in her stomach. And the longer his body rested against hers, the more conscious she grew of his body heat invading her bloodstream, of the way it was curling warm little tendrils of longing deep within her. And the scent of his after-shave was making her think utterly absurd thoughts—thoughts about lying on a forest floor with him amid bark and pine needles.

She stood looking at him, her eyes memorizing the planes and angles of his strong, shadowed profile and sending a message to her fingers about how much they'd enjoy tracing it.

"I envy you the sound of those waves," he offered, glancing at her again. "They must help put you to sleep at night."

She merely nodded, unable to hear any sounds of the night over the hammering of her heart.

And then he smiled down at her—a devastating smile that made her legs feel weak. Without conscious thought, she slipped her arm around his waist and snuggled even more closely against him.

"Hey, that's nice," he murmured, shifting his arm, moving so that she was in front instead of beside him.

He stood gazing at her for one more long, bewitching heartbeat. Then he wrapped his other arm around her waist and drew her to him, bending to kiss her—lightly at first, his tongue merely teasing at her lips until she parted them, inviting the excitement of a deeper kiss.

The thrust of his seeking tongue sent hot shivers through her. The heat of his body, strong yet pliant against hers, was so tantalizing that she pressed more closely against him, loving the feel of her breasts crushing against his chest. He smoothed his hands down her back, then up beneath the bottom of her sweater, and began to caress her behind, pulling her closer yet.

The pressure of his hardness against her lower body sent a surge of increased desire through her.

She began moving against him, and he broke their kiss with a moan, nuzzling her throat, his mouth hot and hungry. Breathlessly, she caught the back of his neck with one hand, splaying her fingers against the corded muscles and drawing his lips back to hers, silently entreating him to continue the exquisite probing of his tongue.

His kiss was hard and eager, his arms around her were strong and reassuring. And his hands... the way he was caressing her made her long for his touch everywhere.

He kissed her until she could barely breathe, until she didn't care if she ever breathed again, until all she cared about was his nearness, his touch and the incredibly erotic sensations he was arousing in her.

Finally he drew back. But only a fraction, only far enough to look at her. His body was still melded to hers, the heat of his arousal still burned against her.

He was, she thought, gazing up at him, the most ruggedly gorgeous man she'd ever seen. Moonbeams were highlighting the angles of his face and dusting his hair with a silvery glow. She reached up to brush a stray lock from his forehead, turning slightly in his arms. And then her hand froze midreach and her body went rigid.

"What?" he murmured.

She tried to speak. The words didn't come out.

"What?" he repeated.

She pulled away and stared down into the yard, trying to see more clearly what she'd only caught a glimpse of from the corner of her eye. There was nothing. Only darkness and moonlit shapes that could be a hundred different night things. But she knew exactly what she'd seen.

"What is it, Lisa?" Dan was gazing downward, too, now. And the tone of his voice had changed from curious to concerned.

"Someone's out there," she whispered. "Someone's watching."

FINALLY DAN looked up from the dark yard to the balcony, and gave an exaggerated shrug. Then he started back toward the house. Lisa headed into the living room, uncertain whether she felt relieved or anxious that he hadn't found whoever had been watching them.

She should have gone down with him and helped look. But he'd been adamant that she stay in the apartment. "If there really *is* someone out there," he'd said, "I want you near the phone, to call the police."

If there really is someone out there. Well, she had twenty-twenty vision, and there wasn't a doubt in her mind that there'd been someone out there, whether Dan had seen him or not. And there wasn't much doubt who it had been. So waiting near the phone hadn't made a lot of sense because she wouldn't have called the police on her own brother.

She and Roy might have fought tooth and nail as children, like cat and dog as teenagers, and even now they didn't always see eye to eye. But he was still her little brother. And deep down, she loved him. Sometimes, though, the love was *so* deep down she could barely find it. This was the second of those times within a week.

And love him or not, she was going to kill him for this. He hadn't spied on her that way since he'd been about fourteen. At least she hadn't caught him at it since then. But a twenty-five-year-old man playing voyeur with his own sister! She was absolutely, literally, going to kill him...if it had actually been him down there. But what if it hadn't?

She almost wished she hadn't started thinking about the man who'd engineered Fiona's fall. Almost wished she hadn't remembered that, whoever the creep was, he was still on the loose. Kurt Kusch might not have turned out to be Detective Moron, but he apparently wasn't any Sherlock Holmes, either. As far as she knew, he still didn't even have a prime suspect. Aside from her and Carl Gustavson, of course.

She stood in the living room, wondering why Dan was taking so long. Eventually, she heard his footsteps on the staircase and threw the door open.

"You didn't know it was me," he said sternly, taking the final two stairs in a single stride. "You shouldn't just open the door without checking who's out here."

"I...well, who else would it have been? And what took you so long?"

"I went out front—to see if the gray Dueler that was parked there had left."

"And?"

"Not a car on the street now, except for mine."

"So...you think it was Roy?"

"Lisa, I didn't see anyone at all. Are you positive there even was someone? Could you just have seen a shadow?"

She shook her head. "Shadows don't move. I saw a man. But I had such a brief glimpse of him. Dan, I'm going to phone home and check whether Roy's there."

"Good idea." Dan stood watching as she dialed. She looked upset as hell, which was hardly surprising. He only hoped it *had* been her fool brother out there.

"Line's busy," she said, hanging up.

He glanced at his watch. "It's almost midnight."

"Well, when there's union trouble brewing, Dad's sometimes on the phone all night. But I . . . I hadn't realized it was so late."

Dan eyed her closely, hoping she wasn't hinting he leave, but seeing that she was. The passion that had been shining in her eyes earlier was gone, replaced by an anxious, worried look. He wanted to cuddle her in his arms and reassure her, but something in her expression told him not to.

He cleared his throat, wishing that simply looking at her didn't arouse him. She obviously wasn't in the mood to pick up where they'd left off. "I . . . do you want me to stay awhile?"

She hesitated, then slowly shook her head. "Thanks, but it's late. And I'll be okay. It was probably Roy down there, doing his best to make an idiot of himself again. And if it wasn't . . . well, I've got good locks. And a guard cat, remember?" She almost managed a smile, but it didn't quite come off.

That made him want, even more, to take her into his arms. "You know, I still haven't caught a glimpse of the mighty guard cat. If I hadn't seen his dish, I'd be starting to think you made him up."

"Trust me. He really does exist. And I'll be fine. I'm not even going to think about anyone lurking. Honestly, I'm not."

Dan took a small, reluctant step backward. "We left that full bottle of wine on the balcony," he tried.

"So we did. I . . . I could put the cork back in and it would be all right until tomorrow night."

A ripple of relief rolled over him, washing away the fear that she'd decided kissing him had been a major mistake. "Tomorrow night?" he repeated.

"Well . . . if you have nothing better to do."

Just offhand, he couldn't imagine anything in the world that would be better to do. "Nothing that comes to mind," he admitted, trying to sound casual but certain he wasn't succeeding. "I'll call you. And dinner tomorrow is on me."

"Dinner." She nodded, smiling.

He slowly backed the rest of the way to the door, then paused, silently asking her to come across the room and kiss him good-night.

Instead, she merely smiled again. "Night, Dan. Talk to you tomorrow."

He opened the door and forced himself to step out onto the landing. "Don't forget to put the dead bolt on."

"I won't. Night." She gave him a tiny wave.

The lock clicked behind Dan, and Lisa sank onto the couch. She hadn't lied when she'd told Dan she wouldn't even think about whether anyone was lurking in her yard. She was ninety-nine percent certain that Roy was her lurker. And there'd be time enough to think about him when she was one hundred percent certain. Right now, she had someone far more important to think about. Mr. Dan Ashly.

She was scarcely able to believe she'd managed to let him walk out that door when she'd so desperately wanted him to stay.

Don't try to kid yourself, a little voice whispered in her ear. All right, then, she'd wanted far more than merely to have him stay. She'd wanted to make love to him. She'd wanted to take him into her bedroom and never let him escape from it. She was in love with the man, and she wanted to make love to him. It was as simple as that.

Dr. Hershberg had been right. There was no fighting Cupid. Even the ton of chocolate she'd eaten hadn't prevented her from falling faster and harder for Dan than she'd ever fallen for a man. Anything she'd felt before had been kid stuff compared to this.

And it had taken every bit of willpower she had, plus some she hadn't known she possessed, not to start kissing him again tonight. But if she'd done that, she'd have ended up kissing him forever—or at least until morning. And she just wasn't the type of woman who jumped into bed with a man without thinking the situation through.

"All right, Saint-John," she murmured. "So start thinking. Exactly what have you got here?"

Well, what she had was that she'd fallen head over heels for a man who half of Walkerton wanted to string up, a man her own father suspected of being part of a plot to destroy Plant W. But that wasn't really a problem. It was merely a misunderstanding. Everyone simply had the wrong impression. Dan had made that clear tonight. So all she had to do was tell her father how things actually stood.

She grabbed the phone from the end table, pushed the redial button and listened to the numbers clicking off.

Rats! The line was still busy. But it wouldn't be busy forever. And once she'd set Dad straight, he'd set the union membership straight, and voilà, Dan would love her for it.

She hugged herself, thinking about Dan loving her. Of course, he hadn't said anything about love, but the way he'd been looking at her since the first moment they'd met...and what she felt for him was so strong that it couldn't possibly be one-sided.

Okay, so where was she thus far? No problem with Dan's study, no problem with unrequited love, no...

Oh. There was that little detail of Dr. Benny, of her plot to make Dan look like a fool on *Fiona*. She winced at the recollection of that. She'd have to do something about it. But what?

She thought rapidly and the answer struck her. When Dr. Benny came for his preinterview tomorrow... well, actually he was coming later today if she was being technical. Whichever, though, when they were discussing the segment, she'd lay down the law about how he was to behave on it. That would do the trick.

Okay. No problem with the study or unrequited love or the show. Anything else?

A minor matter of geography, maybe. She wasn't at all sure she'd like to live in New York. But maybe she was getting just a touch ahead of herself. Dan would be in Walkerton for a few more weeks. So they could proceed slowly...see how things developed. But not too slowly, of course. After all, they'd already wasted the best part of a week.

The phone was still sitting on her lap, so she tried her father again, then sat listening to the busy signal for a moment, deciding whether she should keep trying tonight or wait until morning.

Tiger poked his orange head into the living room—tentatively, as if making sure the coast was really clear.

"Come here and see me, you unsociable cat."

He leaped onto the back of the couch and stalked along its length. She put the phone back on the end table but, instead of curling into her lap, Tiger sat down beside her head and nudged her cheek with his cold little nose.

She ruffled his fur. "You know, I think you'd better start getting used to Mr. Ashly being around here."

"Merrowh," Tiger complained.

"Cats don't have any say in matters like this," she said, rising and reaching for him. "So let's just lock up, put that wine away, and go to bed. I'll worry about getting hold of Dad in the morning."

The cat snuggled against her shoulder and kissed her cheek with his moist, rough tongue.

"Not the best kiss I've had tonight, Tiger," she murmured. "Not even close."

"BRRRINNG...BRRRINNG..."

Lisa woke with a start, the most delicious dream she'd ever had immediately beginning to fade. She buried her face in the pillow, trying to cling to the gorgeous image of Dan Ashly, trying not to lose the tingle his imaginary touch had engendered. But the dratted ringing was demanding every bit of her sleepy attention.

She groggily fumbled in the general direction of the bedside table. Tiger meowed in panic when she almost squashed him beneath her arm, then scurried to safety at the bottom of the bed.

Sightlessly, she found the alarm and clicked it off.

Brrrinng... brrrinng...

Phone, something in a tiny corner of her brain told her. Phone? At...oh, geez, six-thirty, she saw, squinting through the dim morning light at the clock.

She reached past it for the phone, silently swearing at whoever was calling. She and Dan had been on the verge of making love, and that glorious dream had been interrupted by what had to be a wrong number. Everyone who knew her knew that she wasn't a morning person.

Well, maybe not quite everyone, she realized, simultaneously grabbing the receiver and breaking into a smile. She could certainly forgive Dan for waking her up to say "good morning." Heck, she could probably forgive Dan for anything.

"Hello?"

"Morning, Lisa, sorry to wake you."

"Dad?" Dad, not Dan? Dad, at six-thirty in the morning? "Dad, what's wrong? Is Mom all right?"

"Yes, yes, she's fine. Look, baby, I have to talk to you. Can you come over to the house for breakfast?"

"Ah..."

"It's important. I'll call a cab for you, okay?"

"Ahh...okay. Dad, what's up? Roy hasn't gotten himself into trouble, has he?"

The slight pause told her that whatever this was about, her brother was involved.

"No, Roy's not in trouble, Lisa. And there's nothing for you to worry about. It's just...it's just that I have to talk to you about something."

"All right. I'll be ready by the time the cab gets here."

"Thanks, baby."

She rolled out of bed, wishing she could lie there instead—lie there and think happy thoughts about Dan. But what on earth was wrong at home? Regardless of what Dad had said, she'd just bet that her brother—

Roy! How could she have forgotten what he'd done? Forgotten even for a minute that her brother was a voyeuristic spy? She should have thought to ask her father whether Roy'd been out late last night.

Well, she'd find out soon enough. And if he'd been out late last night, he'd darned well better be at home this morning. She'd get her hands around his throat and never let go. That's what she'd do.

But what if...no, Dad had said Roy wasn't in trouble...but what if he actually was? What if he'd been picked up for drunk driving last night?

If he'd spent the evening at the Silver Dollar, that would explain the nonsense in her yard. Not excuse it, of course, but explain it. Then, after she'd spotted him, he'd probably driven off and been stopped. And Dad had bailed him out. And her mother would be incredibly upset.

She scooped her pink sweater and jeans off the floor and grabbed clean lingerie from the drawer. She'd have to come back to shower and change before work, but given the anxious sound of her father's voice, she'd better make it to the house as soon as she could.

CHAPTER EIGHT

LISA WAS ONLY halfway up the walk when her father appeared on the front porch dressed in a three-piece suit and conservative tie. His worried expression hastened her step. Whatever was wrong was darned serious.

"Morning, Dad," she murmured at the door, kissing his cheek.

"Morning, baby."

"Well?" she demanded when he didn't volunteer anything more.

He smoothed his graying mustache with his forefinger, a sure sign he was upset. "Go on in, Lisa. This is as much Roy's story as mine."

She headed along the center hall into the kitchen. Her mother was fidgeting with a handful of cutlery and, as Lisa had expected, looked incredibly upset.

Her hair was pulled back into its standard French knot, but she hadn't bothered to weave the gray strands beneath the brown. Her blue eyes were troubled, and the tiny wrinkles beside them seemed to have grown deeper over the few days since Lisa had last seen her.

"Hi, Mom." Lisa managed a smile.

Her mother barely managed a nod.

Roy, sitting at the table, his hands wrapped around a mug, looked positively grim.

Lisa slipped into her childhood seat across the table from Roy and glared at him. He glanced at her, his expression guilty, then stared down into his coffee. She resisted the urge to give him a swift, hard kick under the table, the way she'd sometimes done when they were growing up.

"Morning, little brother," she muttered as her father sat down at his regular place. Then she bit her tongue, deciding she'd be unwise to say anything more at the moment.

If their parents weren't here, she'd tell Roy that if she ever caught him playing Peeping Tom again, he'd never be able to make her an aunt. But their parents *were* here. And as long as they were, she wasn't keen on getting into a discussion about what she and Dan had been doing on her balcony.

Her mother slipped a mug in front of her. Today, the sum total of breakfast, which Helen Saint-John truly believed to be the most important meal of the day, was apparently coffee.

"Thanks, Mom," Lisa murmured, looking from her father to Roy, waiting for one of them to speak.

Instead, it was her mother who broke the silence. "Roy, begin by telling your sister about—"

"Just a minute," Bert interrupted. "I started this. Let me finish it my own way."

"Bert, I don't like your way. I told you from the beginning that you shouldn't involve Lisa. Now, will you tell her—"

"In a minute, Helen," he snapped. "Baby," he went on more softly, "what did you and Ashly talk about last night? About Plant W, I mean?"

Lisa glanced at her mother for an instant, just long enough to see that she was wearing the tight-lipped expression that said she totally disapproved of what her husband was doing.

But what *was* he doing? Well, at this precise moment, he was staring at his daughter, waiting for the report she'd promised him on her dinner with Dan.

Apparently, her guess about the police picking up Roy had been wrong. This meeting had been called to discuss Plant W. But why did everyone look so upset?

"You did talk about QM?" Bert pressed. "About the study?"

"Yes. Yes, we talked about the study. And the bottom line is that it's not a put-up job, Dad. If the company's trying anything underhanded, Dan doesn't know about it. As far as he's concerned, he's here to give them an impartial analysis of the operation. And to assess the future market for the Dueler. And that's it. He...he's a good guy. You have nothing to worry about from him."

"You're sure of that, baby?"

"Yes. Dad, Jake told me at the start that Dan wouldn't be in QM's pocket. And he was right. We jumped to the wrong conclusion, that's all."

"Baby...baby, just take a minute and think through your conversation last night. Did Ashly say anything...I don't even know what I'm asking you for, but did he say anything that surprised you? Ask any questions that struck you as strange? Tell you anything you didn't already know?"

She shook her head, rerunning the conversation in her mind. "Nothing. He didn't say anything suspicious, if that's what you're getting at. I mean, he's even trying to be helpful, Dad. He even asked me to mention to you that Woody figures you're taking too hard a line with the company, that it may backfire on you."

Bert leaned forward, resting his elbows on the table.
"Exactly what did he say about that, Lisa?"

"He said...just let me recall...his exact words were
that Woody thinks you're pushing Detroit too hard
with the illegal strike threat. That the company might
decide to call your bluff, not give you the answers today and see if you actually walk."

"That's all he said?"

"Pretty well. I mean, he suggested you might be wise
to delay doing anything, even if you don't get what you
want."

"He did, did he?" Roy muttered.

"Yes. And it made sense, Roy. He said Woody figures that Dad backed Detroit into too tight a corner.
And the company won't like that. But if the union
eased up on its ultimatum, then you'd get all the answers you want in due course. Without the membership suffering the cost of a strike."

"Anything else, Lisa?" her father asked. "Anything else you can tell us?"

"I...Dad, what's going on here?"

He reached into his pocket, produced a sheet of paper and unfolded it. "Roy got hold of this a couple of
hours ago," he said, passing it to her.

A couple of hours ago? As in about 5:00 a.m.? Roy
had certainly been a busy boy lately. She stared at the
paper for a moment, uncertain what she was supposed
to make of it.

"It's a photocopy of a hotel statement," she finally
said, looking across at her brother. "The Pritchard
House."

"Where your friend is staying," he pointed out,
managing to turn the word *friend* into an obscenity.

"And that's part of his bill. It shows the latest trans-actions."

"Dammit, Roy! You mean you haven't only been spying on me? You've been spying on Dan, too? Who the hell do you think you are? James Bond?"

"You should be glad that *one* of us is actually find-ing out what's going on," he snapped back at her. "Because, given what I saw last night, you obviously got thrown right off track."

Oh, Lord. Roy'd never been very circumspect, but surely he hadn't made the balcony scene common knowledge in the Saint-John household. She glanced at her father. He was studiously examining his tie. And her mother was eyeing her coffee mug with apparent fascination.

Rats! Roy *had* told them. She glared at him so fiercely that her face began to hurt.

"Lisa, instead of looking at me with murder in your eyes, why don't you take a gander at the room charges? Look at that long-distance phone call Ashly made to Detroit last night. Or, I suppose 1:10 a.m. is really first thing in the morning. Lisa, he left your place, went back to his hotel and phoned the president of QM. On his personal home line. In the middle of the night."

The president of QM? Lisa barely heard anything past those words. But they couldn't be true, because it would mean Dan had lied to her, that when he'd taken her out he'd been doing it for the company. "Roy, how can you know whose number that is? I don't believe for a minute that Mr. Wireton's personal home number is listed."

"No, baby," Bert said quietly, "it isn't. But I have it on file."

She simply stared at her father, trying to figure out exactly what they were telling her.

"Sis," Roy said more gently, "what you said, about Dad backing Detroit into too tight a corner? That he should ease off? Well, Ashly was obviously giving you a message the company wanted Dad to have. And after he'd given it to you, he hightailed it back to his hotel and reported in, told the president that he'd accomplished his mission. And...and they'll likely figure in Detroit that Dad will be amenable to easing the union position because of those supposedly innocent comments Ashly got you to pass along to him."

"That Dad will be amenable," Lisa whispered as this whole awful scene suddenly made sense, "because Dan Ashly sucked in the union president's daughter."

She looked down at her coffee, suddenly nauseous, certain that if she took even one more sip she'd throw up. Dan had been using her. The company didn't want a wildcat strike, and he'd been using her to convince her father it would be a bad move. Gradually, anger began to mingle with the sick feeling that was churning inside her. What had Dan said the QM workers thought of him? The words came to her. They'd decided he was a dirty rotten bastard. Well, the workers were a damned sight smarter than she was, then, weren't they? They'd pegged him perfectly while she and her fool instincts had...

Damn. She'd been a total idiot. She'd misread Dan Ashly and let him worm his way right into her heart, and he'd turned around and used her and hurt her and...yes, one of those fifteen different painful emotions swirling around inside her was definitely hurt. A really terrible, knife-in-the-stomach hurt that was making her throat ache and her eyes burn with tears.

Dan Ashly had sucked her in all right—hook, line, sinker, and then some. And while he'd been merrily using her, he'd have been only too happy to go to bed with her if she'd invited him. Thank heavens she hadn't! Lord, calling him a dirty rotten bastard was letting him off far too easily.

Her father covered her hand with his. "Baby, I didn't mean to get you into—" he paused and cleared his throat "—into any sort of . . . of emotional mess. When I asked you to get close to Ashly I didn't mean that you should . . ."

She blinked fiercely. "I didn't. I didn't get as close to him as Roy apparently implied. And I didn't get into any emotional mess."

"Lisa," Helen murmured. "Honey, calm down and—"

"I'm perfectly calm!"

"Baby, baby, listen. I'm sorry. Your mother's right. I should never have involved you in this. But I do appreciate what you've done. Very much. We learned exactly what we wanted to learn. Ashly's been bought and paid for by QM. There's just one more thing, Lisa. Don't tell the guy we're on to him. His not knowing might prove useful."

Her father continued speaking, but she stopped listening. Don't tell the guy they were on to him? Hell, she wouldn't be telling him the time of day. She was never going to see the man again, let alone speak to him. Dan Ashly was pond scum. He was out to get her father and Roy and the other workers, and he obviously didn't care what he did or said or who he used along the way.

And . . . and she'd fallen in love with him. And she'd thought he was falling in love with her.

A trickle of tears escaped, and she rubbed at her eyes, hoping no one would notice, furious at herself for feeling as if her world had just collapsed.

Well, she'd darned well pick up the pieces and put Dan Ashly out of her mind and never see him again and . . . and she had that damned show to do with him on Friday.

She couldn't. She simply couldn't. But she was going to have to. And not only was she going to have to do it, she'd have to be civil to him. Otherwise, he'd realize they were on to him. And, aside from that, Jake certainly wouldn't put up with her misbehaving. Lord, the powers-that-be had turned against her. All of them. En masse.

Her father finished whatever he'd been saying and rose. "I've got to get down to the union hall. It's going to be a busy day. Want me to give you a ride home, baby?"

She merely shook her head, not trusting her voice.

"And I've got to get to the plant," Roy said, so eager to escape that he bumped the table, scrambling to his feet.

"Look, Sis," he added, backing out of the kitchen. "I was just trying to watch out for you. And don't say anything to anyone about that copy of the hotel bill, huh? Someone could lose their job for giving it to me."

Seconds later, the front door closed soundly behind the Saint-John men. Another few moments and two car engines roared to life in the driveway. Lisa pushed back her chair and forced herself up. "I'll just call a cab, Mom," she managed to say.

She had the number half dialed when her mother tentatively touched her arm. "Lisa? Honey, are you okay?"

"Oh, Mom," she murmured tearfully, hanging up the receiver. "How could a man seem so wonderful and actually be so rotten? And knowing how rotten he is, how can I feel this awful? I just want to curl up and die."

"It'll be all right, honey," Helen murmured, wrapping her arms around her daughter. "It'll be all right. You'll see."

Lisa buried her head against her mother's shoulder and let her tears flow. Until today, she'd never have believed a man could make her feel so miserable. And hurt. And humiliated. She'd been such a fool, thinking he was sincere when he'd merely been turning on the charm for QM's benefit. "I hate him," she said between sobs. "I hate him more than I've ever hated anyone."

Her mother didn't reply. She merely patted Lisa's back and held her while she cried.

BENEDETTO STELLE shot yet another dazzling smile across Lisa's desk. She swallowed over the lump in her throat, deciding it had become a permanent fixture, and tried to make the corners of her lips curl up. But Dr. Benny's expression told her she was only succeeding in looking as sick as she felt.

Not long ago, that smile of his might have had some effect on her. Because he was every bit as good-looking as his photo, every inch the personification of the handsome Latin lover. But this wasn't not long ago. This was now. Now, as in after Dan Ashly had walked into her life and trampled her heart to a pulp.

Whoever first said "better to have loved and lost than never to have loved at all" must have been the masochist of his century.

Well, never mind the saying about loving and losing. She'd concentrate on the saying ''don't get mad, get even.'' Because getting even was the only thing she could think of that might possibly make her feel better. Although, deep down, she doubted there was anything in the world that could make her feel better.

But regardless of whether seeing Dan have a rough time on *Fiona* did anything to lift her spirits, putting him in a negative light could only help Plant W's cause.

Benedetto cleared his throat, drawing her attention back to him.

''Sorry,'' she murmured. ''Between my assistant being on vacation and Fiona in the hospital, I've got too much on my mind. Where were we?''

Concentrate, she ordered herself as he began speaking again. *The harder you concentrate, the less you'll think about Dan.*

''You were talking about the show, Lisa. But you are certain that you want me to tell how dull I find analysts who play only with numbers? I have the tendency to get carried away and make the insults. I am trying lately not to be so...abrasive, is the word, no?''

She nodded, hoping abrasive was indeed the word, hoping that Dr. Benny would be as abrasive as he knew how.

''And some television programs I have been on,'' he continued, ''the host has not...how do you say...has not appreciated my bluntness.''

''I want you to be entirely yourself, Benedetto. At least blunt isn't boring. And I'm afraid Mr. Ashly is one of those dull men who does play only with numbers.''

"Ahh, but if Plant W walks out, then perhaps he shall have a more interesting topic. The strike deadline is this afternoon, no?"

"Yes. Six o'clock."

"And you think this illegal strike will happen, Lisa?"

"I . . . I don't know."

"No. I do not know, either. I have not had time to consult my charts, to see what the heavens predict."

She eyed him closely, wondering if he actually believed the astrological nonsense he spouted.

He grinned at her—a conspiratorial kind of grin that made her think he wasn't actually as nutty as his reputation had led her to believe. In fact, she wouldn't be surprised to learn he wasn't nutty at all, that he merely enjoyed making fun of people who took themselves too seriously.

Well, he could make all the fun of Mr. Dan Ashly he cared to. "I have the impression," she offered, "that whether the plant shuts down or not, Dan isn't at liberty to say anything really meaningful about what's happening at QM. So the viewers might not find him very interesting. But I'm certain they'll be fascinated to hear about how the stars influence companies' successes."

"Not influence, Lisa. Control. Corporate fates are entirely controlled by the zodiac. Just as are human fates. Nothing matters at all except the movements of the heavens."

He grinned at her once more, and this time she almost managed to smile—by visualizing how upset Dan was likely to get when he heard that line. Then her gaze fell on the tiny stack of phone messages from Dan and any trace of a smile vanished.

She'd be forced to speak to Dan again. During the show, if not before that. But she certainly wasn't going to return those calls. She'd been managing to keep her tears at bay by focusing on how angry, rather than how hurt, she felt. But she definitely wasn't up to talking to him.

Besides, she knew what he wanted. He was calling about tonight. About dinner. And about the Chablis in her fridge, the wine he expected to drink with her.

Fat chance of that. She'd break the blasted bottle over his head before she'd share it with him.

"And this other guest?" Benedetto said. "This Dan Ashly? You have told him I will be on the show also?"

"Yes, I've told him."

"And he will not become upset if I make the predictions based on what the planets say? He will not mind if I tell him that his analytical methods do not make the predictions as well as mine?"

"He's looking forward to guesting with you," she lied. "In fact, he told me that he's seen you on other talk shows and thinks your approach is refreshing."

"Really?" Benedetto's raised eyebrow said he found that difficult to believe. "I will look forward to meeting this Mr. Ashly, then. Because I have appeared with many analysts who did not think my approach was refreshing. In fact, I have appeared with one who—what is the phrase—ah, yes, one who poked me in the nose."

"Really? On camera?"

Benedetto nodded.

"Oh," she murmured. Oh, indeed. Probably it was unrealistic to hope that Dan might physically assault Dr. Benny on live television. If he did, though, it certainly wouldn't do much for his credibility. It might even land him in jail.

But, good grief, what was she thinking? She should be ashamed of herself. "I'm sure Mr. Ashly won't poke you in the nose," she said firmly.

"Did I hear my name?"

Her heart stopped beating at the sound of Dan's voice. Slowly, she turned away from Benedetto, praying she was merely hearing things.

No such luck. The last man on earth she wanted to see was standing in her office doorway...smiling at her...making her feel as if someone was gleefully twisting that knife she was certain was lodged in her stomach.

She was sure she couldn't speak. Fortunately, Dan didn't wait until she tried. Instead, he glanced at Benedetto, a flicker of recognition crossing his face. "Dr. Stelle," he said, extending his hand. "I've seen you on television. I'm Dan Ashly."

"Ahh, *sì*." Benedetto rose and shook Dan's hand. "Please call me Benedetto. Lisa has just now been telling me about you."

Dan flashed her another smile, as if he assumed she'd said complimentary things.

"I am so looking forward to the show with you," Benedetto offered, leaning casually against the wall.

Dan nodded. "I expect it'll be interesting. Sorry to disturb your meeting," he added, turning back to Lisa, "but I've been trying to get hold of you all day, so I decided to drop by for a couple of minutes. I guess you haven't been picking up your phone messages."

She took a deep breath, grateful she'd had even a brief minute to compose herself.

Be calm, a tiny, imaginary voice reminded her. *And keep control. After Friday, you'll never have to see this*

*man again. But in the meantime, Dad doesn't want him
to suspect what you know.*

Okay. She was going to make it through this scene if
it killed her. "You're right, Dan. I haven't even
thought about phone messages. The station's been absolutely crazy today. Jake has everything turned up-
side down so we can go live to Plant W the moment
there's any news."

"Yeah. They should be hearing from Detroit soon.
I've got to get right back, but I could pick you up here
once we know what's happening. Or we could leave for
dinner from your place if you'd rather."

"Dinner?" Benedetto leaned forward slightly, away
from the wall, looking puzzled. "But you are having
dinner with me, Lisa. At Trattoria Ricci, no? You have
not forgotten."

She closed her eyes in relief. Not every single power-
that-be had turned against her, after all. She might
manage to get through the rest of this scene, but never,
in a million years, could she have gotten through the
evening with Dan. And she'd just been handed a perfect out.

Not that she intended to have dinner with Benedetto, either. Trying to slip even a bite of food past the
lump in her throat would choke her. All she wanted to
do tonight was go home and have a good, therapeutic,
five-hour cry. But she'd worry about getting out of one
date at a time.

Dan was looking at Benedetto. Then he gazed back
at her, obviously waiting for her to tell the other man
that he was out of luck.

She forced what she hoped would pass for an apol-
ogetic expression. "Oh, Dan, I'm sorry. I *did* make
dinner plans with Benedetto. Yesterday afternoon we

decided we'd go to Trattoria Ricci. I . . . I forgot all about it."

Dan merely stared at her. She pulled her gaze from his and looked unseeingly at the surface of her desk.

Finally he cleared his throat. "There was something about some Chablis later. Is that still on?"

She fought down the urge to scream at him, to tell him he could cut the act, could stop pretending he was disappointed, stop pretending he actually wanted to see her again. Well, maybe he did. Maybe he had more spying to do for QM.

Be careful what you say or it'll all come rushing out, that imaginary voice whispered to her.

"I . . . I think I'd be smarter to get an early night tonight, Dan." She sat gazing at her desk, feeling his eyes on her.

The silence lengthened. She bit her lip, willing him to leave.

"I see," he eventually said. "Well . . . I guess I'll see you both on Friday, then."

She listened to his footsteps fade down the corridor, unable to hold back a few stray tears. When she finally looked up, Benedetto was sitting in the chair once more, watching her. She sniffed, terribly embarrassed. He must think she was an emotional basket case.

"I had the suspicion there was more that bothered you today than having absent staff," he offered quietly. "I should not have said about dinner. I did not realize when I spoke."

"It's all right. I . . . it's too long a story to get into, Benedetto."

"I see."

"There is," he continued a few moments later, "a Spanish saying that I am thinking of, Lisa."

"You aren't Spanish," she managed to say.

"In Europe we learn many languages. And the saying is *Quien bien te quiere te hará llorar.* Whoever really loves you will make you cry."

She shook her head. "I'm afraid you couldn't be further from the truth. Dan doesn't love me. In fact..." She ended with a shrug, unable to keep her voice from quavering.

"I would not be so sure, Lisa. The way Dan Ashly looked at me I feared I might get that poke in the nose we spoke of. And the way he looked at you...I would not be so sure at all.

"Perhaps," he added after a pause, "you would prefer to go to Trattoria Ricci another time?"

"I...I think that would be best. Thank you for being so understanding."

Benedetto nodded and was halfway out of his chair when Crystal breezed into the office. He looked at her, sank back into the chair and kept right on looking.

"Oh," she said, stopping midstride, her long blond hair still swaying for a second after she ceased moving. "Sorry. I saw Dan leaving and thought you were alone, Lisa."

"It's all right. We're done. But you haven't met Professor Stelle, Crystal. He's going to be our second guest on *Fiona* this Friday."

"Not Professor Stelle. Benedetto," he corrected, rising and taking Crystal's hand in both of his. "I am so pleased to meet you, Crystal."

Lisa sat watching them gaze at each other until she began wondering if Benedetto was ever going to release Crystal's hand . . . if either of them was ever going to move again.

"Ahh . . . did you want anything special, Crystal?" she finally tried.

Crystal glanced across the desk, her blue eyes vacant, as if she were in a trance. Suddenly, she snapped out of it and, clearly flustered, pulled her hand free from Benedetto's. "Yes, I did want something . . . but I can't remember what it was."

Crystal blushed.

Benedetto smiled. "Forgetfulness," he said. "That is a common trait in a Libra."

Crystal gazed at him with a puzzled expression. "How did you know I'm a Libra?"

"No woman could be so beautiful but a Libra. You have even a Venus dimple."

Lisa glanced back at Crystal. Darned if she didn't have a dimple.

"I . . . Lisa, it was something about *Love* I wanted to ask you about," Crystal stammered.

"Love?" Benedetto repeated. "Italians know much about love. Perhaps I might help?"

"No. I mean it's not about love. I mean not the emotion. *Love* is the name of the show I host, *Love in the Afternoon.*" Briefly, Crystal explained the talk show's format.

"But . . . but I shouldn't be going on about *Love,*" she finally said. "It's not the type of show men are interested in."

"Only American men are not so interested in love." Benedetto gave her one of his dazzling smiles. "I would like to hear more of your show. My colleagues talk only about business. I wonder . . . ?"

"Yes?" Crystal prompted.

"I wonder if you have a husband waiting for you at home?"

"No. No husband."

"Ahh. Then would you join me for dinner? Lisa has—how do you say—she has stood me up."

Crystal shot Lisa a "have you lost your mind?" look.

She shrugged. "Something came up. But we were only going out to discuss the *Fiona* segment," she added quickly, seeing the uncertainty in Crystal's eyes. "And if you go, I won't feel guilty about Benedetto having to eat alone."

"I do so hate to eat alone," he added.

"Well . . . if you're sure, Lisa."

"I'm sure."

Benedetto took Crystal's arm, settling the matter. "Ciao, Lisa," he said. "Do not be sad tonight."

"Sad?" Crystal repeated, glancing back, looking concerned.

"It's nothing. Go. I'll tell you about it tomorrow." She wouldn't, though. If Crystal asked, she'd brush off the question. She never wanted to talk about Dan Ashly again.

"Well, ciao, then," Crystal said with a tiny laugh, smiling up at Benedetto as they left.

Lisa sat at her desk for a long while after they'd gone. The way Benedetto had looked at Crystal when she'd walked into the office had struck a memory chord. It was the way Dan had looked at her the first time she'd seen him.

Dan's look had been a lie, though. She hoped, for Crystal's sake, that Benedetto's hadn't been.

Finally, she got ready to leave, feeling empty and melancholy. Melancholy...such an old-fashioned word but such a perfect one to describe her mood. The hurt and anger she'd been feeling all day had melded into a dull, aching sadness that filled her heart.

Dr. Hershberg had been right. You couldn't help who you fell in love with. But she'd give the world to have fallen for Mr. Right instead of Mr. Wrong.

She turned off her office light and started down the hall. Maybe she should stop on the way home and buy a five-pound box of chocolates to give Crystal in the morning. But the way Crystal had been looking at Benedetto, chocolates wouldn't do *her* any good, either.

CHAPTER NINE

KEN WOODY looked at his office clock for the tenth time in as many minutes, once more distracting Dan from thoughts of Lisa. Ken Woody was a damned irritating man.

Her image had just reappeared when the plant manager muttered something about it being 5:45, almost deadline time. The image instantly vanished again.

But why in blazes, Dan asked himself, *did he even want to think about Lisa?* She'd clearly decided she preferred to be with that Italian stargazer. That *crazy* Italian stargazer. Talk about a blow to the ego. Dan Ashly had been thrown over for the nutty professor.

Well, Lisa was obviously flighty as hell, so he was better off rid of her. And Benedetto Stelle was welcome to her. In fact, he hoped they had a wonderful time tonight at...at Trattoria Ricci.

Damn. The way Dr. Benny had pronounced the name, his accent suggested they were off to a restaurant in Italy, rather than just down the block. And the menu would be loaded with all those stupid pastas that slipped off your fork when you tried to eat them. And they'd undoubtedly drink Chianti instead of Chablis.

Chablis. He wished he could get his mind off that Chablis. Last night, he'd dreamed about that bottle of wine. Well, actually, his dream had been more about what would happen after he and Lisa had finished drinking it. But now she'd probably invite the Latin lunatic in to share it with her.

He could feel his anger growing red-hot all over again at the thought of his Lisa and that nut bar being alone together in her apartment. Of course, she wasn't *his* Lisa at all. It was just that last night, the way she'd been kissing him, the way he'd been liking it...well, far more than liking it, but, at any rate, he'd started thinking of her as *his* Lisa.

He was definitely going to stop thinking of her that way, though. Lisa Saint-John was nothing more than a damned flirt. She probably played her game with every man she met. But he was done playing with her.

Not that he figured she'd invite him back for a rematch. If she did, though...well, he had her pegged now. And he wasn't having anything more to do with her, even if she asked him to. Which she probably wouldn't.

But why hadn't Jake warned him what she was like? He'd had only good things to say about her. Of course, Jake never was much of a judge of women.

Woody looked at the clock again. "Ten to six. Detroit's certainly leaving this till the last minute."

As if on cue, the phone rang. Woody grabbed it.

The conversation was a quick one, with Woody doing almost none of the talking. But his expression said that the company wanted him to tell the union to go to hell.

He hung up and shrugged at Dan. "Guess we're going to find out how serious Saint-John was about his strike threat. If they walk, will I be seeing you tomorrow?"

"Sure. There's a fair amount of information that I can get whether the plant's operating or not. Let's hope it is, though."

"Yeah, let's hope," Woody muttered, heading into the hallway and turning in the direction of the plant's union office.

Dan stood gazing out the window, trying to imagine the ensuing scene. Bert Saint-John would be waiting with the other top union executives. They'd come over from the union hall earlier. Maybe some of the stewards would be with them. Probably Roy, for one. Maybe some members of the in-plant negotiating committee, as well.

And when Woody told them Detroit wasn't going to open up about the study, they'd either give the afternoon shift the word to hit the bricks or they'd back off. He certainly hoped they'd back off. Strikes might be the only serious weapon unions had, but a wildcat never did either side any good.

Well, he'd done what little he could to help by raising the issue with Lisa. Now it was simply a matter of waiting to see. He paced the breadth of Woody's office a couple of times, feeling like a caged lion, then headed out. If there was going to be any action, it would be on the plant floor.

DAN STOOD on a catwalk that stretched from one side of the engine dress-up line all the way across to the body-build area. The sheer size of the nation's large auto plants never ceased to amaze him. Plant W covered close to sixty acres, and workers had to use bicycles to get from one area to another.

He glanced once more at the double doors leading to the office wing. A good twenty minutes had passed since Detroit's call, and he still saw no sign of Bert Saint-John or his crew. Maybe that was good news. Maybe it meant the union was going to give Detroit some time to come around.

Almost directly beneath him, a foreman stopped and checked his watch, no doubt thinking the same thing Dan was. The supervisory staff knew that if there was going to be trouble it would likely come about six.

The foreman walked on, and Dan gazed back out over the expanse of conveyor equipment. If the various assembly lines were stretched out, instead of coiled in and around themselves like gigantic mechanical snakes, they'd extend for almost twelve miles. And the cacophony of their combined clanks and clatters made normal levels of conversation impossible.

Below, to one side, a slow-moving belt was bringing tires from the storage area, every fifth one a mini-spare. They thudded rhythmically along, each clinking onto an inflator, then whirring their way through the balancing equipment, all the while making the air smell of new rubber.

Dan turned to check the doors again, just in time to see them opening.

Bert Saint-John stepped onto the plant floor, flanked by the two younger union officials who'd been with him on Monday. Then Roy and a couple of men Dan didn't know appeared. The group began making its way across the plant, dispersing to various areas as they walked.

None of them said a word. They simply nodded to the workers.

One by one, as the union officials passed, switches were turned off, machines were silenced, lines stopped moving, and the noise level began to drop.

Dan followed Bert with his eyes until the president disappeared behind the fire door of the tire storage area. A moment later, the belt below the catwalk slowed to a halt, leaving one tire poised halfway on a now-inactive inflator.

Within another minute, Plant W's equipment was totally silent. Men and women who were holding tools or parts put them down. Bert Saint-John reappeared and wordlessly led the workers toward the series of huge overhead doors off the finishing area.

A few jeers rang out, directed at the supervisors, but for the most part, the thousand or so workers filed quietly from the plant. Dan stood watching until the last of them had straggled out, until the only people left were the foremen and supervisors who were beginning a systematic check to ensure all the equipment had been properly shut down.

Slowly, Dan walked along the catwalk, headed down the stairs and started across to an exit. There was no point in checking in with Woody until tomorrow. For the next few hours Woody would be up to his ears, trying to sort out this mess. He was probably on the phone right now, reporting the union's walkout to Detroit. Then he'd be meeting with his managers and foremen.

Dan opened the door, stepped out into the freshness of the early-evening air and surveyed the scene.

Roy and the other men who'd accompanied Bert had apparently been named picket captains. They were passing out placards and organizing the afternoon shift into a picket line.

The union had prepared thoroughly. Already, fires were burning in oil drums. Unnecessary on a warm

September evening, Dan thought absently. Unnecessary but part of the ritual.

He started for the parking lot, not really looking at the strikers. Since Monday, he'd seen the occasional fellow he knew from his student days, not men he'd ever considered close friends, but good acquaintances all the same. Guys who'd normally have stopped to shoot the breeze with him. Not now, though. Now they looked straight through him, as if he didn't exist.

In the past three days, he'd learned how a ghost must feel. And after the first few cold shoulders, he'd stopped acknowledging people he recognized, had stopped setting himself up for the sting of being ignored.

Involuntarily, he looked at the man walking toward him. Craig Bradstock, who'd refused to shake his hand Monday morning. That had been more than just a sting. Craig *had* been a close friend.

Craig hesitated, glancing around. They were alone in the driveway between plant and parking lot, and, when Dan gave a stiff nod, the other man stopped.

"Ahh...it's been a long time, huh, Dan?"

"Sure has. Over ten years." He wished he could say it felt good to be back. It felt anything but, though. "How's life been treating you, Craig?"

"Not bad. I'm married...three kids. And you?"

"No, not yet. I'm still looking."

Craig nodded, eased along a few steps, then stopped again. "Look, Dan, about the other morning..."

"Yeah, I understand. I didn't expect to win any popularity contests. I just...well, I guess I was just hoping there wouldn't be so much hostility, that everyone wouldn't jump to conclusions. Despite the rumors, I'm really not here to cause grief."

"Just doing your job," Craig said with a rueful smile. "But people . . . well, you were gone before we had the long strike, Dan. But we all remember how tough that year was. And we all know how bad things would be if Plant W shut down permanently. When you've got kids to support . . . when your entire life has been in Walkerton . . . well, you'll be leaving again in a month or so, but we'll still be here."

Dan shook his head. "I'm not here to destroy people's lives. I'm really not."

"Yeah, just doing your job," Craig said again. "Well, see you."

Dan watched the other man head on down the driveway, feeling uncomfortably like the Grinch who stole Christmas. Most of the workers were married. Most probably had kids to support. If only there was something he could say, something he could do . . . if only he could simply pack up and leave.

Craig disappeared into the crowd of picketers, and Dan stood surveying the scene for a moment. A large WALK mobile trailer was parked by the main entrance, and, to one side of it, Bert Saint-John was being interviewed. Dan started quickly in the other direction, hoping no one on the camera crew would spot him. He could do without another session in the limelight.

He reached the road and took a final glance back at Bert, wondering whether Lisa had passed on the suggestion that the union ease off its hard line. If she did, her father obviously hadn't bought the logic.

Shoving his hands into his pockets, Dan strode through the early evening crispness, wishing he hadn't begun thinking of Lisa again, unable to stop.

SIMULTANEOUSLY, Lisa's phone rang, and Crystal walked into the office, wearing a mile-wide grin.

"Hi." Lisa motioned Crystal to sit down and answered the phone, thankful for her busy job. The past few days, it had kept her thoughts from dwelling morosely on Dan. Well . . . at least it had kept her from dwelling on him for more than twenty-three hours out of each twenty-four.

"Lisa, it's Gloria," the voice on the other end of the line announced. "Detective Kusch wants to take all the *Fiona* tapes to view over the weekend. He says he'll bring them back first thing Monday morning. Is that okay?"

"He wants all of them? Six months' worth?"

"It's only a couple of dozen. Anyway, he says *all*. He's leaving for his cottage straight from here and thinks he might want to replay some he's already seen. So is it okay?"

"Well . . . I guess. Thanks for checking with me."

"It's called covering your backside," Gloria said, laughing. "While I've got you, though, good luck with the show tonight. We'll all be watching your debut."

"Thanks. I just hope I don't fall flat on my face."

"You won't. You'll be perfectly fine. But even if you weren't, none of the viewers would notice. No female ones at least. Not with those two hunks you have lined up as guests. I can't decide which of them is more gorgeous."

Lisa swallowed hard. Every time she managed to get her mind off Dan, it took about two seconds before something happened that made him pop right back into her thoughts. And she didn't want to think about him. It hurt far too much. And if simply thinking about him hurt so badly, how was seeing him again going to affect her?

She'd soon find out. It was almost five, and the guests were due into makeup at six-thirty.

"Well, bye, Lisa."

"Bye, Gloria."

"Problems?" Crystal asked as Lisa hung up.

"No. She just wanted me to okay Kurt Kusch taking the *Fiona* tapes out of the station."

Crystal made a face. "That guy gives me the creeps. You know, I'm positive that, for a while, he actually suspected me of having something to do with what happened."

"Join the club. By now, I think he's been suspicious of everyone who works here, except maybe Fiona herself."

"But are there any real leads yet?"

"Not that I've heard about." Lisa paused, wondering why Crystal looked so darned happy. "Well," she finally prompted. "What's up?"

"I think I've got it, Lisa. A way to boost *Love*'s ratings."

"Terrific. What?"

"Well, I don't know why it didn't occur to me the moment I met him, but what about Benedetto?"

Lisa gazed blankly at Crystal.

"What if we brought him on my show as a regular for a few months? To talk about the influences of astrological signs on romance? We could have a call-in segment, and people could ask whether their signs are compatible with whoever they're romantically interested in. Benedetto's incredibly funny. And entertaining. And so good-looking. I bet he'd bring in viewers like crazy."

Lisa nodded slowly. "I wouldn't be surprised if you're right. Why don't we see how he comes across tonight and then maybe talk to him about the possibility?"

"Well . . . actually, Lisa, he and I have already discussed it. In fact, we came up with the idea together. Last night, I was telling him about my problem with ratings, and we just sort of realized he might be a possible solution. I said I'd have to see what you thought of it, though."

"Last night," Lisa repeated, looking closely at Crystal and almost hating her for the love-struck look in her eyes.

Crystal's smile grew even broader. "Oh, Lisa, isn't he something? And he seems to want to spend every spare second with me. Last night he took me to a film festival on campus. And later, we sat talking until two in the morning. And we're having dinner after tonight's show. I'm going to stay for it. You won't mind if I'm in the audience, will you? Or would you prefer I watched from the control room?"

"No, of course not. I'll be glad of a friendly face."

Crystal eyed Lisa for a moment, her expression growing serious. "Are you okay about doing *Fiona* tonight? I mean, you're not nervous, are you?"

"A little. It's been awhile since I've been on the lens end of the camera."

"You'll be fine. Perfectly fine."

"That's exactly what Gloria just told me. I must sound like I'm in need of reassurance."

"Ahh . . . well . . . you haven't exactly been looking like yourself lately."

"Oh?" Lisa forced a smile. "And exactly who have I been looking like?"

"Well... well, you just haven't been your normal, cheery self. Look, if there's anything you want to talk about, if you need a sympathetic ear..."

Lisa swore silently. She'd almost convinced herself that she'd been doing a good job of hiding her misery. So much for that bit of self-deception.

She gazed at Crystal for a moment, feeling as if she could drink up a million gallons of sympathy. But now wasn't the time to start in on the subject of Dan Ashly. Not with barely three hours to air. Not when she didn't think she could talk about him without crying. The last thing she wanted was to become any more upset than she already was.

Maybe she'd confide in Crystal later. At the moment, though, the further she kept the conversation away from Dan, the better. "I've been worried about what's happening at Plant W," she said.

And that was the truth. Maybe not the whole truth, but certainly not a lie. "I mean about the way Dad's playing hardball. He's up in Detroit right now, but I just know he isn't going to give an inch. And with the strike being illegal, the company's liable to begin firing people, starting with the union officials."

"I'll bet you're worrying for nothing, Lisa. Benedetto says the reason there's a stalemate is that your dad took Detroit by surprise, that QM was counting on the union backing down. So management was thrown for a loop when the workers actually walked."

Lisa merely nodded. She knew only too well why Detroit had been counting on the union backing down. Because Dan Ashly had told them he'd sucked in Bert Saint-John's daughter.

"But," Crystal went on, "Benedetto figures Detroit's going to be forced to give in and tell the workers whatever they want to know. He says that, since Plant W's the only plant producing Duelers, they have to get the workers on the job again, that if orders from their dealers start backing up, QM will lose millions in sales to the competition.''

Lisa started to reply, then paused, hearing someone thundering down the hallway.

A moment later the someone stormed into her office. Jake...his face purple. Fleetingly, she hoped he'd remembered to take his blood pressure medication.

''Lisa, you aren't going to believe what those bastards have done.''

She tried to decide which to ask first—who the bastards were or what they'd done—but Jake went on before she could make up her mind.

''They've put a gag order on Dan! They're meeting with your father right now, trying to hammer out an agreement that'll satisfy everyone. But until there is one, Dan's not to say a word about either his study or the strike.''

Lisa's mind raced, filling in the blanks. ''They'' were obviously the QM bigwigs in Detroit. And if Dan wasn't allowed to say a word, then he couldn't be on *Fiona* tonight.

That realization set her hovering between relief and panic—relief that she wouldn't have to see Dan, and panic that she and Benedetto would have to carry an entire hour of live television between them, when they'd counted on interaction with Dan.

Lord, she was going to have to wing it on the first show she'd hosted in two years. Only...only she was far more likely to die out there than successfully wing it. Yes, that's exactly what would happen. She'd die right in front of camera one, with half of Walkerton watching.

Jake snapped his fingers, a signal he'd come to a decision. "What we'll do is save the segment till next week. Surely they'll have come to an agreement by then. Tonight, we'll run a tape of an old *Fiona*. How about the one when she interviewed that stunt man? It got good ratings. What was the guy's name? Frank something, wasn't it?"

A tape. Oh, no. If Jake started yelling at her for letting those tapes out of the station, she'd die right here and now. "Jake...Jake, we can't broadcast a rerun of *Fiona*. Not *any* of them. Every single *Fiona* tape is halfway to cottage country."

Jake began sputtering, and Lisa rushed on before he could recover his speech. "Jake, Kurt Kusch took them. On official business. So we'll either have to go live with just Dr. Benny and me or use a file tape of a different show."

"Dammit, Lisa! After we've run special promos to entice people to tune in to *Fiona* tonight? What are you suggesting? That they should tune in and find us airing an ancient episode of *Gilligan's Island*? We'll have to go live. Do you know anything about astrology?"

She shook her head.

"About financial analysis?"

"Even less than about astrology. I was counting on simply acting as facilitator and letting the two guests carry the load."

Jake stood glaring at her, running his fingers through his thinning hair as if he were tempted to pull it out by the roots.

"I'll go and call Dan," he finally snapped. "QM didn't actually say he couldn't appear, only that he wasn't to talk about either his study or the strike. So we'll just tell Dr. Benny those topics are off limits. Then the two of them can discuss financial analysis or the car industry in general—or whatever."

"Jake, will you talk to them about that for me? You and Hank? I . . . I want to catch a bit of rest before we go on."

"Sure. Hank and I will handle it. And I'll tell them that if things get really desperate," he added, his voice dripping sarcasm, "they can chat about what they did on their summer vacations." He wheeled around and stomped back out of the office.

Crystal smiled weakly. "It'll be okay, Lisa. You'll see. Benedetto's a great conversationalist."

Lisa merely shook her head. Those blasted powers-that-be had all turned on her again. Not only would she have to face Dan, after all, but the segment was going to bomb. The only possible good outcome would be if Dr. Benny succeeded in making Dan look like a fool.

For some reason, though, that no longer struck her as the wonderful prospect she'd once thought it was. She told herself that Dan was the enemy and that her father would like to see him discredited. But she couldn't help remembering how Dan had rescued her from Kurt Kusch that morning in the hospital . . . and how he hadn't told Jake she'd alerted Dad to the study. And then she started remembering how Dan had kissed her . . . and that his kiss had taken her halfway to heaven.

But his kisses had meant nothing, she told herself fiercely. He'd simply been using her.

"Try to look on the bright side, Lisa," Crystal murmured.

She tried. But she couldn't even think what the bright side might be, let alone look on it.

ONCE THE MAKEUP LADY was finished with her, Lisa hid in her office, almost until airtime, until she decided Hank would be getting worried that he'd have no host to direct.

When she finally walked onto the set, his relieved smile told her she'd appeared far too late for his comfort.

Dan and Benedetto were already seated on the guest couch, chatting with each other. The moment she saw Dan, a fresh lump formed in her throat. But all she had to do was make it through this one hour. Then she'd never have to see him again.

Crystal and Jake were sitting together in the front row of the audience. Crystal smiled and gave a little wave of encouragement. Jake simply sat there, his expression saying he was certain he was about to witness *Fiona*'s good ratings going straight down the tubes.

Lisa slipped into the host's chair and managed to exchange pleasantries with the guests. Benedetto was all smiles, clearly a born showman. Dan was looking at her with murder in his eyes, not a trace of warmth in their steely blue.

The lump in her throat diminished a little, and she consciously unclenched her fists. How could she have let thoughts of this man upset her so much? He had to have about a hundred times more gall than anyone else in the world. The nerve! Glowering at her like that when he was the one who'd been up to dirty tricks, not she.

Well, maybe she'd ventured into the gray zone, she admitted. But a little attempted spying for her father hardly counted. Dan Ashly, on the other hand, had been a total snake-in-the-grass. He'd wined her, dined her and wooed her, then phoned Detroit to report that he'd talked her into telling her father to call off the strike. And now he had the audacity to sit there, glaring at her. As if *she'd* betrayed *him*. Damn him. She hoped Dr. Benny did make an idiot of QM's esteemed outside analyst.

"We're almost on air," she murmured when Hank began dropping his fingers one by one, signaling the final seconds. "Don't forget that Dan's study and the strike are off-limits," she added to Benedetto.

"Proibito," he agreed.

Hank pointed at her, and she smiled into camera one, then welcomed the viewers, explained who she was and thanked everyone—on Fiona's behalf—for the flood of cards and flowers they'd sent.

"Of course," she went on, "we're all hoping Fiona will be back soon, but, in the meantime, we'll continue to bring you shows on topics of local interest. With special guests like the two gentlemen I have with me tonight."

The camera swung to the couch while she introduced Dan and Benedetto, then back to her.

"Dr. Stelle," she said, smiling at Benedetto, "I understand you prepare an annual list that predicts winners and losers on the stock market."

"*Sì*, it is called Dr. Benny's Stars and Stinkers."

"That's a wonderful name. And your predictions have been amazingly accurate, haven't they?"

"*Sì*. That is because I do not use the traditional analytic tools. They are so limited. I use, instead, the light of astrology to see. I . . . how do you say . . . I reach for the knowledge of the stars."

"And by that you mean you use astrological charts to predict companies' futures. Isn't that right?"

"*Esattamente.* Quite so. I use the natal dates of the companies. Then the planetary indications tell me which stocks to recommend and which to not."

"Natal dates? You mean the companies' birthdays?"

"*Sì,* the date and the place of incorporation are... what is the word... ahh, *critical,* is it."

Lisa took a deep breath and turned to Dan, pasting a phony smile on her face. "And, Mr. Ashly, you analyze companies by those traditional methods that Dr. Benny claims are limited, don't you?" *Go ahead,* she added silently. *Start coming across as Mr. Stick-in-the-Mud. Make the viewers love Dr. Benny and decide you're a deadly bore.*

But instead of elaborating on the traditional methods he used, Dan simply nodded.

Lisa felt her smile freezing. If he pulled the silent guest routine, she'd kill him. But surely he wouldn't do that. He knew Jake was counting on him.

"Don't you agree that orthodox methods are awfully dull in contrast with Dr. Benny's?" she goaded. "And isn't it true that Dr. Benny's predictions have a better track record than those of most traditional financial analysts—those who rely on number crunching?"

Dan gave the camera a slow, devastating smile that rivaled Benedetto's at its best. "I think Dr. Stelle's methods are fascinating, Lisa. But we should point out that, just like traditional analysts, he also relies on numbers. After all, astrology is based on numerical astrological concepts. Astrological charts are divided into twelve houses, and the sun's cyclical relationship to the earth is divided into twelve signs of the zodiac."

"Ahh," Benedetto interjected, "but it is the North Node of the Moon that is symbolic of the future. That is what reveals future events."

"The North Node of the Moon," Dan repeated, making it sound like something from a fairy tale. "Well, I can't claim I use your methods, Benedetto, but I certainly wouldn't argue against a scientifically logical basis for astrology. I just wonder if you shouldn't broaden your horizons. Or perhaps I should rephrase that. I wonder if you shouldn't broaden your horoscopes."

A sense of unease rippled through Lisa. Dan wasn't saying what he was supposed to say at all. He was supposed to stiffly defend the stodgy world of financial analysis against the lunatic Dr. Benny. He was supposed to come across as a jerk. Instead, he'd obviously done his homework on astrology and was playing along.

She shouldn't have told him beforehand that Benedetto would be on the segment. But, of course, she'd had to.

"Broaden my horoscopes?" Benedetto said, eyeing Dan curiously. "What is the meaning of that?"

Lisa glanced at the audience. They were watching in apparent bemusement, but were clearly intrigued.

"Well," Dan said slowly, flashing another smile. This one sent half the female audience members inching forward in their seats. "I can see a company's incorporation date paralleling a birth date, but how do you determine the precise time of birth? Surely that isn't a matter of record as it is with a baby."

"*Sì*, that is true. So I use noon as birth time for each company."

"So... what you're saying is that every company incorporated on the same day, in the same general geographical area, would have the same chart. That's a little mundane, isn't it?"

Benedetto frowned. "It is not possible to determine the specific time."

"Right. That's why it seems to me you might want to consider a wider range of astrological factors."

"Such as?" Dr. Benny peered at Dan, his expression skeptical.

"Well, I thought maybe the geographical natal sign might be a factor. For example, Michigan became a state under the sign of Aquarius, right?"

Lisa almost groaned. Dan hadn't merely done his homework, he'd prepared for exams. He was going to out-Benny Dr. Benny.

"*Sì*, Aquarius," Benedetto agreed, looking as if he didn't actually have the foggiest idea when Michigan had become a state. "That is fitting, no?" he added, quickly recovering his equilibrium. "Michigan is surrounded by the Great Lakes and Aquarius is the water bearer." A slow smile crept onto Benedetto's face as he spoke. He'd clearly decided to go with the flow.

Dan grinned back at Dr. Benny. "Right. The water bearer. And I also figured that Aquarius being ruled by the planet Uranus would probably impact the charts of... oh, say the auto companies situated in Detroit."

Aquarius ruled by Uranus? Lisa glanced from one man to the other, wondering if they knew what they were talking about any more than she did.

"*Sì*, the ruling planet. Its eighty-four-year cycle around the sun is most significant. How perceptive you are, Dan... for a traditional analyst."

Dan grinned again. "And then there are the astrological signs of the companies' chief executives. Those must influence business successes and failures as well."

"*Assolutamente.* Absolutely."

"For example," Dan went on, "the new president of one of the German carmakers is a Taurus. And we all know that Taurus men are a load of bull."

Benedetto chuckled loudly, and a wave of laughter spread through the audience.

"Of course, I'm not referring to the car model with that name," Dan added. "*That* Taurus was actually conceived under a different sign. And it's a great car. But the German president we won't identify on air...."

Oh, Lord, Lisa thought despairingly, Dan's charming the pants off them. That wasn't what was supposed to happen.

"And then there's the Chinese Zodiac to consider," he continued. "Particularly for companies in the North American auto industry, I'd say. I mean, they have so much competition from Asia that you can hardly ignore the Chinese Animal Signs."

"Definitely not," Benedetto agreed emphatically.

"After all, the phenomenal success of Ford's Mustang was probably due, at least in part, to its conception in the year of the Horse."

"*Sì,* no doubt a major influence."

"And then there was the Volkswagen Rabbit."

"The year of the Rabbit," Benedetto supplied.

"And the Audi Fox," Lisa tried, feeling she should contribute at least something.

Both men looked at her as if she had the brain of a kumquat.

"The Chinese Zodiac," Dan informed her with an out-and-out smirk, "does not have a year of the Fox."

She bit her tongue to keep from asking him whether it had a year of the Rat. And whether he'd been born in it. Or maybe the year of the Snake. She glanced at the audience again. People were grinning. And the widest grin of all belonged to Jake.

Lord, the segment was working far better than she'd realized. Her guests might be conspiring instead of clashing, but the audience loved their act.

She sat watching and listening as they grew sillier and wittier. They didn't need a host at all. They were a two-man vaudeville team.

Much to Lisa's relief, but to the obvious disappointment of the studio audience, nine o'clock finally arrived. She thanked Benedetto, then mumbled her way through thanking Dan, not looking him in the eye, afraid that if she did, what little composure she'd maintained would desert her.

She managed a smile when Jake and Crystal congratulated her.

"So what do you think?" Crystal pressed. "Wasn't Benedetto as great as I predicted he'd be? Do I have your okay to invite him to be a regular on *Love?*"

"Terrific idea," Jake declared.

"Terrific idea," Lisa echoed. "Go with it." She turned and fled to her office. She'd wait there until the station cleared . . . until it was safe to come out . . . until there was no risk of running into Dan.

CHAPTER TEN

"SAINT-JOHN! Are you in there?" Jake hollered, pounding on her office door. "I've got great news."

Lisa pushed back her chair and rose. So much for her office being a refuge. But how could Jake have gotten news—great or otherwise—in the ten minutes since the *Fiona* segment had ended?

"Come on, Saint-John. Hurry up.

"QM and the union have reached an agreement," he announced the moment she opened her door. "Plant W will be back to normal operation on Monday."

"Oh, Jake, that *is* great news. I've been so worried about Dad and Roy with the strike being illegal and—"

"No, no, it's not the agreement that's the great news. I mean it is, but there's more. The union's going to co-operate as far as Dan's study goes. And in return, the company will give the union a written rationale for why Plant W is being analyzed."

"That sounds fair."

"Wait, I haven't gotten to the best part. Your father demanded that QM keep the workers current on what Dan's doing. So he's going to be giving a weekly public update on how his findings are coming together."

"Terrific. That's terrific, Jake."

"Saint-John, will you stop interrupting and let me get to the point? Aren't you curious about how I know this?"

"Ahh ... sure."

"Well, when I went back to my office after the show there was a message waiting, asking me to call QM in Detroit. And it turns out they'd like Dan to give his updates on *Fiona,* sort of a Friday wrap-up of his week's progress. It'll just take a few minutes of each segment, but we'll hook a lot of people who'll tune in to see him, then end up watching the entire show."

Lisa stared at Jake, feeling ill, wondering if this could possibly be a cruel joke but knowing, deep down, that it wasn't. It was for real. But how was she never going to see Dan again if he was sitting on her set for the next few Friday nights?

"I wonder," Jake was muttering, "whether we should use him as the lead and risk losing viewers when he's done? Maybe we'd be smarter to save him for last and hope people tune in at eight, anyway. What do you think?"

She shook her head. Jake didn't really want to know what she was thinking. "I'm not sure which would be better, Jake. Let's talk about it on Monday."

"Yeah, right, we have all week to decide. Well, I've gotta run, Saint-John. Just wanted to share the good news."

"Jake, before you go... does Dan know about this yet?"

"Yeah. Yeah, the message was for both of us to call Detroit."

"And what did he think?"

"He didn't say. QM asked me if I liked the idea, and when I said I did, they simply told him that's the way they wanted it handled. There wasn't much for him to say, but I guess he thinks it's okay. Why wouldn't he?"

Lisa shrugged. That was another thing Jake didn't really want to know.

"So, see you on Monday, kiddo. And you were sensational tonight. And the idea of having Dr. Benny on *Love* is inspired. You and Crystal just might pull that show out of the fire." Jake gave her a quick grin and was gone.

She stood listening to his footsteps fade down the hall, telling herself that Dan's study was going to take only another two or three weeks. So a few minutes with him, on a couple of segments, wasn't going to kill her. After all, she'd just made it through an entire hour. But it had been an absolutely miserable hour. And she didn't want to have to go through that few minutes for even a couple of segments. She just wanted to start forgetting Dan Ashly.

"Lisa?"

She jumped at the sound of his voice. He was standing outside her office and, when she didn't say anything, stepped in. "Jake tell you about the weekly update?"

She nodded.

"Well...look...I just came by to say that there won't be any problem with it. I...I know I was snarky with you on tonight's show. But that was only my bruised ego talking. I mean...well, I guess I read more into what happened between us than I should have. And since I had Benedetto figured for a crackpot, your throwing me over for him...well, at any rate, I realize now that he's not a bad guy."

Lisa gazed at Dan as he spoke, all the anger she'd felt toward him suddenly surging through her again. The only thing that had really happened between them was that he'd used her. So why was he still playing games? Why didn't he simply leave her alone?

"Knock it off," she snapped when he finished. "Just knock it off, okay?"

He eyed her curiously. "I was," he finally offered stiffly, "merely trying to be friends."

"Oh? Well, listen to me, Dan Ashly. You're going to come in and do your thing on *Fiona*. And while you're here, I'll be as polite to you as I can manage. But I don't want to be your friend. I don't have liars and users as friends."

"What in blazes are you talking about?"

Lord, he was managing to look so sincerely confused that she wanted to scratch his eyes out. "Dammit, Dan, forget the innocent act. I know exactly what you did."

"Oh? Well, maybe you'd like to tell *me* exactly what I did. Or what you *think* I did, because I sure didn't do anything that would give you reason to stand here yelling at me."

"I am not yelling! And don't lie to me again. I've had enough of your damned lies to last a lifetime."

In the hallway, a man cleared his throat. Both Lisa and Dan wheeled around. Benedetto was standing there, Crystal on his arm and an embarrassed expression on his face.

"Sorry," Crystal murmured, "we thought you two might like to join us for dinner. But I guess we thought wrong."

"There is a . . . a confusion between you?" Benedetto asked.

"A confusion?" Lisa repeated. "No, there's no confusion. The odd lie, courtesy of Mr. Ashly. But definitely no confusion."

"Lie? But you are an Aries, Dan, no?"

"Ahh . . . yes. How did you know?"

"You have the forehead and eyebrows of a ram. I know an Aries . . . how do you say . . . at first sight. And Aries do not lie," he added, glancing at Lisa.

"Benedetto, I think we've had enough astrology for tonight," she snapped.

"Come on." Crystal tugged firmly at his arm. "We have to go."

He shrugged. "Aries do not lie," he offered once more. "It is against their nature."

"Bye, Lisa. Bye, Dan," Crystal said, dragging Benedetto away from the doorway.

"Ciao," he called as they disappeared from sight.

Dan stepped across to the door, closed it, then stood leaning casually against it, his arms crossed over his broad chest, one long leg bent slightly at the knee. In his charcoal pinstripe, his white-on-white shirt and gray silk tie, he might have been posing for *GQ*.

He didn't move, didn't speak; he simply watched Lisa.

She tried to pull her gaze from his, but couldn't. The blue depths of his eyes were mesmerizing. And despite what he was and what he'd done, despite the fact that it was absolutely ridiculous, she found him so desirable it took her breath away.

She felt an almost overwhelming urge to flee. She didn't want to be alone with this man, didn't want to want him. But her office had become a trap. And he was guarding the only way out.

"I . . . I have to go," she tried.

He ignored the statement. "When I saw Crystal with Benedetto, it took me a couple of seconds to realize what was going on. You and he aren't . . . ?"

She shrugged, ordering her heart to stop pounding. But her heart was ignoring her brain. And Dan's nearness was reminding her of all the things she could scarcely bear to be reminded of. How being in his arms felt, how arousing his touch was, how passionate his kisses were . . . how much she'd wanted to make love to him only a few nights ago.

"You and he aren't . . . ?" he repeated.

"We never were. We didn't even have dinner together on Wednesday." The words simply slipped out. She bit her lip in case more tried the same trick. First, her heart wouldn't listen, and now her voice was double-crossing her.

"I see," Dan murmured. "No, actually I don't see. Lisa, let's get back to what it is you're so upset about."

"No, Dan, let's just forget it, okay? I really do have to go and—"

He suddenly stepped forward and placed his hands firmly on her shoulders. His touch sent hot shivers through her, shivers she wished he didn't make her feel . . . shivers she loved feeling.

"Look, Lisa, I don't know if Benedetto was right about all Aries not lying, but I know I don't. When I told you I didn't do anything that would give you reason to yell at me, it was the truth. So let's hear what on earth you think I did."

She stood looking up at him, intensely aware of his hands touching her, of their heat sending the warmth of desire through her.

It wouldn't hurt to tell him . . . to see what he says, a tiny voice whispered.

She took a deep breath, then cleared her throat for good measure. "You left my apartment on Tuesday and then called the president of QM. In the middle of the night. At 1:10 a.m., to be precise."

Dan nodded slowly. "Yes, I did. Should I ask how you know that?"

"No. I wasn't even supposed to tell you I knew."

He almost smiled. "Sort of like you weren't supposed to tell anyone about my study, huh? You really aren't an award-winning secret-keeper, are you?"

"Earlier," she pressed on, ignoring his sarcasm, "you'd suggested I tell Dad that a wildcat would be a bad idea. I didn't realize it at the time, but when...well, the point is you wanted me to pass along a message from QM. Then you called Detroit to report that you'd given it to me. And if doing that wasn't using me, I don't know what would be." She shrugged his hands off her shoulders and took a step backward, feeling the initial hurt all over again.

He dropped his arms slowly to his sides. "You really believe I tried to use you?"

She merely nodded, no longer certain she had her emotions under even the slightest control.

"Would you care to listen to the truth?"

She blinked hard, willing back threatening tears, sure there couldn't be a truth. There'd only be more lies.

"I phoned Bill because, when I got back to my hotel room, there was a message waiting from him. A message that asked me to return his call no matter how late it was."

"Bill," she managed to say. "You're on a first-name basis with the president of QM."

"He wasn't always the president of QM. After I'd finished university here, when I went to graduate school back East, he was one of my professors—taught business strategy. And he was also my thesis adviser. We go way back. And he trusts me. Which is undoubtedly the reason he wanted me to be the one to do their damned study for them.''

"And why... why did he want you to call him... no matter how late it was?''

Dan shrugged. "Because we go way back. Because he trusts me. Because your father's deadline was getting close and Detroit had only Woody's reading of the situation. Bill simply wanted to see what I thought, get my impression of how serious the strike threat actually was.''

"And what did you tell him?''

"I said I couldn't be any real help. That I didn't know Bert Saint-John well enough to read him. But that I'd feel a whole lot better if they *did* tell the union exactly what my study was all about.''

"And... and what did you say about me? About what you'd asked me to tell Dad?''

"Not a thing. Suggesting you tell your father to ease off was my own idea. I just figured that, if he did, it might help resolve the situation. As far as I know, Bill isn't even aware that you exist.''

She stood gazing at Dan, a hundred different emotions swirling through her, trying to decide whether he was telling her the truth or whether she simply wanted to believe what was, in reality, the latest of his lies.

The silence lengthened.

Finally, Dan reached inside his suit jacket and produced a notebook. He flipped through the pages, then stretched across her desk and pulled the phone to him. "Can I make a long-distance call on this line... to Detroit?''

She nodded, then watched him dial and listened to him speak.

"Hi Bill, it's Dan. Sorry to bother you, but I have a friend here who I need you to talk to. You're going to think both she and I are crazy, but just answer any questions she wants to ask you, okay?"

Wordlessly, he extended the receiver. Wordlessly, she took it.

SLOWLY, HER HAND trembling, Lisa replaced the receiver and simply stood beside her desk, certain her face was the color of an American Beauty rose. But she didn't care about the embarrassment. Hearing what Bill Wireton had said had been worth all the embarrassment in the world. What she did care about, though, what she cared immeasurably about, was what Dan must think of her.

She'd jumped to wrong and awful conclusions about him. Despite what she felt for him, she'd taken that damned circumstantial evidence of Roy's for gospel. If Dan had even half a brain, he would probably walk out of here right now and keep walking...right out of her life. And if he did, she was going to die.

She looked across at him. He'd retired to a chair and was sitting, gazing at her.

"I've never before felt this mortified," she murmured. "I'm sorry...I can't say how sorry...both for what I thought and for what I said to you."

"Apology accepted," he offered quietly.

She watched him, not daring to breathe, hoping he'd say something more. Accepting her apology and forgiving her for being a complete twit—forgiving her to the extent that he'd ever have anything to do with her again—were two different things.

Silently, she prayed he'd give her a second chance. Because without him, the past few days had seemed like an eternity in hell.

"I can see," he finally said, "why you might have concluded I was trying to use you. But why didn't you ask me why I phoned Bill? Why didn't you give me a chance to explain?"

Why hadn't she, indeed? Because she was an idiot, that was why. And her idiocy had cost her dearly. "I... well," she tried, "there seemed to be only one logical conclusion. And... and, as I said, I wasn't supposed to tell anyone we knew you'd made the call."

Dan slowly shook his head. "I assume part of that *we* is your infamous brother."

She shrugged miserably.

"So...you didn't ask me to explain because Roy, the great detective, had the facts adding up to me using you. But what was it that you thought I'd lied to you about?"

She bit her lip, wishing he'd stop asking questions. But at least his asking questions was better than his leaving. And if she could only manage to make him understand, then just maybe...

"Well," she said with an uneasy little glance at him, "after I decided it was a QM message you'd wanted me to give Dad, I thought you'd probably lied to me about the study. About Detroit not telling you what your recommendations should be, I mean. About your intending to do an honest analysis. I figured you hoped I'd convince Dad of that, too. And—"

She caught herself as the rest started slipping out and forced a smile, hoping against hope that Dan hadn't noticed the *and*.

"And?" he pressed, dashing her hopes.

She looked down at the floor.

"And, Lisa?"

She shook her head. What if she told him, and he didn't feel even remotely the way she did? What if there was no way in the world he'd truly forgive her?

"Lisa, don't you think I deserve to hear it all?"

"I...I guess maybe you do." She paused, screwing up her courage, then let the words rush out. "I also thought you'd lied about your feelings for me. Not that you actually said anything much," she hurried on, "it just seemed...I mean, I had the impression that you..."

She couldn't continue. All she could do was stare at the floor. When she'd finished talking to Bill Wireton in Detroit, she'd merely felt more mortified than she'd ever been in her life. Now she'd progressed to the most mortified anyone could possibly feel.

Dan rose from his chair, and she risked glancing up. He caught her gaze, crossed the few steps between them, then placed his hands on her shoulders once more.

Those delicious hot shivers began racing through her again. And this time she didn't wish they weren't. Surely, when he was standing here touching her, there was a chance he'd truly forgive her.

"You had the impression that I what?" he asked softly, leaning forward, leaning so close that she felt the warmth of his breath, smelled the woodsy freshness of his after-shave.

She couldn't answer. But he didn't seem to mind. He simply folded her into his arms and began kissing her as if he intended never to stop.

When he finally did, she pressed her cheek against the warm breadth of his chest and clung to him, not certain her legs would support her. If that hadn't been his way of forgiving her, she couldn't imagine what it had been. And she couldn't imagine a more marvelous way. She felt like laughing with joy and crying with relief all at once. It would be impossible to feel happier than she felt this moment.

"Glad we cleared up the misunderstanding?" he murmured, nuzzling the top of her head.

"Glad doesn't even come close," she whispered.

"Then let's clear up something else. That impression you had, the one you didn't finish telling me about...?"

She silently nodded against his chest.

"Lisa, if the impression you had was that I was falling in love with you, it was two million percent accurate. I've been a complete emotional wreck the past few days."

Tears filled her eyes and throat, making it impossible to speak.

Dan tucked one finger under her chin and tilted her face upward. The tears escaped and began streaming down her face.

He gazed at her uncertainly. "You don't look exactly happy. Should I be worried about that?"

"No." She hugged him so tightly and for so long that her arms began to ache. But she couldn't get enough of the wonderful sensation of his body pressing hers, couldn't actually believe he was here, that she was holding him once more.

"No," she finally managed to say, "you shouldn't be even a tiny bit worried. I always cry when I'm happy. And I've never been happier."

He cuddled her head against his chest and began stroking her back, not in a sexual way, but as one would soothe an upset child. Yet his touch was incredibly arousing.

And then he bent and began nibbling warm, moist kisses down her neck, making her feel as if she was melting in his arms, as if her body was turning liquid with longing. A deep, aching throb began within her, and she snuggled even closer to him, feeling his desire, instinctively moving against it, wanting him.

He made a low, moaning sound and shifted her in his arms, sliding his hands down to stroke her hips, then exploring his way slowly, possessively, back up her body to her breasts. He grazed her yearning nipples with his thumbs, sending electric shocks of arousal through her.

His hardness against her made the throbbing within almost unbearable. And each intimate caress made her want him more...made her want more of him than she could safely have here, in her office.

"Dan," she murmured, "Dan, let's go."

"Where?" he whispered.

She kissed his shirtfront, wishing there were no clothes between them. "I think it's time you and Tiger had an official introduction."

He drew away a fraction and gazed down at her face. "I thought you told me," he teased gently, "that when there's a stranger in the apartment Tiger always hides in your bedroom."

"Yes. Always."

LISA CLICKED THE LOCK behind them, then turned. Her apartment was a silvery wash of moonlight, and pale shimmers were playing on the angles of Dan's face, highlighting his strong jaw, deepening the hollows beneath his cheekbones.

He slowly smiled at her, making her feel as if she'd just drunk a magnum of champagne and that every one of its little bubbles was dancing inside her heart.

Dan Ashly was the once-in-a-lifetime man she'd thought she'd never meet. She was absolutely, deliciously insane about him, and she'd almost lost him because of her foolishness. But now he was with her. And she was never going to doubt him again. And she was never going to let him go.

He cleared his throat. "Want me to turn on a light?"

"No...I like the moonlight...I like the way you look in the moonlight."

"I like the way you look in the moonlight, too," he said, smiling at her. "Your hair turns silver."

They stood gazing at each other for a long moment. And then he reached out and stroked her cheek, gently brushing back a lock of silvered hair.

Her entire body reacted to his simple touch. Her heart began hammering, her nerve endings came alive, and she could scarcely catch her breath.

"Second thoughts?" he murmured.

She shook her head. "It's just that I'm twenty-eight years old, and right this instant I feel sixteen," she admitted quietly, glad of the dim light hiding whatever emotions were written on her face. "I...I should be better at this. But I haven't been involved with many men...and I've never wanted anyone so much."

"Lisa...Lisa, I've never wanted anyone so much, either. You...you're special, Lisa. Incredibly special. I think I've wanted to make love to you since the first moment I saw you. And it's going to be better than anything's ever been...just because it's you and me."

His words eased her nervousness. She took his hand and silently led him down the dark hall and into her moonlit bedroom.

Tiger was lying in his usual place on the center of a pillow. He sleepily raised his head and meowed a greeting, then spotted Dan and scurried away, vanishing off the far side of the bed.

"Lisa?" Dan said quietly, drawing her into the circle of his arms.

"Yes?"

"Lisa, can we please save my official introduction to Tiger until later?" He gave her the sexiest smile she'd ever seen, then bent and kissed her as if she were the most delicate creature on earth. And then his kiss became more passionate, began delectably probing, and he slid his hands across her shoulders, across the back of her dress.

His touch, his kisses, her anticipation, combined to make her want him impossibly more. She slipped her hands beneath his jacket, over the firmness of his back muscles, easing his shirttail up as he unzipped her dress, finally exposing the bareness of his back and smoothing her palms possessively across it.

"Mmm," he murmured at her touch. "For a producer, you make a wonderful masseuse."

She smiled up at him in the moonlight. "Promise you won't tell Jake that. Adding duties to my job description is one of his favorite pastimes."

"I won't breathe a word. I don't want you touching any man but me."

And she didn't want any man touching her but Dan...not ever. She wanted him, though, to touch her all over.

His kisses moved hungrily to her throat as he slipped her dress from her shoulders. He began caressing her breasts, lingering at her aroused nipples, gently stroking them through the wisp of her lingerie, making them ache for his mouth.

"I'm glad," she whispered, "that you turned out not to be the enemy."

"How glad?" he teased gently, easing her dress lower until it fluttered, with her slip, to the floor.

"On a gladness scale of one to ten?" she managed to say, suddenly finding it difficult to speak, finding it difficult even to put words together. Her entire being wanted to focus on the incredibly delightful sensations Dan was making her feel.

"All right," he agreed, "on a gladness scale of one to ten."

"I think, so far, I'm at about a hundred and six."

"Let's try for two hundred," he murmured, stepping back and shrugging out of his jacket and shirt, letting them drop in a heap on the floor.

She watched him with anxious anticipation. The moonlight played on his pale expanse of chest hair, revealing a lean, muscular upper body that was as sexy as she'd known it would be. Then he stripped off the rest of his clothes, exposing the full, erect hardness of his desire.

He reached out and took her hand, smiling at her—the most reassuring smile she could ever have imagined.

It banished the last traces of her nervousness, and she smiled back. "I think I'm getting close to two hundred."

"I think," he said quietly, "I'm already at two thousand."

A moment later he was easing her onto the bed, was lying beside her, smoothing his hands down her back, quickly removing the rest of her clothes and drawing her onto her side, fitting her naked body to his, making her quiver with the excitement of being close enough to him that they were almost one.

"This feels so right," he murmured, his breath hot against the hollow of her neck, "so absolutely right. I meant what I said, Lisa. It's going to be better than anything's ever been. Just because it's you and me. Because we're right together. If we weren't, we'd never have made it through all the nonsense that kept coming between us."

She nuzzled his neck, loving him. All the nonsense, he'd said. Yes, that was exactly what it had been. And she'd almost lost him because of it. But she hadn't. He was here with her. And that felt perfect.

She murmured something unintelligible. Rational speech was no longer possible. Her senses were focused entirely on her pure, animal needs. She felt as if her skin was burning against his, as if her blood was about to boil, as if wildfire was sweeping through her, threatening to consume her.

She buried her fingers in his hair and drew his lips to hers, opening her mouth to his seeking tongue, urgently returning his deep kisses until he moved lower beside her and began moving his tongue in moist, swirling motions on her nipples, sending fresh waves of desire crashing over her, making her breathing a series of short gasps, making her whisper a string of tiny, pleasured "ooohs."

His tongue continued to work its magic while his hands slipped downward and began touching her so intimately, so exquisitely, that she moaned with rapture and started to move against his hand. At last, she reached to encircle his erection, no longer able to bear not having him inside her.

He eased her closer to him, crushing her breasts against his chest, kissing her mouth as if he might devour her.

She arched toward him, her body needing his, her hands urging him even closer, vaguely aware of how fast and short her breaths were, intensely aware of the delicious torture of his being this near yet not near enough. "Dan . . . Dan, please."

When he entered her she was so ready, so aroused, that her climax was almost instantaneous, sending her to the brink of ecstasy and beyond as Dan thrust harder and deeper, finally groaning with his own release.

He lay beside her, still part of her, his breathing ragged, while a final tiny series of shivers shook her. Then they lay quietly, the warmth of their body heat intermingling, the warmth of his breath caressing her throat.

Finally, he nuzzled her cheek. "Was I right?" he murmured.

"Mmmmm . . . definitely. About what?" she added lazily.

"Was it better than anything's ever been?"

"Mmmmm . . . double definitely."

"Good, because . . ."

He paused, stroking her hair, and she silently filled in the blank with the words he'd used earlier, *Because it's you and me. Because we're right together.* But when he finally spoke again, he said something different.

"Because I love you, Lisa Saint-John," he whispered, cuddling her even closer, making her happiness complete.

CHAPTER ELEVEN

LISA LAY in Dan's arms, absently thinking about a future in which she'd be wakened, every day, by his caress. Absently thinking it would be heaven.

Unlike last night's frantic passion, their lovemaking this morning had been slow and gentle, had lasted a wonderfully delicious forever.

She glanced down to the bottom of the bed, where Tiger had discovered Dan's big toe peaking out from beneath the quilt and was tentatively poking at it with one paw.

Dan was watching him through sleepy eyes. "That cat's solid orange," he finally said, sounding puzzled.

"Very observant," she teased.

"My point, Ms. Smarty, is that tigers are striped."

"You're simply a fountain of knowledge, Dan. But his name's not *Tiger,* as in the animal. His full, official name is Tiger Lily, as in the flower."

"Lord, I sure hope you haven't told his friends. That's a darned sissy name for a tomcat."

"Well, I'm not certain he qualifies as a tom anymore. I had him fixed."

"I doubt he sees it in quite those terms," Dan muttered. "Ouch," he added, quickly moving his foot.

Lisa grinned lazily. "He sometimes forgets he has claws."

"Yeah? Well, I think I liked it better when he figured I was a stranger."

"He could hardly," she murmured, "mistake you for a stranger now."

Dan drew her even closer and whispered something against her throat.

"Pardon?" she said, unable to make out his words.

He propped himself up on one elbow, and the sheet fell away from his naked chest. She resisted the urge to nuzzle her way down it. Her body was already aching, and she'd discovered that Dan needed no encouragement . . . and almost no recovery time.

"First, I said that I love you."

She smiled. He could tell her that twelve times a day for the rest of her life and she wouldn't grow tired of hearing it.

"And second, I asked if you realized we didn't eat dinner last night."

"Oh . . . that's true, we didn't. Should I take it you're hungry?"

"Hungry isn't the right word. In fact, it's not even close. We're talking famished or ravenous or weak with starvation."

"Do you have the strength to get dressed?"

"I was hoping," he said, caressing her hip, "that I could persuade you to get up and serve me breakfast in bed."

She captured his hand. "If you keep doing that, all you're going to persuade me to do is stay right here. But unless a generous goblin's snuck in and stocked my fridge, I'm afraid breakfast would consist of cat food. Washed down with Chablis that was uncorked days ago."

Dan gave an exaggerated groan. "At least coffee, then. You must have coffee. I saw some the other night."

"That was the other night. It ran out yesterday. I was going to go grocery shopping this morning...and I wasn't expecting to have a starving man in my bed."

"Sorry that you do?" he teased.

"Sorry isn't the right word. In fact, it's not even close," she added, stealing a quick kiss, then rolling out of bed as he grabbed for her.

"You know," he said, watching her walk naked across the room, "as much as I like the way you look in moonlight, I like the way you look in daylight even better."

She grabbed her robe from the closet and quickly pulled it around herself. "Still?" she asked, grinning back at him.

"Anyone ever tell you that you're a spoilsport?"

"Yes. When we were kids, Roy used to say that all the time." She paused, thinking about Roy and his damned, faulty detecting. She'd better have a talk with little brother. As soon as possible. And explain the facts about Dan's late-night phone call to her father, as well.

"Got a robe for me, too?" Dan asked.

"Nope. I thought I told you last night. I don't generally invite men into my bed. You're special."

"Come on back here, then, and show me exactly how special."

"Uh-uh. It would take the rest of the weekend, and I have to get to the grocery store today."

"Well, if that's the way you're going to be, get dressed and I'll take you out for breakfast. But after that, as much as I'd rather spend the entire day with you, I have to go into QM for a couple of hours."

"Oh?"

"Yeah. Detroit wants to use some of the data I've started collecting—to prepare that statement for the union. And last night, I agreed to pull it together today."

"I didn't know outside analysts got stuck doing overtime."

"We don't. At least, we don't get to call it overtime. It's just known as working till you drop. But after that wildcat, I think the sooner I can wrap things up, the happier the company will be."

Lisa felt a sharp pang of alarm. The sooner he wrapped things up, the sooner he'd be back in Manhattan. Quickly, she reminded herself that New York State was hardly the end of the earth. It would even be Ohio's next-door neighbor if Pennsylvania wasn't sitting between them.

"Of course," Dan went on, giving her a long, appreciative look that almost sent her racing back to his arms, "when I agreed to work today, I didn't know I'd have something so much better I could be doing." He swung his long legs over the edge of the bed and sat staring down at the wrinkled heap of his clothes.

Finally, he picked his jacket off the floor and appraised its sad condition. "This suit isn't ready to face the world again without a trip to the cleaners. So why don't we just head over to my hotel? We can try room service and have that breakfast in bed I wanted."

Lisa had a sudden, disquieting premonition. Whoever'd given the copy of Dan's hotel bill to Roy would show up with their room service order, then report directly to her brother.

"Dan...Dan, instead of breakfast together, why don't we each get what we have to do out of the way? I'll catch something to eat at my parents'. That way, I can straighten out Dad and Roy about your phone call. Until I do, they're going to keep right on considering you the enemy, no matter what the company says in its statement."

"That's probably a good idea. I'll drive you."

"No, that's probably *not* a good idea. In fact, it's definitely not a good idea. Your dropping me off, first thing in the morning, wouldn't leave much to my family's imagination. Especially," she added, glancing in the mirror, "when my lips are swollen from kissing you and my face is red from whisker burn."

Dan grinned at her. "Your lips are going to be swollen and your face is going to be red whether I drop you off or not."

"Well, maybe no one will think anything of it. But they'd sure think something if they saw me getting out of your car. And with you and your study and Dad and the union and my hotheaded brother...well, a little advance warning about us would be a good idea."

"Us," Dan repeated. "You know, that has a nice ring."

Lisa rewarded him with a smile. *Us, us, us,* she silently chanted, heading for the bathroom, almost hugging herself for joy. Until last night there'd been no *us*. But today Dan loved her. And she loved him. Today was the beginning of the best of her life.

"LISA, WHAT a nice surprise," her mother said, pulling the door fully open. "And you're just in time for breakfast."

"Good. I was hoping I would be. Are Dad and Roy home?"

"Yes—both sitting at the kitchen table." Helen eyed her daughter closely. "Have you been in the sun, dear? Your face is red."

"Ahh . . . I think the camera makeup irritated it last night. And the hot lights. Did you catch the show?" she asked, quickly switching topics.

"Of course. Roy and I were glued to the set. And I taped it for your father because he was on his way back from Detroit when it aired. You were wonderful, dear. Just wonderful."

"And your motherly opinion is totally unbiased, right?" Lisa teased, starting down the hall, the aroma of bacon and eggs making her mouth water.

"Morning, you two," she said, breezing through the kitchen doorway ahead of her mother. "I hear you got all the concessions you wanted from the company, Dad," she added, sitting down across from her brother. "That's great."

"Well, we had a major advantage. Detroit desperately wanted us back to work." Bert took a sip of coffee, then glanced at Lisa once more. "Your mother says your show was great."

Lisa grinned. "As I was just telling her, she isn't exactly impartial."

"Oh, you did pretty well," Roy offered. "Too bad Ashly landed on his feet, though."

"The idea of making him look bad didn't work out, huh, baby?" her father asked.

"No. But that's just as well, because it turns out we jumped to the wrong conclusion about that phone call he made."

"You told him you knew about it?" Roy demanded sharply. "I specifically asked you not to."

"Look, little brother, what you specifically did was add two and two and come up with a hundred and seven."

"Which means?"

"Which means that the only reason Dan phoned Mr. Wireton in the middle of the night was because there was a message asking him to call."

"Oh, come on, Sis! You don't expect—"

"Listen to me, Roy. Just listen. It wasn't that Dan was reporting on his evening with me. And it wasn't because he'd been trying to use me. He didn't even mention me during their conversation. Or mention that he'd suggested Dad give the company more time. And that, by the way, was entirely Dan's own idea. And he was simply trying to help."

"That's what Ashly told you, Sis? And you believed him?"

"Yes, I believed him."

"Oh, Lisa, have a brain, will you? You didn't expect him to admit the truth, did you?"

"Roy, *you* have a brain. I'm not an idiot. I didn't just say, fine, if that's what you tell me, I'll believe you, Dan."

"Oh? Then how did he convince you?" The expression on Roy's face said that he had a darned strong suspicion about how Dan had convinced her. Well, at least the blush she could feel spreading over her cheeks wouldn't show for the whisker burn that was already there.

"It wasn't Dan who convinced me, at all," she finally said, unable to think of anything to tell them except the truth. "I talked to Mr. Wireton last night. And

I asked *him* about that call, about their conversation."

Roy and her father exchanged glances, then focused on Lisa once more.

"You talked to Mr. Wireton, baby? You do mean *Bill* Wireton? In Detroit?"

She nodded.

"How did that come about?"

"Dad, it's a long story and . . . well, I don't want to get into a lengthy discussion about it. But when I didn't buy Dan's explanation, he called Mr. Wireton and asked him to tell me whatever I wanted to know."

"And you believed him?" Roy snapped.

"Dammit, Roy, you're sounding like a broken record!"

"Now, children," Helen murmured, slipping a plate of bacon and eggs in front of Lisa, "don't squabble."

She took a bite of egg, told her mother she was the best cook in the world, then turned to her father. "Dad, what Dan's been saying all along is the truth. He's doing an unbiased study of the plant's operations. And a projection of what he sees as the Dueler's future market share. Period."

Her father and brother exchanged glances again.

"You two still don't believe that?"

"Baby . . . baby, I've got to admit that I've heard so many half-truths and downright lies from QM over the years that I find it hard to believe anything they say."

"But it's not just the company that's saying this, Dad. It's Dan, as well. And he doesn't lie. It's not in his nature. He's an Aries."

"Oh, right!" Roy hooted. "What did you do? Catch the astrology bug from Dr. Benny?"

"Roy, that's enough," Helen said sharply.

Lisa glared at him, then turned to her father again. "Dad, what's going to happen when you tell the workers to cooperate with Dan? They'll listen, won't they?"

"Yeah. They'll listen."

"And they'll be pleasant to him? Right now, he feels like a leper."

"Baby, I can tell the brothers and sisters they have to cooperate. But I can't force them to act as if they like the guy."

"But will they at least be civil?"

"Lisa," Roy muttered, "would you feel like being civil to some jerk who was going to cost you your job?"

"Dammit, Roy, that's not the way things are. Is your head full of rocks? Haven't you been listening to me? The study is going to be fair. And Dan's report will be honest and objective."

"Let's say, for the sake of argument, that it is," her father offered quietly. "But what if this honest and objective report recommends shutting down Plant W? Baby, until that report is in, the workers are going to view Ashly with suspicion."

"But...but..." She paused uncertainly. She'd been completely caught up in her relief that Dan wasn't in QM's pocket, after all. But Dad was right, of course. Just because the study was objective, that didn't mean the damned report might not say something negative. If there was anything negative to be said . . . and if Dan was honest . . .

If? He was a blasted Aries. And according to Benedetto, that made Dan one of the most honest men this side of the Pacific. So his report would tell it the way he saw it.

She gazed at her father, swallowing hard. He was fifty-three years old. If Plant W was shut down, would he find another job? Not likely. Certainly not in Walkerton, when half the town would be suddenly unemployed.

She glanced at Roy. His worried frown was a duplicate of Dad's. Her brother was young and single, though. He could easily pull up roots and go into different work. Maybe even go back to school. But her father had spent his entire adult life in the auto industry. So what would become of him? Of her mother?

"Bert?" Helen murmured, reaching across and patting his hand. "Maybe everyone's just thinking the worst. Lisa's a good judge of people. And if she's right about this fellow being honest, then his report should say good things, shouldn't it? I mean, the Dueler's a top-selling line. And Plant W's efficient, isn't it? You've told me the industrial engineering people are happy with its production."

Lisa breathed a little more easily at her mother's words. Of course. The entire town was overreacting, thinking negatively. But, logically, why would Dan recommend closing the plant?

Bert shrugged. "We hear we're doing a good job, Helen. But there are always rumors about how the company might cut costs."

"Like eventually moving all assembly offshore," Roy interjected.

"But...but I don't think Dan's report is going to get into that sort of issue," Lisa protested.

"Baby, who knows what issues hotshot Wall Street analysts get into? I'm an autoworker. Hell, I didn't even go to college."

"Dad, that doesn't make you a dummy."

"I know it doesn't, Lisa. And I keep up. When it comes to QM, and to the auto industry in general, I know twenty times more than the average line worker. But I don't know what variables Ashly might take into account. Just at yesterday's meeting, Detroit was tossing around phrases like, 'global marketing means global production,' and 'labor costs versus sociological considerations.'"

"But don't you see, Dad? Even if Dan *is* supposed to get into things like that, he's not going to recommend anything that would cause dire economic problems for Walkerton. That's what they mean by 'sociological considerations.' Dan's final report simply won't contain anything that might jeopardize Plant W's future."

"We'll see, baby. We'll see."

Roy tilted back in his chair and grinned teasingly across the table. "You know, Sis, anything you can do to influence Ashly's report would be okay with us."

"Roy," Bert said sternly, "watch your mouth."

"Well, hell, Dad. If you and I have to put up with snide remarks about Lisa hanging out with the enemy, then at least—"

"What snide remarks?" she demanded.

"Nothing, baby. Word just got around that you and Ashly were at the Cajun the other night."

"Dad! Don't say that as if you disapprove! Not when the reason I went there with him was because you asked me to see what I could find out."

"Was that why you were in Central Park with him later?" Roy asked. "Word also got around that the two of you were holding hands there."

"Lord, is there no privacy? Sometimes I hate small towns."

Bert shrugged. "Well, you know how it is, Lisa. Then a few of the boys...well, you know."

"No, I don't know. What?"

"The workers," Roy said, "have been giving Dad and me a hard time about you and QM's hired gun. That's what."

Lisa took a deep breath. "Well, I'm sorry they have. But get it through your thick head that Dan Ashly is not QM's hired gun. Because I'm going to tell you both something. I like Dan. And...and I'm going to be spending more time with him."

Her brother rolled his eyes. "Oh, that's terrific. Hell, Lisa, I won't be able to show my face in the Silver Dollar without someone insinuating that my sister's—"

"That is enough!" Helen snapped. "In the first place, the less time you spend in the Silver Dollar, Roy, the better. And in the second place, who your sister chooses to date is her own business. Besides, I've seen Dan Ashly both on the news and on *Fiona,* and he seems like a fine man. So if Lisa likes him...well, you and your father would be better off spending your time thinking up good replies for those workers than sitting here trying to make her feel guilty."

The two men began studiously poking at the remains of their breakfasts, and Lisa mouthed a silent "thanks" to her mother. She darned well wasn't going to feel guilty. And she'd learned her lesson about giving Dan a chance to explain things to her. She'd asked him all about his study. And she just knew he'd tell her there was no need to worry about his report.

THE OPENING CREDITS for *Sunday at Ten* began rolling across the screen, and Lisa snuggled more closely against Dan's bare chest. Moving the television in here, so they could watch it in bed, had been one of his better ideas. Not that they'd ended up doing much watching.

"I guess," he said, stroking her hair, "that I'll have to head back to the Pritchard House when the news is over. Much as I'd love to, sleeping here *every* night probably wouldn't be a good idea."

"No?" she murmured. It sounded like a perfectly good idea to her.

"No. I imagine that our call to Bill was enough to clue *him* in that something's going on between us. I know he won't worry about my integrity, though. And I can trust him not to say anything. But I wouldn't want the word getting back to any other QM brass. They might think I'd let you influence my report."

Lisa ordered her mind into alert. Yesterday, she'd meant to ask all about his study. But one thing had led to another... well, actually, one thing had led to more of the same. At any rate, she hadn't gotten around to asking. And now he'd offered her a perfect opening.

"Would you?" she tried.

"Would I what?"

"Let me influence your report."

"If you tell me," he said, grinning, "that you've only been making love to me in hopes of influencing my report, my ego will be totally destroyed."

"Be serious, Dan. I mean... well, you know how much what happens at Plant W matters to my family. So... would you?"

His grin slowly faded. "Lisa, I'm getting kind of tired of telling you this, but I intend to do an honest job."

"I know you do, but..." Her words trailed off as Dan's faded grin was replaced by a frown.

"Lisa, why are you going on about this? Would you really want a guy who'd compromise himself?"

"No, of course not." *Not under most circumstances,* she added silently.

"Good, because you don't have one in me. Hey, come on," he said less sternly, tucking his fingers under her chin. "You're lucky it was me who QM hired. They could have given the job to someone like Dr. Benny. Then you'd have had to worry about how the planets were aligned when the first Dueler rolled out the door. At least with me you've got fair, rational and objective. You can't ask for more than that, can you?"

"No, of course not," she murmured again, pressing her cheek against the softness of his chest hair, listening to the rhythmic beating of his heart.

"Dan," she tried, a few minutes later, "Dan, tell me about what your report will cover."

He shrugged. "I've already told you sixty-three times."

"No, I mean tell me more specifically. Are you looking at...say...sociological considerations?"

"I'll be looking at everything I feel is relevant. But I can't tell you specifically what that'll be. Not yet, at least. What I'll be looking at in the final stages will depend on what I've found by the time I've collected all the data I need from the plant."

"Oh. But you'll tell me what you're doing as you go along?"

Dan shifted so that he could see her face. "Lisa, we'll be airing those updates on *Fiona.* I'll be telling everyone what I'm doing as I go along."

"No, I don't mean just little snippets of information. Jake said those segments are going to be brief."

Dan looked at her for a long, silent minute, until his gaze began making her uncomfortable.

"What?" she said.

"Lisa, let's make a deal."

"What deal?"

"Let's make a deal not to talk about my study."

"But why?"

"Well, just think about what's happened between us. When we first met, you didn't want anything to do with me because I was the one conducting the blasted study. Then you put me through three days of hell because you jumped to the wrong conclusion about my objectivity. And right now, I'm getting more than a little annoyed by this third degree you're giving me. So steering clear of the topic makes a lot of sense."

"But, Dan, I'm really interested in what you're doing."

He gave her a slow, cat-that-swallowed-the-canary grin. "I know you're really interested. And so are a lot of other people . . . including your father."

"Dan!" She sat up and glared at him. "You aren't suggesting that—"

"Lisa, what I'm suggesting is that you and I will be safer staying away from the subject. Aside from anything else, I don't want to take any chances on saying something that could be misconstrued if you repeated it."

"Oh, Dan, I'd never repeat anything you said. Never. Not a word."

"Really?" he teased, his grin broadening. "But aren't you the same woman who promised Jake you wouldn't breathe a word about the study? Then turned around and did? And aren't you the same woman who promised Roy you wouldn't tell me you knew about that late-night phone call to Bill? Then told me? And aren't you the same woman who I've already concluded isn't exactly an award-winning secret-keeper?"

"Dan, that's not fair!"

"All's fair in love and war," he whispered, pulling her back to him and kissing her neck. "And I'm not going to risk having that damned study cause any more problems between us. So, except when we're on the set of *Fiona,* let's make this our final discussion of it, okay?"

"I...well...okay." She began drawing tiny circles on his chest, catching at its pale hair with her finger. Maybe he was right. Maybe they'd be better off not talking about Plant W.

Besides, she really had no reason to be concerned. Despite what he said about not compromising himself, he loved her. And that meant he couldn't help but be influenced by her feelings, whether he was conscious of it happening or not.

But even without any subconscious influence, a man like Dan would never do anything that he realized would ruin people's lives. Whatever his findings, in the final analysis she knew his primary consideration would be how vitally important Plant W was to Walkerton.

Just as she'd told her father, that was what sociological considerations were all about. Just as she'd told her father, Dan's report would contain nothing that might jeopardize Plant W's future. Because she could never love a man who had it in him to destroy her hometown. And she certainly loved Dan Ashly.

She reached up and wrapped her arms around his neck, drawing his lips down to hers, feeling an urge to show him precisely how much she loved him.

CHAPTER TWELVE

"BENEDETTO ONLY TEACHES an afternoon class on Tuesdays," Crystal offered. "So how would tomorrow be?"

"Fine," Lisa said. "Why not have him come in first thing? And I think we'll try shooting the promos without a script. There's so much chemistry between you two that it's bound to come across on the screen. Just chatting naturally about what he'll be doing on *Love* will probably work better than anything we could write."

Crystal smiled one of her mile-wide smiles. "The chemistry really *is* obvious, isn't it? Benedetto says that's because he's a Leo and I'm a Libra. Oh, Lisa, I can't believe how quickly things have changed. When Jake told me he was thinking of canceling *Love,* I was devastated. But now I'm floating on air. I just know having Benedetto on the show is going to give my ratings the boost they need. And suddenly I have this wonderful man in my life and..." She paused for a moment, then went on. "Speaking of things changing, Benedetto was telling me that you and Dan are...?"

"That Dan and I are what?" Lisa teased.

"Well, that there's something between you, something serious. After Friday, after that argument we walked in on, I could scarcely believe he knew what he

was talking about. But he was so insistent. He said he
realized it the first time he saw you together. And he
said your signs are perfectly matched, one of the best
astrological combinations there is."

"Crystal, you told him when my birthday is?"

"Not really. He knew. He said, 'Lisa's a Sagittar-
ius, isn't she?' I simply confirmed it."

"Honestly?"

"Yes. He can tell practically anyone's sign within a
few minutes of meeting them. And he said a Sagittar-
ius will be immediately drawn to an Aries, and that
they get along wonderfully. You're both fire signs,
which apparently makes for awfully hot... I mean...
well," she concluded with a laugh, "you know what I
mean."

Lisa tried unsuccessfully to repress a grin. She didn't
believe in Dr. Benny's astrological mumbo jumbo. Not
for a minute. He had to know a trick about figuring out
people's signs. Still, he was bang-on about the awfully
hot sex. The weekend had been an absolute scorcher.

Crystal smiled. "Benedetto's right, isn't he? There
is something going on. And I'll bet, given the Chesh-
ire-cat grin you're wearing, that whatever was wrong
on Friday isn't wrong any longer."

"Well, I could truthfully say it was a good weekend." In fact, she could truthfully say it was the best
weekend of her life, but while she was deciding whether
she wanted to get into a game of true confessions,
someone knocked on the office door.

"Yes?" she called.

The door opened halfway and Kurt Kusch stuck his
head in. "Morning, ladies. Lisa, I just wanted to let
you know that I've returned those *Fiona* tapes."

"Great. Thanks."

"And I thought you might be able to tell me where Carl Gustavson is. I checked the janitor's room but it's locked."

"Carl's taking a couple of days off, Kurt. He and a friend went fishing."

"Do you know where?"

"No, he didn't say."

"Think anyone at the station would know?"

"I doubt it. He doesn't talk much about his personal life."

"He got a wife who'd know?"

"No, he's a widower. Kurt, is there anything I can help you with? Is something wrong?"

He merely shrugged. "Lisa, how were the *Fiona* ratings last Friday? Did they shoot up after what happened?"

"Ahh...we don't have official numbers. But Jake's informal survey said they were really high. Why?"

"Just checking. And, Lisa, you produced every one of the past *Fiona* segments?"

"Right."

"And that fellow in the audience, the one who stretched the trip wire?"

"Yes?"

"You haven't had a brilliant flash about him looking familiar, have you?"

"No. Sorry."

Kurt rubbed his jaw. "He didn't...he didn't remind you of one of the guests you've had on the show, huh?"

"No. No, he really didn't remind me of anyone, Kurt. Why? You saw someone on one of those tapes? You think you've figured out who the guy in the audience was?"

"Well...it's hard to tell with the disguise, but it might have been one of your earlier guests."

"Which one?"

"I can't tell you that right now. But there was something on a tape that made me wonder.... Well, at any rate, I have to question Carl again. Even if my hunch is right about the guest, there still had to be an inside man at the station. You said he'll be back in a couple of days?"

"Yes. On Wednesday."

"I hate things hanging," Kurt muttered, shaking his head. "'Specially when we're talking attempted murder. Guess it's not worth scouring the state for the guy, though. Well, I'll let you two get back to work. See you, Lisa. Crystal." He closed the door, leaving them staring at each other.

"He thinks it was Carl," Crystal whispered. "He thinks Carl was the inside man who had access to the studio and sawed that board."

"I know," Lisa whispered back. "Crystal, why are we whispering?"

Crystal shrugged, then slipped out of her chair, opened the door a crack and checked the hall. "Coast's clear," she announced, shoving it closed and sitting down again. "Do you think Carl realizes he's a suspect?"

"Definitely. He talked to me about it last week. And he was awfully upset."

"Lisa, he's going to be awfully, awfully, awfully upset on Wednesday. Kurt's liable to haul him off to jail for attempted murder."

"But you don't think Carl could possibly have had any part in it, do you? He's such a sweetie."

"I know, but Kurt's obviously decided he's the one."

Lisa shook her head. "Poor Carl. It just can't have been him. But if Kurt figures Carl's his man, he's probably not going to look any further."

"He'll try to stick Carl with a bum rap. That's how they'd say it on a cop show, Lisa."

"You know, maybe I'd better view those tapes and see if anything prompts that brilliant flash Kurt was hoping I'd had. Carl simply can't have been the inside man. And if I could figure out which guest Kurt suspects, maybe I'd remember if he knew anyone on staff at the station or—"

"Lisa, Fiona's been here since last spring. She's done at least a couple of dozen shows. At an hour each, you'd still be viewing when Carl gets back."

"You're right. I guess that's not such a hot idea. But if that creep in the audience has really been a guest, surely all I need is something to jog my memory and I'll realize who he is. You know, I'm going to go over to the General at lunchtime. If Fiona and I go through the list of guests, maybe something will strike one of us. And she probably wouldn't mind a visitor."

Crystal grinned wryly. "She might not mind *some* visitors, but I doubt you make her approved list. After you hosted such a terrific show on Friday, you'll be lucky if she doesn't tear your hair out."

DAN WAS DRIVING into the WALK lot when he spotted Lisa at the bus stop in front of the station. He wheeled the Dueler around, pulled up in front of her, and shoved the passenger door ajar. "Need a lift, lady?"

The way her face lit up when she realized it was him made Dan feel warm inside. How could he have been so damned lucky as to have met Lisa Saint-John?

Finding her was the best thing that had ever happened to him.

"What a nice surprise," she said, getting in.

He drew her to him and kissed her. The enticing scent of her perfume and the lush softness of her mouth made him want to whisk her back to her apartment. Lord, he was crazy about this woman.

"How did you escape from the plant?" she asked when he released her.

"I was in the midst of retrieving data from a computer when it crashed. There's a techie working on the problem, but I figured there wasn't any point in sitting and watching him. Especially not when I could be taking you out for lunch, instead."

"Lunch, huh? How do you feel about hospital cafeteria food?"

"It's certainly not what I had in mind."

"And how do you feel about visiting Fiona?"

"That's certainly not what I had in mind, either. Why? Is that where you're headed?"

She nodded. "And I could use your moral support. Crystal figures Fiona's going to be upset that I didn't fall on my face on Friday."

"Then why visit her?"

"I have to. I've got to talk to her about something. You don't really have to come in with me, though. You can just drop me off. I know you're not going to want to sit and listen to us."

He shrugged. Sitting and listening to Lisa was better than not sitting and listening to her. "I don't mind. Maybe your talk won't take long and we'll still be able to catch a decent lunch."

"Oh, Dan, I don't know. I've really got a problem. Kurt Kusch was in this morning and he has a totally ridiculous theory."

Dan shifted the Dueler into gear and started off, listening to Lisa tell him about Kurt suspecting the station's janitor of conspiring with some unidentified *Fiona* guest to murder the host.

"You're absolutely positive Kurt couldn't be right?" he asked, turning into Walkerton General's parking lot.

"Absolutely. Carl's really a darling. He'd never do anything to harm anyone. Not for a million dollars. So I just *have* to help him."

Dan cut the engine and sat gazing at Lisa for a moment. *I've really got a problem,* was how she'd begun this story. When it wasn't actually *her* problem, at all. If he was ever in serious trouble, he certainly hoped he'd have someone like her on his side.

They headed up to the General's seventh floor and along to Fiona's room.

"I hope she isn't too upset with me," Lisa said anxiously, as they neared the door.

"Take a deep breath before you go in to face her."

"It smells as if we're standing outside a florist's," she whispered after the breath.

"Well, if Fiona throws a vase at you, feel free to hide behind me."

"Thanks. I knew your broad shoulders would come in handy for something."

Fiona actually smiled when she saw them. She was still in traction but, aside from that and a few fading bruises, looked her normal self.

Instead of a hospital-issue gown, she was wearing a silky black creation that clung suggestively to her breasts... and every other bit of her. Dan consciously forced his gaze up past her neck.

Her red hair seemed freshly washed, and, despite her one sprained wrist, she was fully made-up.

"Visitors," she gushed. "I never thought I'd be so happy to have visitors as I've been lately."

Lisa visibly relaxed. "Even ones who are filling in on your show?" she teased.

Fiona's smile slipped, but only a little. "You did a very competent job, Lisa," she offered stiffly. "Both of you," she added, nodding to Dan. "You were both fine. So, sit down and tell me what's happening in the real world. What's going on at WALK?"

"Oh, Fiona," Lisa said, sinking onto the bedside chair, "that's what I've come to talk to you about."

"It's not bad news, is it? Jake hasn't come up with some harebrained scheme that's going to affect my show, has he?"

"No, no, it's nothing like that."

Dan wandered across to the window and stood looking at the street below, absently listening as Lisa began explaining why she was here.

"Fiona, Kurt Kusch watched all the tapes of your shows, and he's decided the fellow who ran the trip wire was once your guest."

"What?"

Fiona's voice cracked on the word, and Dan turned to look at her. The color was rapidly draining from her face. Despite her makeup, by the time she spoke again, she was as white as the pillowcase.

"Which guest?" she whispered.

"I don't know. He wouldn't tell me."

"Has he talked to the guy yet?"

"I don't think so. I got the impression he wanted to talk to Carl Gustavson first."

"Carl?" Fiona's voice cracked a second time. "Lisa, did Kurt say *why* he wanted to talk to Carl?"

"Oh, Fiona, it's ridiculous, but he's decided that Carl and this guest were in cahoots. I know that can't possibly be true, but Kurt's going to accuse Carl of trying to murder you, and Carl's going to be so incredibly upset, and I thought that if you and I could figure out who the fellow in the audience was, then we might be able to figure out who the actual inside man at the station was."

As Lisa spoke, Dan watched Fiona curiously. Her expression was growing more and more frightened.

He glanced at Lisa for a second. She was eyeing Fiona as if she couldn't understand the intensity of the woman's distress, either.

"Carl's taken a couple of days off work," she continued. "But come Wednesday morning, Kurt's going to—"

"Lisa...Lisa, you have to help me." Fiona grabbed Lisa's hand. "You have to help me. Kurt knows."

Lisa turned to Dan. He shrugged and refocused on Fiona. This was getting more intriguing by the moment.

"Kurt knows what?" Lisa asked.

"He...either he knows or he suspects. And when Carl tells him...and when he talks to Frank, Frank will tell him..." Fiona swallowed, her gaze sweeping the room, lingering on Dan.

"Ahh...you want me to leave, Fiona?" Damn. He was dying to hear more, to learn who the hell Frank was. And what he and Carl were going to tell Kurt.

Well, Lisa would fill him in later. At least there was *something* to be said for her inability to keep secrets.

"No, don't leave, Dan," Fiona finally answered him, her voice quavering. "I need your help, too. Oh, Lisa...Dan...I need all the help I can get. And you and Jake are friends, Dan. You can help Lisa make him agree."

"Agree to what?"

"To talk to Kurt. Oh, if he does that, everything will be all right," she rushed on, clearly trying to convince herself as well as them. "Jake's an important citizen in Walkerton. If he talks to Kurt, if he explains how things are in the industry, how crucial ratings are, if he tells them it would be bad for the station's image, then the police won't press any charges. And my job, Lisa. We've had our differences, but you know I'm a good host. You have to tell Jake that. I love my show. Losing it would kill me."

Dan shook his head. "Fiona, I don't understand what you're talking about."

"The fall, Dan. The attempted murder. It wasn't."

"Fiona, for heaven's sake make sense. What wasn't what?"

A tear trickled down her cheek...a second one followed, leaving a tiny trail of mascara.

"Fiona?" Lisa said softly. "Fiona, tell us what's wrong." With her free hand, she reached across and brushed Fiona's cheek dry.

Fiona sniffed and her lower lip began trembling. "I...I did it," she whispered.

"You did what?" Lisa murmured.

"There was... there was no murder attempt, Lisa. I...I was the inside man. I sawed the board. Frank and I...we planned the whole thing."

JAKE SLAMMED his fist down onto his desk again.

This time, Lisa didn't jump. But she wished he'd stop before he gave her a headache.

"Jake, for God's sake," Dan snapped. "Quit pounding the desk. You're going to break your hand."

"But how could she do such a damn fool thing?"

"I told you," Lisa said. "For the ratings. She figured an attempt on her life would send her ratings soaring. And she was right."

"Ratings! Who the hell cares that much about ratings?"

Lisa resisted the impulse to say she'd always thought *he* did.

"Idiot. Goddamned idiot. She could have killed herself."

"Hell, Jake," Dan muttered, "she wouldn't even have been injured if it wasn't for Carl."

"He was only doing his job," Lisa said quickly.

Jake shook his head. "No one's blaming Carl for taking the cartons away, Lisa. How the hell was he supposed to know that a pile of empty boxes had been put there for a reason?"

"But he must have realized after she fell," Lisa murmured. "That would explain why he was so upset. Remember? The camera caught him when he was helping Dan keep the crowd back, and he was white as a ghost. But why on earth didn't he say anything about cartons having been piled behind the seating stand? If he had, we'd have known from the start that her fall was a hoax."

"Probably," Dan offered, "he was terrified that he'd be blamed for moving them. I mean, from what I saw of him, I'd say he's not the brightest man in the world. And people who aren't too bright learn that keeping quiet sometimes keeps them out of trouble."

Lisa shook her head. "If only he'd spoken up, everything would have made sense. You know, now that the truth's out, I can remember Fiona's interview with Frank Hockly practically word for word. One of the things he specifically talked about was stuntmen using empty cardboard cartons to break their falls."

"But why the hell did this stuntman character get involved in Fiona's half-baked scheme?" Jake demanded.

"Jake...do you really have to ask?" Lisa said. "Fiona did her man-eater number on him. After she'd gone out with him a couple of times, she could probably have convinced him to help her with anything."

"Well, she's damned well not convincing me to help her," Jake snapped. "You two can knock off pleading her case. I don't care how good a host she is. I'm not having a lunatic working for me. And as far as I'm concerned, Kusch can charge her and her stuntman with whatever he wants. The police force has probably spent a fortune investigating this damned travesty."

Dan nodded. "Yeah, that's likely true. I wonder...?"

"What?"

"Well, Jake, in New York a hefty donation to the police association's benevolent fund would take care of something as minor as a public mischief charge. And I imagine that's the only one Kusch could lay."

"A donation? A *hefty* donation? Surely you don't mean from me?"

"Not you directly. I was thinking about the station."

"Dan, I *am* the station. And you're talking bribery."

"No, I'm talking a donation to a worthy cause. Hell, Jake, it's tax deductible."

"That's beside the point. Why should I throw away money because Fiona was an idiot?"

"It might take care of your problem, Jake."

"I don't have a problem. Fiona has a problem. Her stuntman friend has a problem. Not me."

"Jake," Lisa tried, "don't you think Fiona might be right? Don't you think, if word of what actually happened gets out, that it'll be bad PR for WALK? I mean, Fiona's awfully popular with the viewers. So people might not want to believe she thought up the idea on her own. They might suspect that it was your scheme, and that you made her go along with it. Or worse yet, that you arranged it without her even knowing, and then the plan got screwed up."

"What?" Jake sputtered.

"Anything's possible," Dan offered. "But setting aside whose idea viewers might think it was, I sure wouldn't be too hasty about firing her. A lot of people would figure you for a real jerk. I mean, what sort of man would fire a woman who's lying in a hospital bed?"

"But . . . but . . ."

"At least give some thought to keeping her on," Dan continued. "And think about that donation, too. You just can't be sure how your viewers would react to a scandal, not to mention what the network honchos would think. Or the licensing board."

"The network? The licensing board?" Jake's face was rapidly turning fuchsia.

"Jake," Lisa said gently, "Jake, relax. What's happened has happened. And Fiona didn't really do anything *that* awful. You're always going on about how important ratings are. And she just got carried away. And she's the only one it really hurt. And...well, Jake, she's obviously been suffering, emotionally as well as physically. I think she's already been punished enough. So why not take time to think things through before you decide whether to fire her? And why not do what you can to keep the facts about her fall from surfacing?"

Jake stood staring at the wall, his color gradually fading to pink. Finally he turned to Dan. "How much do you figure a hefty donation is?"

"Well, let's see. This is Walkerton, not New York. I'd say you could see how Kusch reacts to the idea of five grand."

"Five grand? Five big ones?"

"Could save you a lot of grief," Dan said.

"I think I'd rather save five thousand bucks."

Dan shrugged. "Your decision. We're only trying to help. Well, listen, I've got to get back to the plant. Talk to you for a minute, Lisa?" he added, nodding toward the hall.

She followed him out and pulled the door shut behind them. "What do you think?" she whispered.

"I expect he'll come around. But you know, I'm still not entirely convinced Fiona doesn't deserve to be charged."

"Dan, you agreed that her logic made sense."

"Yeah, I guess. If the truth comes out, Jake *could* find himself in a darned uncomfortable position. And I imagine, when he calms down, he'll realize the quieter this is kept, the better."

"What about Fiona's job? Do you think he'll ever let her back into the station?"

"That's a whole different matter, isn't it? I wouldn't blame him if he didn't."

"Oh, Dan, how can you say that after seeing her today? The poor woman is—"

"The *poor* woman," Dan interrupted, grinning wryly, "is a damned bitch. And *you* are a damned softie for feeling sorry for her. If Jake does let her keep her job, you'll probably end up kicking yourself."

"Maybe...maybe she'll turn over a new leaf."

"Sure. Maybe. Look, let's forget about Fiona. I was thinking that it's hardly worth my going back to the plant today. Can you sneak out early? I know this terrific apartment with a gorgeous view of the river...and the most comfortable bed."

Lisa smiled. "How about meeting me there later? I can't leave yet. Roy called earlier—he's coming by to see me after his shift."

A distinctly unhappy expression appeared on Dan's face. "Roy? What's he want? He dig up some new incriminating evidence against me?"

"If he did, I'll ignore it."

"Promise?"

"Yes. And I also promise to get home as soon as I can."

"Eager to sit out on the balcony with me? Enjoy the view?"

"That's not what I had in mind doing...or enjoying."

"HI," ROY SAID from the doorway.

Lisa smiled across at him. "Hi, little brother. Come on in." She watched him close the door and settle into a chair. His hair was tousled, lending him a boyish air, making it hard for her to believe he was almost twenty-six. But there was no doubt he'd grown into a man. He was a younger version of Dad now, a little taller, but with the same dark good looks.

He wiped his palms along his jeans and cleared his throat.

"What's up?" she prompted.

"I . . . Lisa, I came to apologize."

"Oh?"

"About the things I said when you were at the house Saturday. You'll be glad to hear that Mom did quite a number on me after you left."

"Mom did quite a number on you while I was there."

"That was nothing compared to later," he said, grinning. "Mom always did like you best."

Lisa laughed. Roy had been using that old Smothers Brothers' line on her practically since he'd learned to talk.

"At any rate, I'm sorry about the remarks. It's none of my business what guys you date. And . . . and I never intentionally spied on you. Honest."

Oh, right, her brother the spy. She hadn't been thinking about that. But now that she was, she began feeling angry at him again. "You want me to believe it was an accident that you were lurking in my yard? Twice?"

"Lisa, give me a break, huh? The first time, I didn't know Ashly would be bringing you home. Hell, I didn't even know who he was, remember? I just figured you might have heard more about the study."

"And the second time? When Dan and I were on the balcony and you were playing Peeping Tom?"

"I...well, that night I did know you were going out with him. But I thought it was only an information retrieval mission for Dad, so I assumed you'd say goodbye at the door again, and then I could find out what he'd said. But look, after he went in with you, I was simply hanging around on the riverbank, waiting for him to leave. It wasn't what you thought."

"Dammit, Roy, then why did you tell Mom and Dad about me kissing him?"

He shrugged, looking so downright miserable that her anger began to dissipate. "I shouldn't have. It just slipped out. I guess because I was upset...upset about Ashly's study and you being with him like that...I don't know, Lisa. Whatever it was, I'm sorry." He started to rise. "I'll stay away from your place from here on in, okay?"

"Roy, no, wait a minute. I don't want you staying away. I hardly see you anymore as it is." And they hardly talked anymore, so she didn't want to miss an opportunity to learn what was going on inside his head. She knew he hadn't been happy for the past few months. And there was his drinking that Mom was so worried about.

He slumped down into the chair again.

"Roy, why are you so upset about Dan being here? I mean, what's the worst thing in the world that could result from his study?"

"You know," he said, shaking his head, "for a smart lady you sometimes ask really dumb questions."

"No, Roy, I mean let's assume the worst actually happened. Say QM shut down Plant W."

"Lisa...do you know anything? Has Ashly told you something?"

"No, I don't know a darned thing. And I'm not going to, either. Dan and I don't even discuss what he's doing at the plant. So I won't know a single fact that anyone can't learn by watching his updates on *Fiona*."

"Then there's not much point in us talking about what's happening with the company, is there?"

"Roy, I don't care about the company. But I do care about you. And what I'm getting at is that there's no law saying Roy Saint-John has to work for QM for the next thirty-five years."

"Oh? And what do you suggest I do? Get a job pumping gas? At minimum wage?"

"Roy, you could do anything you put your mind to. You're an intelligent man."

"Right. I'm an intelligent man with a high school diploma. Period."

"Roy, you could—"

"Don't give me the lecture about how I could have gone to university if I'd wanted, okay? I wasn't you. I wasn't scholarship material."

"Dammit, Roy, you're smarter than me. You just didn't apply yourself in school."

He shrugged. "Maybe I didn't. But the bottom line is that I didn't have a scholarship, and, by the time the long strike was over, my college fund was gone and Mom and Dad were in debt."

"You could have worked for a year, then gone back to school."

"Well, I didn't, did I? So let's forget this, okay?"

"Roy...Roy, I didn't mean to get onto what you could have done years ago. What I meant to do was suggest that maybe you should think about going back to school now. You don't like what you're doing all that much. You've told me so."

"It's an okay job."

"Roy, you could do better than okay."

"Oh, hell, Lisa, I couldn't go to university now. I'd be an old man by the time I got out—an old man starting at the bottom with a bunch of kids."

"You're exaggerating, Roy. You know you are. But I'm not saying you *have* to go back to school at all. I just said you should think about it. Or think about changing fields. Working in the auto industry isn't your only option."

"It was good enough for Dad."

"I'm not saying being an autoworker isn't good enough, Roy. I'm saying you don't seem happy with it."

"It's what I know, Lisa."

"Fine. It's what you know. So say Dan's report tells Detroit that everything is fine at the plant. And say you just stay where you are. In that *okay* job. What happens if, when you're forty-odd years old, with a family to support, QM does decide to pull out of Walkerton?"

"Then I'll have a problem, won't I?"

"Damned right you will. So don't you think you should at least consider doing something else with your life? Something that you'd like better than okay? Something that wouldn't leave you up the creek if the worst happened?"

"Oh, hell, Lisa, I'm an autoworker. And I can live without you sounding like Ginny." Roy leaned back against the chair and took a deep breath, as if merely mentioning Ginny's name had pained him.

Lisa bit her lip. He'd been so closemouthed about his broken engagement that even Mom hadn't been able to drag any details out of him. But Mom was certain it was the reason Roy had begun spending so much time at the Silver Dollar.

"I really liked Ginny," Lisa offered tentatively.

"Yeah. So did I."

"So what went wrong?"

"Nothing. We just decided getting married would be a mistake, that's all. Look, can we drop this?"

She almost said yes, then changed her mind. Ginny was perfect for her brother, and maybe there was still hope for them. "No, Roy. We can't drop this. Because you owe me one."

"What the hell does that mean?"

"It means you've spent the last little while with your nose wedged firmly in my personal life. And now I deserve a turn at yours. I take it that remark, about me sounding like Ginny, means she was concerned about your future, too?"

"That's one way of putting it. But I'd say it was more that she was concerned about her own. More like she decided she could get a better husband than a line worker at Plant W. And since I wasn't about to put my life on hold for the next half century to become a doctor or lawyer, she decided to look for greener pastures."

"She never struck me as a gold digger," Lisa said quietly. "Not in the least. Maybe she just thought you'd be happier doing something else."

"Well, maybe people should just stop thinking about what I'd be happier doing! Maybe people should just stick to running their own lives. Look, I've gotta go. See you around," he added, shoving himself up from the chair and stalking out.

Lisa simply sat at her desk after he'd left, wishing to hell she hadn't opened her mouth. Roy found apologizing tough. He always had. So she should have merely forgiven him and sent him on his way. Instead, she'd stuck a knife into him . . . and twisted it for good measure. She hadn't realized he was still hurting so badly. She should have, though. He'd been absolutely crazy about Ginny.

Just as crazy as she was about Dan. If she lost him the way Roy had lost Ginny . . . she couldn't even imagine how awful she'd feel if she lost Dan.

A tiny thought crept out of the recesses of her mind, a tiny thought about Dan only being in Walkerton for a little while. A tiny thought about him going back to New York soon, about the possibility that she *would* lose him.

She shoved the thought firmly back into the cob-webbed recess it had escaped from. Right now, Dan was here. Right now, he was waiting at her apartment.

CHAPTER THIRTEEN

CRYSTAL DANCED into Lisa's office, waving a sheet of paper as if it was a conqueror's flag. "Have you seen Jake's latest unofficial numbers for *Love?*"

"They were the first thing I checked this morning. They're looking good."

"Good? They're looking fantastic," Crystal exclaimed, sinking into a chair. "Benedetto's only been on two shows and our share's already up five. I can't believe how the past two weeks have changed things—or how fast the time's flown."

Lisa merely shook her head. Between filling in as host on a second, then a third *Fiona* segment, keeping up with her regular production schedule, and spending every spare instant with Dan, it didn't surprise her that two weeks had passed like two days.

"Viewer response to the live astrology call-in bit is fabulous," Crystal continued. "Even before I introduce it, the switchboard's swamped. I'm starting to think every woman in Walkerton is worried about how compatible her sign is with her romantic partner's."

"I only hope we don't precipitate a slew of divorces."

Crystal looked taken aback, then laughed. "You're joking. Sorry, I can't get my head past these beautiful numbers. I must be starting to take ratings as seriously as Jake does."

"As long as you don't start taking them as seriously as Fiona did, we'll be all right."

"Oh, I can't imagine getting *that* intense. How is she, anyway? Have you seen her?"

"Dan and I dropped by her apartment a couple of nights ago. She's hobbling around in her leg cast, worrying herself sick that Jake's never going to let her come back."

"Is he?"

"I'm not sure. He's still furious about her costing him five grand."

"You know," Crystal said, grinning, "when Dan suggested that donation, I could hear Jake shouting about it all the way down in my office. That was quite a day, wasn't it?"

"It certainly was." And Crystal only knew the half of it. It had also been the day Roy had come by to apologize, then gone away angry. It had been the day Lisa had realized just how deeply losing Ginny had hurt him. And it had been that realization that had started her thoughts persistently dwelling on the prospect of Dan heading back to New York.

Strange, that none of the issues raised that day had really been resolved. Oh, since Jake had paid his *contribution* to the police fund, neither Fiona nor her stuntman conspirator would be charged with anything. But the future of Fiona's job was still up in the air.

And as far as Roy was concerned, Lisa hadn't even seen him for the past two weeks. The couple of times she'd gone by the house, he'd been conveniently out. Next time, she wouldn't call ahead.

And Dan...the most important issue of all was that he'd be going home soon.

"Your dress arrived over the weekend," Crystal said.

"What dress?"

"For the show...you know...the gown you're going to model on our wedding fashions segment."

"Oh, Lord, I'd forgotten all about agreeing to be one of the models."

"Just what kind of producer are you?" Crystal teased. "We're taping that show in a week. You should be checking that all the details are falling into place, not forgetting them."

"I seem to have details coming out of my ears these days. Besides, I'm relying on you. You're starting to get as involved in the production end of things as Fiona does."

Crystal made a face. "I haven't started acting like her though, have I?"

"Hardly."

"Well, promise that if I do, you'll shoot me. But as long as you're relying on me, I want you to try on the dress...in case it needs alterations. Come on."

Crystal dragged Lisa down to the wardrobe room, threw open the door and flicked on the light. An elegant ivory confection hung before them. "Tell the truth, Lisa. Isn't that the most beautiful wedding gown you've ever seen?"

"I think it just might be. It's absolutely gorgeous. The picture we saw didn't do it justice." Lisa fingered the delicate peau de soie, tracing the pattern of the tiny seed pearls appliquéd on the bodice. "It looks as if it belongs in a fairy tale, as if it was sewn by bluebirds from Disney."

She held it up to herself and gazed at the mirror. "There must be a thousand yards of fabric in the skirt."

"Only twenty," Crystal said, smiling. "Try it on. After all, it probably wouldn't be a bad idea for you to start trying on wedding gowns."

Lisa gazed at the dress for another moment, all her uncertainties escaping to the forefront of her mind. "I . . . I'm not sure about that."

Crystal's smile vanished. "Problems with Dan?"

"Not really. I mean, no. No problems with Dan. He's wonderful. But . . . well, oh, I don't know."

"You don't know what?" Crystal asked softly.

"Oh, I just don't know whether I'm coming or going. Or maybe I should be more literal and say I don't know whether I'm staying or going."

"You mean . . . when Dan goes?"

"Exactly. You know, it's ironic. When I first got involved with him, I was worried I might not like living in New York. And that if we had any future together, I'd have to move there. But the way I feel about him now, I'd go anywhere on earth to be with him."

"Then what's the problem?"

"Crystal, Dan hasn't said anything about the future. Not a word."

"So ask him about it."

"I can't. He knows I love him. And he must know that I'd marry him in a minute, if he asked me."

"You're allowed to do the asking, Lisa. This is the nineties."

"Oh, Crystal, maybe it's old-fashioned of me, but I can't even bring up the subject. I just keep worrying that he has no intention of ever talking about the future. Maybe he's simply planning to say 'nice knowing you' and head home to Manhattan without a backward glance."

"Lisa, it'll be all right. You'll see. Dan's insane about you."

She shrugged unhappily. "I don't know why I'm so upset today. It's probably Dan being in Detroit. Crystal, he went there to get the last bits of data he needs. His study's done, and his report's almost complete. He expects to have the final draft wrapped up by the end of the week. And then . . . and then I just don't know."

"It's funny what love does to people, isn't it, Lisa?"

"What do you mean?"

"Well, remember how concerned you were at first, that Dan's report might bring grief to Plant W? Remember how you said you could never have a relationship with him if you thought it might? Well, lately, you haven't even mentioned the possibility of his report being negative. But I guess," she added with a grin, "you know a lot more about what it's going to say than he's been revealing on his *Fiona* updates."

"I . . . no, actually, I don't. We haven't been talking about his study at all. I guess I just convinced myself that . . ." Her words trailed off. Of course the report would be favorable. She was positive.

That's why she'd managed to stop worrying about it. Well, she'd *almost* managed to stop worrying about it. Dan knew how important the future of Plant W was to her. And he loved her.

But what would she do if his report contained an unpleasant surprise?

"Everything will work out between you and Dan," Crystal said reassuringly. "He's head over heels in love with you. You aren't doubting that, are you?"

"I . . . I don't know what I'm doing. I guess what I've *been* doing, the entire month he's been here, has been trying to ignore the issue of his not being here forever. But I can't do that any longer."

"Lisa, don't worry. He'd be out of his mind to leave Walkerton without you. I only pray Jake finds another good producer."

Lisa managed a smile. She only prayed Jake would need to.

"So come on," Crystal pressed. "Try on the dress. Let me see how it looks."

Hesitantly, Lisa changed into the wedding gown.

Crystal zipped it up, fastened a seemingly endless row of clasps, then stepped around and gazed at Lisa. "It's a perfect fit. Here, I'll put the headdress on you." She fidgeted with the veil for a moment, then smiled. "You look like the bride of the year."

Lisa turned to the mirror and stared at herself. Crystal was right. She'd been transformed from the girl next door into a model for *Brides* magazine.

"All you need is Dan," Crystal murmured.

Yes. Crystal was right again. All Lisa Saint-John needed in the entire world was Dan Ashly.

LISA TOOK ANOTHER bite of lunch—assuming a dry sandwich from the vending machine counted as lunch—and leaned back in her chair. She couldn't stop thinking about how she'd looked in that gown... couldn't stop thinking about Dan.

Her phone rang. When she answered it, his voice sent her adrenaline racing. "Dan, where are you?"

"At the Pritchard House. I wrapped up everything in Detroit earlier than I expected."

"Oh, that's great. I didn't think you'd be back till tonight."

"Well, now that I am, can you play hooky this afternoon?"

"I'd love to, but I don't think I'd better."

"This is important, Lisa. I have to talk to you."

"It can't wait?"

"I don't want it to wait. I can come by and pick you up in ten minutes."

"Well . . ."

"Lisa, it's really important."

Something in his voice told her exactly what *it* was. She closed her eyes and offered up a silent prayer of thanks. *It* was a discussion about their future. "Ten minutes," she repeated. "I'll be waiting out front."

Ten minutes later, Dan pulled up at WALK and shoved the passenger door open for Lisa.

"Hi," she murmured, slipping into the bucket seat. "Welcome back." She leaned across and pecked his cheek.

He resisted the urge to grab her and kiss her properly. Kissing her always made him forget what he meant to say. And he couldn't forget what he meant to say this time. "Want to go for a drive?"

She gazed at him curiously. "I thought you'd want to go back to my apartment."

"No. I meant what I said about having to talk." He started off in silence, mentally rehearsing his words.

"For a man who wants to talk, you're awfully quiet," she offered hesitantly.

"Just thinking."

She gave him a tentative smile that made him wonder for the thousandth time if he could possibly survive in New York without her.

He turned at the stone pillars and drove into the university grounds, still silently repeating his speech, still afraid he was about to make the major mistake of his life. He drove along the familiar, poplar-lined drive, then turned down toward the Misty. When they reached it, he pulled the Dueler to a halt.

Once they were outside the car, the breeze ruffled Lisa's hair, catching at loose strands, offering them to the sun to play with. It dazzled them with golden highlights.

Below, tiny ripples skimmed the surface of the gray water. At their feet, the wind was whisking yellow-and-red autumn leaves tip over stem along the riverbank.

"Plant W looks so different from this side of the river," Lisa murmured, gazing across at the sprawling buildings. "Almost like a toy—a little metal factory in a child's play town."

"My work's done over there, Lisa."

She turned, her eyes fixed on him, her expression unreadable.

"I mean, I'll only be there for a few more days, till the end of the week, till I've finalized my report."

"And then you'll be going home," she said quietly.

"Yes. Then I'll be going home. We...Lisa, we both knew it would come to this."

She gazed at him...silently...her gray eyes luminous.

He reached for her hand. The mere warmth of her skin started his heart pounding. "Lisa, I brought back something from Detroit." He fumbled in his pocket with his free hand, pulled out the tiny blue velvet case, and silently held it out to her.

She simply stared at it. For an eternity. Until he was certain he'd made the worst possible error in judgment.

"Lisa?"

Tentatively, she drew her hand from his. In slow motion, she reached for the case, opened it, stood gazing at the ring.

And then someone pressed Fast Forward. She threw her arms around his neck and began speaking so quickly he couldn't understand a word.

All he knew was that she was hugging him and trying to talk and laughing and crying at once. All he knew was that she wanted to marry him, that he wasn't rushing her too fast, didn't have to face the terrible prospect of trying to live without her. All he knew was that he was the happiest man alive.

He hugged her tightly, loving her warm softness against him, loving the way the fresh scent of her hair was mingled with a hint of perfume.

Gradually, he realized his shirtfront was growing damp. "Lisa? I *do* recall you saying that you cry when you're happy, don't I?"

She looked up at him, smiling through her tears. "Yes, you do recall that. And this time, I may never be able to stop."

He bent and kissed her nose. "Well, try hard. Because I thought this afternoon would be a good time to get blood tests and a marriage license."

She sniffed, wiping her eyes. "Dan...so soon...I..."

"I know it's so soon. But that's not important. What's important is that it's so right. Lisa, let's get married this Saturday."

"Oh, Dan, you can't arrange a wedding that fast."

"Sure you can. When you get a little help from fate, that is. I talked to the manager at the Pritchard House, to see if there was anything he could do for us, and it turns out they just had a cancellation. A couple who were getting married in one of the salons called off their wedding. Which meant there was a justice of the peace suddenly available, too. Lisa, you do believe in fate, don't you?''

"Dan...I...Dan, there are so many things to decide about our future.''

"So we'll decide them. Lisa, we'll decide every last one of them right now if you want to. Just for starters, you don't have a problem with living in Manhattan, do you?''

She smiled. "Not as long as I'd be living with you.''

"That was the perfect answer,'' he murmured, kissing her again, then drawing her even closer, his words falling all over themselves, trying to escape.

"Look, I realize you won't want to leave Jake in the lurch, so I'll take a little time off, stay here for a couple more weeks. We can postpone our honeymoon till Christmas. But I want us to get married right away. I love you. I don't think I realized how much until I was away from you yesterday. And I don't want to be separated from you ever again. I could call my parents. They'd come out from Spokane. Oh, Lisa, what do you say about Saturday?''

He drew back a little and gazed down at her, waiting for her to say yes.

Instead, she hesitated.

"Lisa? What?''

"I...Dan, just this morning, Crystal and I were talking about your study.''

"And?''

"And...and, Dan, tell me there's not going to be anything negative in your report.''

He eyed her uncertainly. He loved her totally, without condition. And he wanted the same from her.

"Lisa, I promised you it'll be fair and objective. That promise stands."

"I know. I know it'll be fair. It's just that my father...Roy...I'd feel so much better knowing for sure that everything will be fine."

A tiny, icy shred of doubt crept into his heart. Did Lisa really love him, or not? He wanted to know she loved him so much that even his damned report couldn't possibly come between them. "Lisa...Lisa, what would happen if there *was* something negative in that report?"

"Dan," she whispered, "I love you. I've never loved anyone even close to the way I love you."

He nodded slowly. She hadn't answered his question. He stood gazing down at her, thinking how much he loved her. And one of the reasons he did was because she cared about people. She simply wanted reassurance because she cared. How could he fault that?

"Lisa, if I tell you what you want to hear, you'll believe me? No more nagging doubts."

She slowly smiled up at him. "You're an Aries. I know you'd never lie to me."

"All right. You win. I promise you that there will be absolutely nothing in my report that could conceivably harm the Plant W workers."

She pressed her face against his chest. "Thank you, Dan. Thank you for telling me that. I love you so much."

And she did seem to love him so much. Maybe it wasn't quite unconditionally. But if it wasn't, he'd just have to make do. Because he couldn't conceive of not having her in his life.

"DAN WAS RIGHT, you know," Crystal said, kneeling down and beginning to carefully wrap a width of protective plastic around the bottom of the wedding gown. "Fate *has* played a part in this. I'll bet nobody else has ever gotten married in a perfect dress on such short notice."

"Short notice?" Lisa said, grinning. "We decided days ago."

"Oh, of course. How silly of me to think *days* wasn't loads of time to plan a wedding."

Lisa laughed. "There wasn't really much to plan. The Pritchard House is looking after the ceremony and reception, and Mom's looking after everything else."

"Oh, Lisa, I still think you should have taken time off to help her."

"She didn't want my help. She made it clear she didn't want me underfoot—said if she had to stop every two minutes to ask what I thought, she'd never get things done. Besides, I owed it to Jake to come in."

"Poor Jake," Crystal murmured, taping a seam in the plastic and starting to wrap another layer. "You know, he's fit to be tied about your leaving. But he can't say much except 'congratulations' when you're marrying his friend. Oh, Lisa, this is all so exciting. Jake, the best man. Me, a bridesmaid. A party tonight and the wedding tomorrow."

"The party's probably excessive, isn't it? But Mom wanted to do something for Dan's parents. They're coming straight from the airport to the house."

Crystal shot Lisa a curious glance. "Your Mom's really thrilled about the wedding, isn't she? I mean, she's not just putting on an act."

"No, she adores Dan. I think she fell in love with him watching him on TV, before she'd even met him.

I . . . I only wish Dad and Roy were as pleased as she is. The plant workers were giving them a hard time when I was merely seeing Dan. And now . . .

"Well, at any rate, Roy's been making an obvious effort not to say anything negative. And Dad keeps smiling at me. It's kind of a strained smile, though. I . . . I know I shouldn't have, but I told them Dan promised me the report's going to be fine. Still, they just . . ."

"They'll just be happier once they've seen it with their own eyes," Crystal concluded, rising from her knees and inspecting her wrapping job. "That should keep it safe on its trip to the hotel. I've arranged to have it picked up first thing tomorrow. It'll be waiting for you in your changing room. Now, let's get out of here. It must be after five."

Lisa glanced at her watch. "Ten past. Dan's already going to be outside waiting for me."

They walked along the corridor, toward their offices. Crystal stopped outside Lisa's door and gave her a quick hug. "Benedetto and I will see you tonight. Around eight?"

"Right. But . . . oh, Crystal, what if Dan's parents don't like me?"

"Not like you? They'll adore you." Crystal flashed a reassuring smile and started off again.

From her office closet, Lisa collected the dress she'd be wearing at the party. Then she skimmed the phone messages on her desk, hoping they could all wait until next week. They could, she decided, except the one asking her to call her mother before leaving.

She dialed and stood absently tapping her desk, listening to the ringing at the house.

"Hello?" Helen Saint-John finally answered.

"Hi, Mom, what's up?"

"Well, I'm sure nothing's really wrong, dear . . . but I'm a little worried about Roy."

"Why? What's happened?"

"I don't quite know. That's the problem. I tried to get hold of him at the plant . . . to remind him about picking up something I need for tonight. But they told me he'd gone home ill. This morning. I mean, he apparently said he was ill and left work. But he hasn't come home. And I can't reach your father. He's in some emergency meeting. So I thought . . . well, dear, I'm just worried about what shape Roy could be in for the party. And you and Dan will go right by the Silver Dollar on your way here. So would you look in? Just in case Roy's there?"

"Sure. Sure, Mom. I'm leaving now. So we'll see you in about twenty minutes."

Lisa hurried out of the station, her anxiety level inching upward with each step.

"It's about time," Dan said, grinning at her as she opened the car door. "I hand delivered the final report to a print shop and stood over the guy until he produced my bound copies. And then I broke ten speed limits getting to the hotel and back here in time to pick you up. And after all that, you keep me waiting."

"Sorry," she murmured, leaning into the back and laying her dress carefully across the seat on top of his suit.

"Hey, I was only kidding."

Lisa slid into the seat and glanced over at him.

"What's wrong?" he asked, the moment he saw her expression.

She forced a smile. "No wonder I'm not an award-winning secret-keeper. My face must be an open book."

He leaned over and brushed her lips with a kiss. "So?" he asked, drawing back and taking her hand. "What's the problem?"

"Hopefully, there isn't one." Quickly, she repeated her mother's story. "I'm not sure whether I want to find Roy at the tavern or not," she concluded. "You know, he never used to drink much at all. Not until he and Ginny broke up. Oh, Dan, I should have made a point of talking to him about her again. I shouldn't have simply let it slide."

Dan squeezed her hand reassuringly, then pulled out into the traffic. "Don't worry. He's probably fine. Maybe he just took off someplace to get his only sister a special wedding gift."

"Maybe. Oh, I hope so." Lisa sat gazing silently at the passing city as they headed toward the Misty, then across the bridge into East Walkerton and along Hastings Street.

Dan slowed when they neared the tavern. "I'd ask if you see Roy's car, but every single one parked around here seems to be a Dueler."

"The Dollar's a Plant W hangout."

"I know. Jake and I spent some of our misspent youth in it."

Lisa smiled. "If you pull up by the door, I'll just run in."

"I'll just run in with you," Dan told her with a wry look. "This place is a dump."

"Well, hangouts aren't normally classy joints, are they? But I'll be fine. Seems to me I've told you before—Walkerton isn't New York."

"Yeah?" Dan said, pulling half onto the sidewalk in front of the door and switching off the ignition. "Well, it seems to me I've told you something before, too."

"Oh?"

"Yeah. I've told you I love you. And that means I'm sure as hell not taking any chances on some jerk hassling you. Either here *or* in New York."

Lisa smiled across at him again. She liked his loving her. No, she loved his loving her.

"Come on," he said, reaching over and shoving her door open. "Let's get this show on the road. We've got a party to get ready for."

The air inside the Dollar's dingy interior was laced with smoke and the stench of stale beer. The ancient hardwood floor was strewn with butts. Lisa glanced around, looking for Roy.

The scarred wooden tables at the front were mostly empty. A few men were sitting at the long bar. In the dimness beyond it, a dozen or so others were lounging around tables laden with beer bottles.

"If he's here, he must be in the back," she murmured, starting forward.

"Hold on," Dan muttered, grabbing her arm. "This isn't a 'ladies first' sort of place."

One of the men at the back table glanced up as they made their way along the bar, then muttered something to his cronies. A moment later, they were the focus of attention.

Dan stopped at the end of the bar, still holding Lisa's arm.

In front of them, a man shoved himself to his feet. "Well, if it isn't *Mister* Ashly. If it isn't the hired gun himself. You've got one hell of a nerve coming in here, Ashly. One hell of a nerve. Especially today."

"What's that supposed to mean?" Dan demanded.

The man smiled an unfriendly smile. "Oh, I guess maybe you don't know what's happened yet. But we sure do."

Two of the other men rose, and Dan's grip on Lisa's arm tightened. She looked nervously around the tables, from one face to the next, finding none she knew.

"Craig," Dan said to one of the seated men, "we're looking for Roy. Have you seen him?"

The man remained motionless for a moment, then shook his head. "No. He hasn't been in."

The man who'd risen first glanced a question at the fellow named Craig. "That's Saint-John's daughter with Ashly," Craig muttered. "Why don't you back off, McGillvary?"

"I don't give a damn about Saint-John's daughter. Now that you've dropped by," he continued, focusing on Dan once more, "I guess we have a chance to show you what we think of your stinking report."

"Let's get out of here," Dan snapped, wrapping his arm around Lisa's shoulders and turning her quickly toward the exit.

"Not so fast, Ashly," snarled a large man sitting at the bar. "Like McGillvary said, we're going to show you what we think of your stinking report." He eased off the bar stool and positioned himself in their path.

He was, Lisa realized, an *extremely* large man.

Without taking his gaze from them, he reached back, picked up his beer bottle by its neck . . . and smashed it onto the bar.

Lisa stared in disbelief as shards of brown glass sprayed across the bar and onto the floor. The broken bottle was now a jagged, beer-dripping weapon.

Horrified, she forced her gaze away from it. Behind the man, beer was lazily spreading into a tiny brown lake on the worn bar surface.

She closed her eyes, praying this was a nightmare, willing herself to wake up.

Then, from behind her, came the unmistakable crash of a second bottle being broken ... echoed by a third ... and a fourth.

CHAPTER FOURTEEN

ANOTHER SMASH. A final bottle shattering behind them. Then nothing. For an instant, the Dollar was shrouded in absolute, motionless silence.

Dan broke it suddenly, shoving Lisa forward. "Get the hell out of here."

"Yeah," the man blocking their way snapped. He shifted a couple of inches closer to the bar and gestured her past. "Get the hell out of here, lady."

"No," she said, her voice merely a whisper. She whirled around, scanning the faces of the men behind them, trying to catch the eye of the fellow Dan knew. He was staring at the floor.

"Dammit, Lisa! I said get out of here," Dan repeated, jerking her toward the door once more.

The large man stepped forward, waving his broken bottle menacingly. Then, with surprising speed, he shoved Lisa to one side, into the wall.

Her shoulder smashed against it. She spun with the impact, turning back once more, terrified of what might happen next.

Dan was lunging at the man.

She tried to scream, tried to tell him to stop. No words came out.

He smashed his fist into the man's stomach, doubling him over. Then two other men grabbed Dan from behind and pinned him against the bar.

The large man straightened up slowly, his expression pained. A moment later, he lurched at Dan, thrusting the jagged edge of the bottle under his jaw.

Lisa's breath caught. She stood stock-still, frozen in terror.

"Now that you're not going anywhere, Ashly," the man muttered, his breathing ragged, "let's talk about the Dueler's *future prospects*. Or maybe we should talk about *your* future prospects. All of a sudden, they ain't lookin' any better than the Dueler's, are they?"

He glanced at Lisa, then grinned a cold, calculating grin. "Maybe it won't be his throat I slit. Maybe I'll slice up another part of his anatomy."

Again, she tried to speak. Again, she couldn't. She had to do something. But her legs felt as if they were going to give out beneath her.

"Rashlin!" an authoritative voice roared. "Rashlin, knock it off!"

Lisa wheeled toward the door, toward the voice, recognizing it but certain she must be wrong.

No. Not wrong. Framed in the doorway, light streaming in from the street and silhouetting him, stood Roy.

"Rashlin," he said once more, his voice ringing along the length of the bar, "get rid of that bottle."

"Go to hell," the large man snarled.

Lisa's gaze left Roy and swept the rear of the tavern. None of the men were sitting. They were all on their feet, standing beside the tables. Craig had moved forward, maybe to help Dan, but now he stood motionless, his eyes on her brother.

"For God's sake, Rashlin," Roy snapped, drawing Lisa's attention back to him.

He was striding alongside the bar. Behind him, the door slowly swung closed, reestablishing the close, gray atmosphere of the tavern.

Roy stopped when he reached Rashlin. "Look, wise up. Ashly's not worth going to jail over."

"No? I ain't so sure about that."

"Well, I am. Let him go."

The two men holding Dan glanced at each other, then at Rashlin, but didn't loosen their grips.

From the corner of her eye, Lisa saw one of the fellows in back put down his broken bottle.

"I said, let him go," Roy ordered. "You aren't doing anyone the slightest good."

"He's right," Craig offered from beside a table. "Slice Ashly up and the cops'll toss every one of us in jail as accessories."

A few faint, uneasy murmurs greeted the remarks.

For another eternity, Rashlin held his bottle at Dan's throat. Then he slowly lowered his hand and let the weapon drop to the floor. It rolled in a tiny, uneven circle on the filthy wood.

"Another time, Ashly," Rashlin muttered. "Watch your ass, because there'll be another time."

Lisa took a long, deep breath as the men holding Dan released him and backed off.

He pushed himself away from the bar, squared his shoulders, and quietly said something to Roy. Then he glanced at her. "You okay?"

She nodded, stepping forward.

Dan wrapped his arm securely around her waist and, without another word, started for the door.

It was the longest walk of her life. She sensed Roy on their heels, between them and the others. But she was certain that, any instant, Rashlin and half a dozen more would have second thoughts and charge.

They finally made it to the door, then out onto the sidewalk of Hastings Street.

Outside the Dollar, the world was a different place— a safe place. The cool, fresh air was a breath of freedom. The late-afternoon sun beamed down assurance that everything was fine. Ironically, just across the street, one of Walkerton's finest stood chatting with an elderly woman.

Lisa vaguely noticed Roy's Dueler—pulled up onto the sidewalk directly behind Dan's.

"That was damned nice timing," Dan offered, extending his hand to her brother.

Roy took it. But hesitantly, she thought. And he was still wearing an awfully grim expression.

"Thanks, little brother," she murmured. "We owe you."

"*Thanks* doesn't come close to covering it," Dan added. He glanced at Lisa and gave her a wry grin. "I hope you're through telling me how much less dangerous Walkerton is than New York."

She merely shook her head, amazed he could see humor in anything about this. If it hadn't been for Roy... "How did you know we were in there?" she asked him.

"We were driving by and I spotted Dan's car."

She checked Roy's Dueler to see who the *we* was. "Ginny," she said, surprised. Ginny's long dark hair had been cut in a short blunt style that made her look sophisticated. But when she waved, she was the same friendly Ginny who could tease Roy out of his darkest moods.

Lisa waved in return, then refocused on the men.

"With that rental company's slogan splashed across the rear window," Roy was saying, "your car's pretty hard to miss. And I figured the Dollar wasn't a good place for you to be. Especially not..." He ended the sentence with a shrug.

"What's Ginny doing here?" Lisa asked. "Are you two back together?"

"I...yeah. Yeah, we are."

"So that's where you've been all day," she concluded, grinning.

"Well...yeah. Something happened this morning that made me want to talk to her. And the more we talked..." Roy ended the sentence with a smile.

A warm, happy feeling banished Lisa's last remnants of fear. "That's good, Roy. I'm glad."

"I'm thinking about going to university," he offered quietly. "Maybe just part-time, but we'll see."

Lisa wrapped her arms around his neck and kissed his cheek. "That's wonderful about you and Ginny, little brother. We'll have a double celebration tonight."

"No, she said we shouldn't steal your thunder, that she wouldn't start wearing her engagement ring again until after tomorrow. So don't say anything to Mom and Dad."

"What? Me keep a secret like this? We don't care about having our thunder stolen, do we, Dan?"

"Not a bit."

"But...oh, hell," Roy said. "I don't think I can keep it a secret, either. Let's head for home. You're going to want to get cleaned up before your guests start arriving," he added, gesturing at Dan's neck.

Lisa glanced at it. There was a little trail of blood trickling down his throat. "My God," she whispered.

"My God, Dan, he cut you." She reached up and gently wiped at the blood, trying to see how serious the wound was, relieved to find it was only a long scratch.

"Am I going to live?"

"Dan, stop joking. This isn't funny. You could have been killed." Just saying the words sent a shiver through her. "Let's get home and fix you up."

"Better tell Mom that's a shaving accident," Roy suggested. "She'll be in Panic City if she hears what actually happened."

"Good idea," Lisa agreed. "See you at the house then, Roy."

"Yeah." He nodded and stood watching as they got into the car.

Absently, Lisa wondered why he didn't seem happier. He'd just been hero of the moment. And he had Ginny back. So why wasn't he floating on air?

"Sure you're okay?" Dan asked. "You took quite a whack from that wall."

"I'm fine." She smiled reassuringly, then sat silently as he drove, hands folded in her lap. They trembled slightly while she replayed the tavern incident in her mind.

Partway through the mental rerun, her memory caught on something one of the men had said, something that hadn't registered in the fear of the moment.

"Dan?"

"Yeah?"

"What happened today?"

"You mean aside from me almost getting my throat slit?"

"No, be serious. That first man who spoke to you in the Dollar…McGillvary, I think his name was. He said you had one hell of a nerve going in there, *especially today.*"

"Did he?" Dan glanced across the car at her, then turned his attention back to the traffic. "My blood was pounding so loudly in my ears that I barely heard a word anyone said."

"But what happened today?"

"Nothing. Nothing that I know about, at least."

Lisa gazed at Dan's profile as his words triggered further recall—crystal-clear recall. The man named McGillvary had said, *"Maybe you don't know what's happened yet. But we sure do."*

She thought about pressing Dan, then decided it was pointless. He'd just finished saying he didn't know about anything happening. And if he didn't, there was no sense in belaboring the issue. She closed her eyes, not wanting to remember anything more. Not wanting to speculate on what McGillvary had meant.

AUNT MARY, one of the first guests to arrive, was taking full advantage of her opportunity to chat with "Lisa's handsome young man."

Lisa smiled politely at her tiny, blue-haired great-aunt, trying to concentrate on what she was saying but hearing only the occasional word.

Something was wrong. Very, very wrong. Not just with Roy, who should be a million times happier than he seemed, but with her father, as well. Something that went far beyond the uneasy feeling she knew they'd both had since she and Dan had announced their wedding plans.

She'd asked each of them several pointed questions, but hadn't gotten any answers. And now that the party was underway, she wasn't going to. *So stop worrying about it for the moment,* she silently ordered herself. *Stop worrying and enjoy yourself.*

Aunt Mary murmured a ninth 'congratulations, dear,' squeezed Dan's hand a final time, then toddled off in the direction of the punch bowl.

"How are you holding up?" Dan whispered.

"I'm a nervous wreck. I wish your parents would get here. Until they do, I'm going to be terrified that they won't like me."

He leaned closer and kissed her nose. "They're going to love you. Exactly the way I do. Well, no," he amended, giving her an exaggerated leer, "I guess not *exactly* the same way."

The doorbell rang once more, this time announcing Jake's arrival. He paused, holding the door open, extending his hand back out to the porch.

"Good Lord," Dan murmured, "he's brought Fiona."

Sure enough. With an elegant black designer cane in hand and a long, full black skirt concealing all but the foot of her leg cast, Fiona entered, smiling sweetly at Jake.

"Mom invited her, of course," Lisa whispered. "But last I heard, Jake was barely speaking to her."

Jake tucked Fiona's arm securely in his, then escorted her across the room to Lisa and Dan, his stride solicitously slow.

"I'm so thrilled for you," Fiona purred, kissing the air beside Lisa's cheek. "So thrilled for you both," she added to Dan.

"You look terrific," Lisa offered. "Not even a trace of bruising left."

Jake nodded. "She looks ready to take back the host's chair, huh, Lisa?"

"Definitely."

Fiona edged Lisa a couple of feet away from the men. "I have you to thank for Jake coming around."

"Oh?"

"Yes. With you leaving in two weeks, he won't have a fill-in host for my show."

"Oh, Fiona, I'm sure that's not the only thing that decided him."

"Well, no, of course not. It undoubtedly had a lot to do with me being so good. But your leaving probably speeded up his decision-making. At any rate, I hope you and Dan will be very happy."

"Thank you."

"I'm sure you'll like living in New York. I really miss it. Maybe I'll come and visit you once you're settled."

"Oh . . . what a . . . a lovely idea."

"You know," Fiona went on, eyeing Jake, "now that he won't have you to run interference for him, I'm going to make more effort to get along with that man. He may not be the world's best-looking guy, but he has a good heart . . . and he has the station," she added, almost, but not quite, under her breath.

Lisa managed not to laugh, and filed the remark away to repeat when Crystal arrived.

There was no need to keep it filed for long. Crystal and Benedetto were the next couple through the doorway. Crystal immediately spotted Fiona hanging on Jake's arm, nudged Benedetto in the ribs, and steered him across the room.

"What's with the boss man and the dragon lady?" she murmured to Lisa.

"Jake's given in gracefully. And not only that, Fiona's considering making him her next conquest."

"No! Jake? No way. He'd run for the hills the minute she crooked her finger at him."

"Crystal, why do you think such a thing?" Benedetto asked. "If there is one man who can...what is the word...ah, yes, who can handle a Scorpio woman it is a Scorpio man."

Dan grinned. "Fiona's a scorpion? Somehow, I don't find that difficult to believe. Jake a scorpion, though? Are you sure, Benedetto?"

"*Sì*. But the sign has also the eagle as a symbol. Perhaps you would believe Jake to be more an eagle?"

"Yeah, I'll buy an eagle."

"Well, that may be. But there is not so much difference between Fiona and Jake as you think, Dan. Both of them *must* win," he explained at Dan's dubious look. "A Scorpio will risk anything to win."

"You mean that explains why they're both so insane when it comes to ratings?" Lisa asked.

Benedetto nodded. "Scorpio is ruled by Pluto. Named for the god of the underworld," he added at her blank look.

That didn't mean anything significant to her, either, but he blithely continued. "Pluto is an awesome planet. Two Scorpios together...always keeping the score, always getting even. *Mamma mia!* If Fiona is truly interested in Jake there will be...how do you say...many contests of will. There will be much fireworks at WALK."

"Terrific," Crystal muttered. "WALK's been bad enough since Fiona arrived. *Much fireworks* will just ice the cake. Lisa, how can you go merrily off to New York and desert me when this is going on?"

"You can always get a break by coming to visit us. Fiona says *she* intends to."

Dan shot Lisa a wry look. "I think we'd better talk about selling my pullout couch."

"You do not have to stay at WALK for the fireworks," Benedetto said, draping his arm around Crystal's shoulders. "You can go anywhere. You might even come back to California with me, no? Look at her, Lisa. The blond hair, the long legs, the beauty. Would she not be a wonderful California girl?"

"Yes, I'm sure she would. Even the Beach Boys would have to agree." She smiled at Crystal. Whatever her friend decided to do, she'd be wonderful at.

"Your parents aren't here yet, Dan?" Crystal asked, surveying the guests.

"Any minute now, I expect. And then Lisa can stop worrying about them not liking her."

"What are their signs?" Benedetto asked.

Dan shrugged. "My father's birthday's at the end of March."

"Ahh. An Aries. Like you." Benedetto smiled at Lisa as if there was no doubt in the world that Mr. Ashly would love her on sight.

"And my mother's birthday is . . ."

Lisa held her breath. Not that she believed any of this astrological gobbledygook but—

". . . is August 4," Dan concluded.

"A Leo!" Benedetto exclaimed. "I am also a Leo."

Lisa breathed again. Given the way Benedetto was beaming at her, a Leo apparently made a good mother-in-law.

"And is she a lioness or a shy pussycat?" Benedetto asked Dan.

"She can be both."

"No matter. Leo is the third fire sign, Lisa. You are all four fire signs—you, Dan and his parents. Fire blends easily with fire. And for the mother, there is no secret of how to make a Leo love you."

"How?" Lisa asked quickly. Never mind her skepticism. There was certainly no sense in taking chances.

"Leos love compliments," Benedetto explained.

"I'll say," Crystal said, grinning at him. "You don't even seem to mind that I can't cook, just as long as I compliment your choice of restaurant."

"*Sì*. True. We all have Leonine vanity. Tell Mrs. Ashly a compliment when you first meet, Lisa. That is all it will take, and she will welcome you to the family with ... what is the expression?"

"Open arms," Crystal supplied.

"With the open arms," Benedetto concluded.

"You promise?" Lisa asked, smiling.

"I promise. You will see."

LISA STEPPED from the overcrowded house into the cool night air. The party was still in full swing and she needed a breather, a moment to herself. She wandered along to the far end of the porch and sank onto the old-fashioned wooden swing that had been one of her childhood hideaways. It creaked a familiar greeting and slowly rocked back and forth a few times, gradually coming to rest.

She gazed out over the moonlit front lawn, thinking this had been one of the best nights of her life. Just as both Dan and Benedetto had predicted, Mr. and Mrs. Ashly seemed to love her. Bill and Sarah, she corrected herself. "Call us Bill and Sarah," her future mother-in-law had said when they'd been introduced.

And she'd smiled so warmly that Lisa had hugged both of them without a second thought.

Yes, this had been one of the best nights of her life. And tomorrow was her wedding day. She smiled to herself, scarcely able to believe she wasn't dreaming.

A motion in the yard caught her eye. Roy and Ginny were walking hand in hand toward the house, deep in conversation. Their getting back together was an added bonus that made the entire world rosy. Before she could call out to them, Ginny's words floated through the night.

"I still think you're making a mistake, not telling her. If it was me, I'd sure want to know before I married him."

Lisa froze, no doubt in her mind who they were talking about.

"Look, I've caused enough problems by opening my mouth when I shouldn't have. And I told you, Dad and I talked it through this morning and agreed that saying anything would be a mistake."

"It's a wonder it didn't all come out in the Dollar," Ginny murmured.

"Well, it didn't. Maybe that was an omen that we shouldn't tell her. At any rate, it's just not the sort of thing you lay on someone a few hours before they're getting married. She's crazy about the guy. No matter what, she's going to marry him. So what good would telling her do? We'd just make her wedding day miserable."

"Roy, I'm not so sure about her marrying him *no matter what*. Honesty is awfully important to Lisa. And if Dan's been feeding her a line . . . well, all I'm saying is, if it were me, I wouldn't want to get a surprise like that after I married you."

"No surprises with me," Roy murmured. "I promise."

He brushed Ginny's cheek with a kiss, making Lisa feel even more guilty about watching and listening. Still, she sat motionless in the darkness, her heart pounding, fearful of what they'd say next yet determined to hear.

"Well," Ginny went on, "Lisa shouldn't be getting any surprises, either. Not like this one, at least."

"Look, we'd just cause grief. Mom would have an absolute fit. Lisa and Dan would have a big blowup. Hell, we'd have a bride and groom saying their vows through clenched teeth."

"You might not have a bride and groom at all."

"The guy's simply doing his job, Ginny. Like it or not, even I've come to admit that. And that's the way Lisa will see it."

"You're sure?"

"In the long run, at least. So we'd be causing problems for nothing. I just wish to hell he'd been straight with her about it."

"About what?" The words simply slipped from Lisa's mouth, then hung in the air as Roy and Ginny stopped in their tracks.

Roy swore quietly and turned toward the porch. "Forget it, Lisa. It's not as bad as it sounded."

She pushed herself off the swing, realizing she was trembling, and rested her hands firmly on the wooden railing. "What's not as bad? Tell me." Lord, her voice was trembling as well.

"Look, Sis, you don't want to know. Not tonight. Forget it."

"No way. You tell me what you think Dan hasn't been straight about."

"Forget it," Roy said again.

"Look, I'm not going to forget a single word! Either you tell me what's up, either you tell me this minute, or I'll go inside and ask Dad . . . right in front of everyone."

Roy stood staring at her for a long moment, then finally shrugged. "It's the report. Rumor says it's going to mean Plant W's closure."

She almost laughed with relief. A rumor. She'd been feeling frantic because of a rumor. "No. No, it isn't going to mean anything of the kind. I told you. Dan specifically assured me there's nothing in the report that could harm the workers."

"I . . . yeah, you told me. So I guess . . . well, I guess what we've got here is just an ugly, unfounded rumor. See? I said it wasn't as bad as it sounded." Roy turned and started toward the front door, pulling Ginny with him.

"Roy?" Lisa called uncertainly, picturing Dan in the tavern, that broken bottle at his throat.

They stopped and looked back.

"Roy . . . how did that ugly, unfounded rumor get started?"

"Who knows?"

Slowly, Ginny shook her head. "Don't you lie to her, too, Roy."

Lisa focused on Ginny, fresh ripples of anxiety washing through her. "What's the truth here?"

"Tell her," Ginny said quietly to Roy.

He scowled at her, then at Lisa. "All right," he finally snapped. "The truth is that someone read Dan's report this morning, a bit of it at least."

"That's not possible. Dan only finished it this afternoon. He barely had time to take it to the printer's before he came to get me at the station."

Roy shrugged. "Well, this guy was walking by Dan's office first thing this morning, the door was open, Dan wasn't inside.... Lisa, he went in and read a couple of pages of the report that were sitting on the desk. They were the start of a section called 'The Dueler: Future Prospects.' And...and they basically said the public perceives all-terrain vehicles, including the Dueler, as toys. That the novelty will soon wear off and therefore they have no future."

Roy's words registered gradually, one by one. The man in the Dollar, the one who'd cut Dan, had used that term: *future prospects*. So that's what he'd been referring to. *But there has to be some mistake!*

"Yeah, there probably is," Roy said.

She looked at him blankly, then realized she must have spoken out loud. "Dan told me everything would be fine, Roy. He wouldn't lie to me."

"Right." Roy gave her a grin that didn't come close to making the grade. "Right, Dan's an Aries. Lying isn't in his nature."

"But this morning...you believed that guy's story, didn't you? That's why you left the plant. That's why you went to talk to Ginny. Because you were so upset."

"Look, Sis, it's like you said. There must be some mistake. Come on, Ginny," he added, turning away, "we'd better get back to the party."

Ginny began to protest, but Roy dragged her along, his voice drowning out hers. "You said to tell her the truth and I did" were the last words Lisa could make out.

She stood gazing through the darkness after them, thinking of Dan . . . and his report. Roy had jumped to the wrong conclusion about that late-night call to Detroit. He'd undoubtedly jumped to the wrong conclusion this morning, too.

Dan Ashly was the man she loved . . . a man she could trust . . . not a man who would destroy Walkerton.

THEY DROPPED Dan's parents off at their hotel. Then Dan drove Lisa home.

"Want me to pick you up tomorrow?" he asked when they reached her door. "Drive you to the Pritchard House?"

"Thanks, but no. Don't you know that it's bad luck for the bride and groom to see each other the day of the wedding?"

"I hope you mean only until the ceremony."

"Of course that's what I mean, silly. Besides, Dad figures it's his duty to drive me. Even though it means he'll have to sit around the hotel in his tuxedo, waiting while I get dressed."

"You know, those are the longest sentences you've managed in the past couple of hours. You tired?"

She simply nodded, still trying to decide whether she should tell him what was bothering her. But why was she hesitating? Whoever claimed to have seen the report had fabricated the story. That had to be it. Probably there wasn't even a section in it called "The Dueler: Future Prospects." And if she just went ahead and told Dan what Roy had said, he'd assure her it was nonsense. Then the nagging little doubt that she felt so guilty about having would vanish.

"I won't come in," Dan said, taking her key and unlocking the door. "Much as I'd like to spend the night, you'll get more sleep if I don't. Besides,'' he added, wrapping his arms around her waist and hugging her to the warmth of his body, "after tonight, we'll have the rest of our lives to be together.''

The rest of their lives. She intended to spend the rest of her life with this man, and she was worrying about passing a stupid rumor by him? She was being completely ridiculous.

"Dan?'' she murmured, gazing up at him, loving the way moonlight made his jaw seem carved from granite.

"Uh-huh?''

"Dan, I found out what happened today.''

"What do you mean?''

"In the Dollar. The remark that guy made about you not knowing what had happened. Roy told me what it was.''

"Oh? What?''

"Some fellow at the plant claimed he saw part of your report. That you'd left it on your desk and he read it. It was supposedly the first bit of a section called 'The Dueler: Future Prospects.'''

Dan didn't speak, but his face tensed.

No, it didn't. She must be imagining things in the dim light. How could a face that seemed carved from granite tense?

"I see,'' he finally said. "Guess I should be more careful about leaving things lying around.''

"You . . . you don't mean there actually *is* a section with that title?''

"Yes, there is. You knew one of the things I'd be doing was trying to project future market share.''

"But, I mean, is that the exact title?''

"Yes, that's the exact title.''

"Oh."

Dan gazed down at her, looking annoyed. Or was she imagining again?

"What does 'oh' mean?"

"I...I guess it means I thought the guy made up his story. But he wouldn't likely have pulled your exact heading out of thin air, would he?"

"No. Not likely." Dan continued eyeing her. "So...what's the problem?"

"Dan, look, I know this can't be right. I told Roy there had to be a mistake. Because this fellow claimed your report said that the Dueler was perceived as a toy, that once its novelty wore off it wouldn't have a future."

"Good."

"Good, what?"

"Good, I'm glad you stuck up for me. I'm glad you told Roy there was a mistake."

She waited anxiously for him to say something further. He didn't. And his silence was making her more uneasy by the second. Why didn't he assure her that wasn't at all what the report said?

"Dan?"

"Uh-huh?"

"Dan...nothing's changed, has it? I mean from what you promised me..." She bit her lip to stop from saying anything more. There was no longer the slightest chance that she was simply imagining Dan's annoyance.

"What I promised you," he said evenly, "was that my report would be fair and objective."

She swallowed uncomfortably. "I know...but you also said there'd be nothing that could conceivably harm the workers."

"Yes, that's what I said."

"So...so you're saying this fellow was lying about what he read?"

Dan slowly withdrew his arms from around her waist, placed his hands firmly on her shoulders, then took a step back. She could feel his tension, could sense that his annoyance had escalated to anger. It made her want to apologize for pressing him, made her want to hug him and never let him go. But his eyes had grown steely cold, making her hesitate. And then he was speaking again.

"You know, Lisa, I'm sure glad the report's done, that my job here is finished. Because every time you get going about it, I can't help wondering where we would be if I'd found a lot of things wrong at Plant W. I can't help feeling that if I'd had reasons to write a negative report, there wouldn't even be a *we*. I can't help thinking that your love for me has always been conditional on what that damned report might say."

Abruptly, he dropped his hands from her shoulders, wheeled around and stomped off toward the front yard, leaving her stunned. How could he doubt her love? She stared into the darkness, her thoughts racing, then started after him. Before she'd taken twenty steps, she heard an engine roar to life and a car screech away.

She began to run. But when she reached the front of the house, Dan's taillights were fast disappearing down Misty Drive. Through her tears, they were two tiny red blurs. She watched them, waiting for the car to slow and turn around. She watched them fade to nothingness.

Blindly, she headed back along the side of the house and up to her apartment. Just as she turned the key in the upstairs lock, her phone began ringing. She raced across the living room to answer it, praying it was Dan, knowing it couldn't possibly be.

It was.

"Lisa, I'm sorry," he murmured.

She sagged onto the coach, relief sending a fresh trickle of tears down her cheeks. "Where are you?"

"At the first pay phone I saw. Look, I'm so damned sorry. I just...well, I just love you so much that it scares me. I keep thinking you can't possibly love me the same way."

"Oh, Dan. Oh, Dan, don't even say that. I love you so much that it scares me, too."

"Yeah?" he said slowly, a grin creeping into his voice.

She could almost see it playing on his lips. "Yeah," she whispered.

"It scares you more than the dark?"

"Yeah."

"Scares you more than *Gremlins?*"

"Yeah."

"More than *Gremlins 2?*"

"More than a *Gremlins 19* would."

Dan chuckled and the last of her distress slipped away.

"And you love me enough to forgive me for behaving like a jerk?" he pressed.

"Enough to forgive you if you behaved like a thousand jerks."

"Enough to still show up tomorrow?"

"Definitely."

"Well, just exactly how much do you love me?" he teased.

"Oh...more than I love pizza...more than Bene-detto loves astrology...more than Jake and Fiona love ratings."

"Bingo. You just convinced me. So I'll let you get to bed now."

"See you tomorrow, love," Lisa murmured.

"See you tomorrow, love," he repeated.

CHAPTER FIFTEEN

LISA GAZED SLOWLY around the elegant Wedgwood blue and ivory salon. Arrangements of pale gold chrysanthemums stood on either side of the double doors, ready to welcome the wedding guests. At the far end, where the ceremony would take place, bird of paradise stalks posed strikingly amid sprays of eucalyptus.

The setting was fairy-tale perfect. And she wished everything about this day could be perfect. But her father was so clearly unhappy that she had a tiny lump in her throat. He'd barely said a word during the drive here and now was looking as if giving her away would constitute delivering her up to the devil.

She should have told him she knew about that rumor the moment she'd gotten into the car, should have told him she'd talked to Dan about it. But something in Dad's expression had stopped her.

They had to discuss it, though. She had to make him believe everything was fine. He'd see that on Monday, of course, once the report was released. But she couldn't stand to have him thinking what he did about Dan today.

"Whoever orchestrates weddings for the Pritchard House does a first-rate job," Bert offered, managing a strained smile. "That's the classiest bar I've ever seen," he added, gesturing at the linen-covered table that held crystal flute glasses and champagne. Each dark green bottle was chilling in its own silver bucket.

"And you're the classiest father-of-the-bride I've ever seen," Lisa told him, fidgeting with the already perfect lapels of his tuxedo.

"Baby... baby, you really do love this guy?"

"Oh, Daddy, I really, really do."

"And you're sure he's the one?"

"Absolutely sure."

Bert nodded slowly. "Fine, then. I just want you to be happy. That's the only important thing. I...I guess it's time for you to go upstairs and change, isn't it?"

"I have a few minutes yet." She stood gazing at him, the tiny lump in her throat growing larger and tears forming in her eyes. He'd been the most important man in her life since the day she was born. And now he believed she was deserting him for the enemy.

"Lisa," he murmured, "don't start crying on me. I'm already having trouble, thinking about losing my baby."

His words sent the threatening tears trickling down her cheeks.

He reached out and wrapped his arms around her, cuddling her to him. "There, there," he crooned, patting her back, making her feel like a little girl.

"Daddy, you aren't losing me," she managed to say. "I'll always be your baby."

"I know you will. It's just hard to share you with another man after all these years.

"Hey, come on," he continued a moment later, taking her firmly by the shoulders. "Keep doing this and you'll have red eyes for your wedding."

She brushed the tears away and cleared her throat. "Dad . . . Dad, I know what's bothering you. Roy told me last night."

Her father shook his head. "I wish he hadn't, Lisa. Whether I like what that report says or not, I'm not blaming Dan personally. At least, I'm trying my damnedest not to. I know he had his job to do. And your wedding day is no time for you to be worrying about Plant W."

"But Daddy, I'm not. And I don't want you to be, either. There's nothing bad in that report."

"Baby . . . baby, I know what I read."

Lisa gazed at him blankly, not comprehending. "What *you* read?"

Bert shrugged slowly. "I'm not proud of what I did, Lisa. You know I'm not the type to snoop. But I was walking by Dan's office and just stuck my head in to say hello. And when I saw those pages sitting there . . . well, I couldn't resist reading them. And then I had to tell the union executive and . . . well, the news obviously leaked out. I'm sorry you had that incident in the Dollar, baby. I almost had a fit when your brother told me about it."

Lisa barely heard what her father was saying. Last night, Roy had said *someone* had read part of Dan's report. But the someone had been Dad. So this couldn't be an ugly, unfounded rumor at all. But Dan had assured her . . .

"Dad . . . Dad," she managed to say, "there has to be some mistake here, some confusion. Tell me exactly what you read."

"Lisa, there's no point. Just—"

"No! Please tell me."

"I...well...oh, hell. The damned thing's as clear in my mind as if I still had it in front of me. It was the first couple of pages from a section called 'The Dueler: Future Prospects.' And it concluded that QM should plan to phase out production of the Dueler and shut down Plant W."

Lisa tried to correlate her father's words with what Dan had told her. She couldn't. Dan had said...just what, precisely, *had* he said? He'd said that yes, there was a section titled "Future Prospects." But he hadn't actually said anything else. Nothing specifically about that section, at least.

"Baby, like I told you, I know Dan's just doing his job."

She shook her head, trying to ignore her growing sense of panic. "Daddy, I have to talk to him. Something's wrong. I don't understand what, but he can't have...he just can't have." She hugged her father hard, kissed his cheek, then forced herself to let him go.

"I'll see you back down here in a while, baby."

"Yes, see you in a while." She turned and ran from the salon and along the corridor to the elevators.

She rode up to the third floor, her mind reeling in confusion. What Dad had read and what Dan had been telling her simply didn't add up. There must be a missing part to the equation. There just *had* to be. Because, if Dan had lied to her...oh, but he couldn't have. Not about something so important.

The elevator door slid open and she hurried down the hall to his suite. She stood at the door for a moment, afraid to knock, afraid of what she might learn, telling herself not to be ridiculous, telling herself there was an explanation. Then, tentatively, she tapped.

No response.

She tried a second time, more loudly. But Dan didn't answer. She stood uncertainly in the hallway, her heart pounding. And then a maid came out of the next room.

"Locked out?" she asked. "Want me to let you in?"

Lisa hesitated for an instant, then nodded. "Please."

"Dan?" she called hesitantly once the door was open. Her voice sounded like a stranger's.

There was no reply, no sound of a shower running, no sound of Dan. Her gaze focused on the far side of the living room, on his desk.

It was a mishmash mountain of books, folders and loose pages. And plopped precariously on the top of the mountain was a stack of blue-covered, spiral-bound volumes.

She stared across at them, instinctively certain they were the copies of his report, and shoved the door closed behind her. Her feet started toward the desk, all on their own volition, with no instruction from her brain. And she'd been right. The volumes were copies of the report.

She grabbed the top one, realizing her hands were trembling, and skimmed the index. There it was. "The Dueler: Future Prospects."

Her eyes leaped across to the page number and her fingers flicked quickly through the pages, locating the section.

She skimmed the preamble of the opening paragraphs, flipped to the next page and proceeded. And then her gaze ground to a halt. She focused on the top of the page once more and began rereading the lines, this time with excruciating slowness:

Naturally, the Walkerton operation faces the same risks as other auto plants, vis-à-vis potential economic recessions and overall industry slow-downs. In addition, since Plant W produces only the Dueler, it is more vulnerable to the whims of consumers than are other Quality Motors assembly plants.

Because the purchasing public perceives all-terrain, sports utility vehicles to be toys, it could be predicted that the novelty of such models will wear off. Should this likelihood materialize, the Dueler would have no long-term future.

Retooling Plant W to produce alternative vehicles would require a substantial capital investment that would be more profitably utilized in other areas of company operations.

The obvious conclusion is that Quality Motors should plan to phase out production of the Dueler and shut down the Walkerton operation.

Lisa stood staring at the print, a sick, sinking feeling mixing with total disbelief. She couldn't actually have read what she thought she'd read. There had to be some sort of disconnect in her brain.

She started at the top of the page again, her eyes traveling slowly along the lines. With each word, her sick feeling grew. Her stomach began knotting and reknotting. Her eyes misted over. By the time she reached the bottom of the page a second time, the report was a complete blur. There was no point in trying to read on. She couldn't distinguish a single word.

SHE HADN'T HEARD the door open, but Dan was standing in the room, silently eyeing her.

Her vision was still blurred and her face still wet with tears. She had no idea, though, how long she'd been staring blindly at the report. She felt completely stunned, utterly devastated.

Wordlessly, Dan took the volume from her and gazed at the page she'd been reading. Then he looked at her once more.

"How could you?" she whispered, almost choking on the words, vaguely aware of a fresh flood of tears starting down her cheeks. "How could you write this report if you love me?"

"Lisa, this isn't what you think."

"It's not what I think?" She paused, swallowing hard. Her voice was working but her emotions were completely out of control. Those final words she'd read were etched in her brain. *The obvious conclusion is that Quality Motors should plan to phase out production of the Dueler and shut down the Walkerton operation.*

This man was going to destroy her father's livelihood...and her brother's...and her hometown. How could she possibly love a man who would do that?

"No, it's not at all what you think," he said firmly.

"Not what I think?" she echoed again, barely able to believe he was actually trying to convince her of that. "Dan, I don't need to think. I can read."

"Lisa, you read about one page. Right?"

She nodded, vaguely aware his voice had taken on an annoyed tone but only partially listening to his words. Her mind was whirling crazily. She was marrying Dan Ashly in less than an hour. But she couldn't marry a man who'd lied to her about something this important. She couldn't marry a man who'd be causing so much grief for so many people she knew, for people she loved.

"About one page," he said again. "And you read it completely out of context. You don't have all the facts. What you read isn't what it sounded like."

"Dan, I saw it with my own eyes. Dammit, I'm not an idiot. Phrases like 'phase out production' and 'shut down the Walkerton operation' can't have very many meanings."

"Lisa, I said you don't have all the facts. You didn't read past that page, did you?"

"I didn't need to! You promised me," she added, her voice cracking. "How could you promise me and then make recommendations like that?"

He didn't answer. He merely glared at her. *He* was glaring at *her*. As if *she* was the one who'd done something despicable.

"If you trusted me," he said sharply, "you wouldn't have felt you had to look at the damned report. And if you hadn't done that, you wouldn't be upset and we wouldn't be having this scene . . . this scene that is absolutely ridiculous because you've jumped to the wrong conclusion."

He snapped shut the report and tossed it back onto the pile. It teetered, for an instant, at an impossible angle, then slithered off the top of the stack and onto the floor. They both watched it hit the carpet. Neither moved to retrieve it.

"Look," Dan finally said, "were you even listening when I said that what you read was completely out of context?"

She nodded. But out of context or in context or beside context, she knew what she'd read.

"And I've told you a hundred times," he was continuing on, "this report won't harm the workers. *I've* promised you that. *Me*. The man you're supposed to love and trust till death do us part. So how about a little of that trust now, okay? How about you stop crying and stop worrying?"

She stared at him, both her thoughts and emotions running rampant. How could he say no harm would come from what he'd done? But...but maybe there was a chance...maybe "out of context" were the key words. Because surely he wouldn't stand here and lie to her, would he? Not when he knew she'd learn the truth. His lying didn't make sense. And she *did* trust him. And once before she hadn't given him a chance to explain when she should have. And she wanted so badly to believe him.

She took a deep breath and cleared her throat, ordering herself to be as calm and rational as possible. "Dan...Dan, I think you'd better tell me exactly how that recommendation being out of context makes a difference. Or maybe I should have a closer look and you can show me what—"

As she made the suggestion, she reached toward the desk. But Dan caught her wrist and stood watching her with an expression she couldn't interpret. Finally, he shook his head.

"No, I don't want you to have a closer look. Not right now. I've told you everything will be fine. I've told you that time after time, and I just told you again, not two seconds ago. Don't you believe me? Don't you trust me?"

"I...yes."

His face told her she sounded as unconvincing to his ears as she did to her own.

"Dan, I just don't understand," she tried, wishing more than anything in the world that she did. She simply wanted everything to be all right. "The report . . . the part I read . . . it was totally negative."

He gazed at her for an eternity, still holding her wrist. When he spoke again, his words were slow and measured. "Lisa, no matter what I say, you keep thinking the worst about me. You want a closer look at the report. You want proof that what I'm telling you is the truth."

"Dan, I merely—"

"Listen to me! You believed your brother about that phone call. And last night you were half believing the word of some guy from the plant. You didn't even know who he was and you half believed him. Yet you just can't accept things I say. And that makes me wonder what the hell kind of relationship we have. This is beginning to sound like a rerun of last night, Lisa, but you've done it to me again. You've got me wondering how much you really love me."

"I . . . I *do* love you. Very, very much. Only I don't see how things can be the least bit fine." Maybe she was stupid or blind, but she didn't understand at all.

"Lisa I want to ask you something."

"All . . . all right."

"It's something else I raised last night, something that got brushed over. But what if I'd found problems while I was studying Plant W? What if I'd felt that, to do an honest job for QM, I had to recommend closure?"

"Then that's it," she whispered. "Dan, that *is* what you're doing. I didn't misread, did I?" She gazed at him, her eyes misting over again. Was that really it or not? She was so damned upset and confused she didn't have the foggiest idea what he was actually telling her.

"I'm saying *what if*, Lisa. What about us if that *were* the case?"

She shrugged a meaningless shrug, unable to think.

"What about us if that were the case?" he pressed.

"I...Dan, I don't know," she murmured miserably, her mind a mass of confusion. "I'd have to think."

"Wrong answer, Lisa," he said slowly. "Wrong answer. It should have been that you'd love me no matter what. It should have been that if I felt obliged to do something you didn't like, you'd at least understand. And that it wouldn't make you love me less. It should have been that nothing could change the way you feel about me."

"But, Dan, I—"

"Lisa, nothing could change the way I feel about you. And...and I thought I could accept less than that in return. I'm so damned crazy about you that I thought it didn't matter if you don't love me as much. But it does."

"I do love you as much, Dan. We settled that, didn't we? I love you so much it scares me, remember?" she added, her voice breaking.

"So much that it scares you, Lisa? Maybe you just scare too easily."

"Dan...Dan, I—"

He shook his head, cutting her off. "Lisa, I'm not going to go through life wondering whether you love me enough. And right this minute, I'm not going to say, 'Look here, read the whole damned report and see everything I've written.' I'm not going to have you reading it so you can decide whether loving me will be safe. Because if you did love me, if you loved me enough, you wouldn't have to pour over the blasted thing to decide whether or not what's in it makes any difference to the two of us."

He released her wrist, picked up the copy of the report from the floor, then scooped the others off his desk. "I'm just going to put these away," he said, turning toward the bedroom.

She stared after him, her eyes full of tears, her throat tight, not knowing what to think or say or do.

A moment later he came out of the bedroom again and simply stood looking at her. "If you can't believe me, Lisa . . . if you don't trust me . . . if you can't have faith in what I tell you, then you *don't* love me enough. Not enough to marry me."

"I . . . I . . ." she couldn't manage any words, still wouldn't have known what to say if she could have. Why shouldn't she get to pour over the report? Why wouldn't Dan let her see for herself? Because of his pride or because of what she'd find in it?

She loved him. Oh, she loved him so much. But what she'd read made a liar of him. And what she'd read would destroy too many of the other people she loved.

"I'm going to change now," he said. "And then I'll be heading downstairs. I love you, Lisa. I want to marry you. If you love me enough, that is."

JAKE LOOKED AT his watch once more. Dan forced his hand to remain at his side, resisting the urge to check his own again.

"Brides are always late," the justice of the peace murmured. "I think Emily Post must have a rule about it."

Dan tried to smile. It felt sick. *He* felt sick. Physically and emotionally ill. What the hell had he been thinking of? He'd pushed Lisa too hard and too far.

He'd wanted her to prove how much she loved him. Instead, he'd driven her away.

She wasn't late. She simply wasn't coming. And he had only himself to blame. He was the stupidest, most insensitive man who'd ever walked the earth. He wished he were dead, would rather be dead than alive without Lisa.

His mother caught his eye and gave him a reassuring little wave. It didn't reassure him in the slightest. Lisa simply wasn't coming.

Well, she was right not to. He didn't deserve her. What he deserved was exactly what he was getting. He was being stood up at the altar. He'd never see Lisa again, and it was his own damned, stubborn fault.

He glanced grimly at the assembled guests. They'd gradually run out of chitchat and an awkward silence hung in the room. They knew. By now, they'd all figured out what was happening. Well, at least most of them had.

Roy, standing up front between his mother and Ginny, still looked unhappy. But he wouldn't be unhappy for long. His sister wouldn't be getting married today, after all.

On one side of the gathering, Benedetto was talking to Fiona, probably telling her how he'd seen in the stars that this wedding would be called off.

At the back of the room near the door, the harpist riffed through a series of chords. And then she began playing the Wedding March.

Dan closed his eyes in total, complete, irrevocable misery. He'd lost the only woman he'd ever truly loved, and, when the music ended, he'd have to tell the guests that and send them home. He doubted he could manage it without breaking down.

"Here we go, old buddy," Jake whispered. "Too late to change your mind now."

A murmur swept the room. Dan opened his eyes and suddenly... incredibly... marvelously... he no longer wanted to be dead.

Crystal was walking into the salon, wearing a long pink dress and a smile that said the wedding was about to begin.

The guests had carefully left an aisle in the center of the room, and she started up it.

Then, amazing as it was, Lisa appeared on her father's arm. And everyone else in the room faded from Dan's sight.

His heart swelled and his throat tightened. He watched Lisa walk slowly toward him. She looked pale and nervous but absolutely beautiful, practically floating up the aisle in a wedding gown that transformed her into a princess.

He smiled at her—a smile that felt as if it might never leave his face. Tentatively, she smiled back. It was just a tiny, anxious smile, but that didn't matter. Everything was going to be all right. No, everything was going to be wonderful. Lisa was going to marry him. She loved him enough.

Lisa took another small step toward Dan, her heart hammering so hard she knew her father could hear it. He squeezed her arm and whispered that she looked gorgeous.

She swallowed hard and met Dan's gaze once more, still trembling with relief. She'd been so frightened that he'd change his mind, that he wouldn't be here waiting for her. She'd been such a fool... such a fool since the first moment she'd met him. It was a miracle that he still wanted her.

But he did. And his being here made her the luckiest woman in the world. She loved him so much. That was what mattered most. And if this damned report didn't say what she wanted it to...well, she'd just have to deal with that. Because regardless of anything else, she could never be happy without Dan.

Just a few more steps and she'd be beside him. Just a few more minutes and she'd be his wife.

"I love you, baby," her father murmured as they neared the front of the room. He stopped, withdrew his arm from hers, and stepped to one side to stand beside her mother.

Lisa stood motionless, her gaze locked with Dan's. But instead of reaching out to her, he turned and spoke quietly to Jake.

She froze at the surprised expression that appeared on Jake's face...stopped breathing when he cleared his throat.

"Ladies and gentlemen," he said, "we'd...ahh... we'd like to ask your indulgence for just another few minutes."

He turned and said something to the justice of the peace, but Lisa didn't even try to hear. She knew what was happening. Her most terrible fears were becoming reality. Dan couldn't go through with this, after all. He didn't want a wife who mistrusted him, who doubted him. She was going to lose him.

He reached out, took her hand, and drew her blindly along with him toward the tiny anteroom where they were supposed to sign the marriage certificate. But they wouldn't be doing that. Instead, Dan was going to tell her the worst thing he could possibly tell her.

She swallowed against the enormous lump in her throat, trying not to cry, feeling numb, barely able to move her feet.

Dan opened the door and guided her into the little room. Vaguely, she realized that Jake was ushering her father and mother and Roy in.

Wordlessly, she turned to Dan, her heart breaking, knowing the words he was about to say would destroy her.

But he was smiling.

She wiped at her eyes, praying her tear-blurred vision wasn't playing a trick on her.

It wasn't. He was shaking his head and smiling at her.

"Hey," he murmured, "for Pete's sake don't go jumping to any more wrong conclusions. All I want to do is make your family happy about this wedding. And make *you* happier about saying *I do.*"

He reached across the table and picked up the book that was lying on it . . . a copy of his report.

"This is supposed to be confidential until Monday," he said, flipping through the pages. "But some things are far more important than going along with QM's damned orders."

Lisa glanced at her father. He was looking uncertainly at Roy. She turned back to Dan.

"Here we are," he murmured, turning to her father. "I'd better start with this bit that's misleading . . . out of context, that is. I was writing about the fact that, since the public perceives all-terrain vehicles as toys, any tightening in the economy might result in declining demand for the Dueler. But let me quote the text. 'The obvious conclusion is that Quality Motors should plan to phase out production of the Dueler and shut down the Walkerton operation.'"

Lisa bit her lip and looked at her family. *Happy.* Dan said he was going to make them happy. But she'd never seen three more unhappy people.

"However," he continued, turning over a few pages, "I go on to explain why the obvious conclusion is all wrong. You see, there's a rapidly developing realization that all-terrain vehicles are just coming into their own. Let me quote again.... 'Far from being a candidate for shutdown, Plant W has a healthy future. Duelers will be in increased demand as the greenhouse effect makes weather patterns more uncertain and causes the southern U.S. deserts to spread. Changing rain patterns, flooding and more intense and frequent hurricanes and tornadoes will also be part of global warming, and all-terrain vehicles will have an increasing role in rescue operations, worldwide.'"

He stopped reading and gazed at Lisa.

Her father and mother and Roy all began talking at once. But she wasn't listening. "Thank you," she murmured to Dan. "Thank you for telling us now."

"There's something else I'd better tell you now, Lisa, before we go through with the ceremony."

She gazed anxiously at his serious expression, afraid to ask what the something else was.

"Lisa, just before I came downstairs, I phoned my boss and resigned. I've decided to set up on my own. There's lots of room for free-lance consultants in New York, and I don't want ever to be forced into doing another job I hate doing. But... well, things might be touch and go for a while. Until I get established, I mean. So if you want to rethink this...?"

"Oh, Dan," she murmured, almost laughing with relief that the something else was nothing at all. "You don't really believe I'd let you escape, do you? Not when you make me as happy as you do."

"I make you happy?" he asked quietly, taking her into his arms.

"Dan, you make me happier than I ever imagined possible."

He smiled down at her...a slow, sexy smile that made her wonder how she'd ever been happy before he'd come into her life.

"Just exactly how happy do I make you?" he teased.

"On a happiness scale of one to ten?" she whispered.

"All right, on a happiness scale of one to ten."

"Let me think...just exactly what number comes after a zillion?"

Harlequin Superromance ®

Come to where the West is still wild in a summer trilogy by Margot Dalton

Sunflower (Coming in June)
Robin Baldwin can't believe she's become the half owner of a prize rodeo horse—Sunflower. But to take possession, Robin has to travel the rodeo circuit with rough-and-tumble cowboy Matt Adams, living with him in very close quarters.

Tumbleweed (Coming in July)
Until she met Scott Freeman, Lyle Callander was about as likely to settle in one spot as tumbleweed in a windstorm. Now Lyle's heart is lost. But who *is* Scott? He's more than the simple photographer he claims to be...much more.

Juniper (Coming in August)
Devil-may-care Buck Buchanan can ride a bucking bronco or a Brahma bull. But can he win Claire Tremaine, a woman who sets his heart on fire but keeps her own as cold as ice?

Praise for Margot Dalton's previous books:

"I just finished reading *Under Prairie Skies* and had to hide my tears from my children. I loved it. What a wonderful story." *A reader*

"A beautifully written story that will tie your heartstrings in knots." *Romantic Times*

"A good, good read!" *Rendezvous*